CASTLE ADAMANT

by

Sally Watson

BookLocker.com, Inc.
2009

Dedicated to Ann and Richard Zimmer

Acknowledgements

With salutations to Annie Feakes Honja
who roamed the ruins of Corfe Castle with me
when she was just a nipper.

and

Thanks--again!

to Gill Freeman, master-researcher!

TABLE OF CONTENTS

POTTED HISTORY

England, lurching toward civil war--oh, roughly since Charles I became king in 1625--was now positively lunging. Everyone was angry; religions and politics divided and squabbled in a dozen directions.

It wasn't always like this. A hundred and fifty years ago everyone simply obeyed the Pope and the King: one religious and one political ruler. There was little choice. But it gave a great stability to life: you knew exactly where you stood, whom to obey and what to believe.

But then--in 1519, to be exact--a certain Martin Luther upset the applicant even more than he'd expected to. He challenged the Pope, demanding that the Church be reformed--thus inadvertently starting the Restoration. This sort of thing proved contagious. Less than fifteen years later, Henry VIII challenged the Pope, too--but what *he* wanted was his first divorce so he could marry Anne Boleyn. When the Pope refused, Henry divorced *him*--thus inadvertently starting the Church of England, a kind of Popeless Catholicism--which was not at all what he'd had in mind. He'd wanted to be Pope, himself.

Well, the English were always a solid tolerant people, slow to anger and slower to violence. All this in itself wasn't too upsetting. What came next, was! When Henry died (in 1547) his heirs were all over the religious map. (And we know how people can get about religion!) First Edward VI, a Reformist, gave the Catholics a bad time for six years. Next his half-sister Mary gave the non-Catholics an even worse time, thus earning the sobriquet Bloody Mary. She also upset England considerably by marrying the ever-so-Catholic Prince Philip of Spain, whose goal was to rescue England from heresy if he had to burn them all at the stake to do it. England had spent the 500 years since the Norman Conquest wresting some civil liberties back from the Normans, and didn't fancy losing them to Spaniards; so when Mary mercifully died after only five years, and the disgruntled Philip went back to Spain, England welcomed Mary's half-sister Elizabeth. An amazingly wise and tolerant young woman (who once said that we all worshipped the same god and the rest was a dispute over trifles), she managed to calm everything down and make the people adore her, and all was well...

Oops! The Catholic countries--especially Spain and France--were *shocked* to find that England went right on being heretics and bound for hell.

They truly wanted to save all their souls--and also to rule that prosperous little country. For its own good, of course. So for most of Elizabeth's 45-year reign and right into the Stuart Dynasty, there were Plots upon Plots to kill or depose that heretic Elizabeth in favor of a French or Spanish ruler--none of which endeared Catholicism to England.

Along came Charles I, in 1625. He started out badly by marrying the ever-so-Catholic Henrietta, Daughter of France, and made it worse by doting on her. He was, England was sure, about to impose Popedom upon them all. When he declared the Divine Right of Kings, they were sure of it. What, *the King above the Law?* Entitled by God to rule autocratically, in any way he liked? To enjoy total instant obedience? Even from Parliament?

Never! Not likely! No way! The people and Parliament had worked long and hard for civil rights and a share in governing England. The House of Lords, who inherited their power and who tended to go to the Church of England (Catholicism with no Pope) didn't mind as much as the House of Commons, who, being elected, were in greater danger of losing their power-- and who, being commoners, were more likely to belong to one of the proliferating Reform religions, now generally called Protestant. Thus nicely mixing religion and politics.

By 1641 bad matters became worse when Parliament hanged one of Charles' First Ministers of State, just to show Charles he couldn't have it all his own way. A year later, Charles decided to arrest five members of the Commons just to show Parliament it couldn't have it all *its* own way, either. Being Charles, he botched it, and had to flee London (which was furiously Reformist and Anti-Catholic) with his wife and older sons. King's and Parliament's armies began arming and thinking up insulting names. The Royalists called the Protestants Puritans (which the Protestants took as a compliment) and Roundheads because the men wore their hair short, just below the ear, instead of falling in long beribboned lovelocks over their shoulders. Parliament responded by scornfully calling Royalists cavaliers-- which in turn was taken as a compliment. Both sides knew insult was intended. Both sides were were now fairly unreasonable, both sides were itching for a war, and in October of '42 at a previously unimportant place called Edgehill, they began one.

Both sides botched that battle, both sides became more unreasonable, both intended to rule autocratically and force the other to worship the 'True' religion--and both sides lived to regret the whole thing, one way or another,

But before all that came about, a certain young sprig of nobility and his royalist escort set out for a place called Corfe Castle...

PROLOGUE: MARCH, 1643

"I warrant this is the place." Major Rawlins drew his troop to a halt on a slight rise and stared across a meadow or two at a large manor, probably built more than half a century ago in Queen Bess's reign, set in wide wintry gardens. "Fairview Manor," he explained to the puzzled silence around him. "Colonel Goodchild's estate"

To his right, a stalwart, ginger-haired sergeant with a weather-beaten face murmured vaguely. On his left, a bland civilian eyebrow in a blunt face aimed a few long hairs into the sky.

"Indeed," murmured its owner with polite detachment.

The major bristled, looking and feeling much like a self-respecting basset hound thrown into unwilling companionship with a cat. He had not wished to escort this arrogant sprig of nobility halfway across England--nor for that matter had Master Peregrine Lennox wished to leave Oxford, which was particularly exciting of late. Incredibly, in this modern and supposedly civilized year of 1643, a civil war had started: a thing that had not happened in England for something like two hundred years. King Charles had quit London in a huff, with his Court and Army and older sons, and simply moved them all to Oxford.

But now, Peregrine had left Oxford.

Actually, as it happened, he did not particularly mind. Learning had fallen apart. The University of Oxford was deeply disrupted by the royal invasion. And when the King took over the colleges, Peregrine had been forced to move in with his draconian grandmama. Almost anything was better than that! Certainly Major Rawlins was.

In any case, the University had proved a disappointment. He was too clever for his own comfort. He found most conversation to be pedestrian and predictable, even at Oxford--and it was hard not to let it show. All of which had made him vain, kind, condescending, and resigned to boredom. His arrogance, however, was altogether unlike that of his grandmama the Dowager Lady Heath, who had never in her life seen the least need for courtesy. Peregrine in his unassailable vanity had never seen the least need to be rude. Not deliberately. People sometimes took offense anyway, which sometimes puzzled but never worried him. He wondered now--just as a matter of mild interest--if Rawlins would manage to stay even remotely civil as far as Corfe Castle. He doubted it.

1

The silence grew thin. So did a late winter wind that aspired to become an early spring wind, blowing damp and chill and gray across southern England. Sergeant Sowerbutts, who admired that-there clever lad but was instinctively aware that he probably should not, looked anxiously from the set face to the tranquil one. Eh, but they was bound to fratch. Happen he warn't that clever, hisself, but sometimes he figured things out, come how. He fidgeted on his horse.

"This--er--Colonel Goodchild," Peregrine asked delicately. "Is he Our colonel or Theirs?"

"Theirs." The major turned to him a ruddy face decorated with a splendid Van Dyck goatee and mustache in imitation of King Charles. "I want to see if he's home."

"Shouldn't think so." Peregrine, who had observed only a very thin line of smoke rising from only one chimney, was all kindness. "I mean, if he's a colonel, and there's a war on, he'd be with his troops, wouldn't you think? You weren't planning a social visit, were you?"

The major grumped, wondering just how insulting that was intended to be, and suspecting the worst. Peregrine, who had not actually intended any insult, saw that the major was itching to pick a fight, but felt disinclined to oblige him. He could seldom bother to quarrel with anyone, not even Madam Grandmama. (Especially not Madam Grandmama!) He smiled. Not appeasingly: that never occurred to him; merely dispassionately. Sergeant Sowerbutts did hoped they'd not fratch. One were aristocratic and clever, t'other a full twenty year older and a major, aside from being that fussed.

"Military business," the major snapped, determined to quench the boy, who, being a cripple, had no right to such arrogance.

Peregrine nodded, unquenched. His self-worth was so complete that it never needed to prove itself: it simply was.

"To be sure." he agreed. "Very logical, for a military man to be on military business. Er--might one ask how long we require to stay here talking about it?"

They moved down toward the manor house. Sergeant Sowerbutts glanced worriedly at his commander's face, seeing with ease that his temper was come all-a-bits under the shuttered expression. The upper classes were champion odd that way, never showing how they felt; but he could tell. The Lennox lad, now, was reet pleased with hisself. Sergeant Sowerbutts sometimes suspected he riled the major o'purpose.

He was wrong. Peregrine would never bother to do that.

CHAPTER ONE

INVASION

"You can't come in!" Verity shouted from behind the door.

She was mistaken. They could and did. Unfortunately for Major Rawlins, it was not quite the dignified and stately entrance that he had intended. In fact, it was with no dignity whatever. To start with, it took his troopers several minutes to break down the solid oak door. Then they fell headlong with their own impetus. The major, staggering behind, found himself facing a pair of furious blue eyes behind a drawn bow. He knew at once that such a young maiden lacked both the skill and the will to be any kind of menace, knew in the next instant that he was wrong on both counts--and dropped flat on his face.

The arrow sped over him and on through the doorway.

"God's ears!" he exclaimed, incredulous.

Peregrine really could not help the tiny yelp of amusement that escaped him. The major's face, normally ruddy, became livid. Conceited sprig! Contempt almost spoke aloud.

Peregrine did not quite shrug. The fact that he too had instinctively ducked the arrow no more wounded that conceit than did his lameness. Why be embarrassed about taking evasive action if it seemed needful? As Major Rawlins rose, Peregrine turned his amused gaze to the girl. She looked like a furious young angel, face stern under the white cap that had come askew, permitting tendrils of silver-gilt hair to escape in a fury of fine ringlets.

Hair was the last thing on Verity's mind. Her face did not hint at the wild pounding of her heart under a modest lawn fichu. She had been well trained in self-control. She groped for another arrow, determined to kill at least one of the enemy--but the second arrow never flew. Robin Hood doubtless could have drawn, placed, aimed and shot in about five seconds, but Verity's archery training consisted of stolen lessons with a tolerant stable-master, unknown either to Father or Aunt Huldah. Nor did she have five seconds. Before she could even settle the arrow in the bow, the officer rose furiously to his feet and slapped her hard across the face, dazing her for a moment. Her training held: she did not cry out or do anything disgraceful. After all, Aunt Huldah had struck her often enough--albeit never this hard on her face. But

3

before she could focus her eyes again, both arms were held firmly by no less than two Royalist soldiers.

To struggle uselessly would have been hideously undignified, and Verity was a great believer in dignity. So although they were hurting her arms quite a lot, she stood still, slim and upright as a young beech tree, cornflower-blue eyes vivid in her narrow face, looking rather like a Protestant Jeanne d'Arc-- and fully aware of it. It was a very dramatic moment in a life that had until today been placid to the point of tedium. Now her wits had began to function again--and crisis seemed to have sharpened them. She narrowed the eye that still functioned, noting that all those fearsome men, even the officer himself, were in fact looking rather shocked. She felt a kind of exaltation--no doubt because her cause was righteous--and began rather to enjoy her own heroism.

"How dare you!" she hissed through stiffening lips. Her voice was unexpectedly throaty, like a blackbird song. "Minions of Satan! 'There is no peace, saith the Lord, unto the wicked!' That's from Isaiah, by the way. How dare you invade my home and lay hands on me?"

Rawlins pulled himself together. "Malapert minx! I suppose you never tried to lay hands on me?"

"Indeed, and well you deserved it, knave! Trespasser! Invader! Anyway, I didn't, exactly. It wasn't hands, it was an arrow. It should have been a sword," she pointed out, "because he who lives by the sword shall die by the sword; but I don't own a sword, so an arrow had to do."

She looked regretful, to Peregrine's fascination. He had never met a maiden anything like this: what kind of jade was she? Personally he thought the slap distasteful and this whole incursion foolish. This Colonel Goodchild was certainly not here, or the place would have been warmer, swept, dusted, and guarded by more than a lone maiden--but as Rawlins certainly did not want his opinion, Peregrine could relax and enjoy the show. He proceeded to do so.

They were in the oak-paneled hall of a fine but neglected estate suitable to perhaps a knight or squire, or just possibly a baronet. Tapestries fluttered and carpets swayed on the walls, and the already-cold room was becoming even colder in the wintry air now pouring in at the shattered door. There was not a servant in sight: only the girl, wraith-thin, puritan-plain, with white apron, cap, and fichu over full blue skirts. But some one here did not altogether scorn worldly beauty, noted Peregrine (who had an artistic eye for dress) for they had very astutely chosen, not gray or brown, but a blue that exactly matched her eyes. Her cheek would, he decided, soon be a similar hue, thanks to her shocking foolhardiness.

Major Rawlins was wondering why unkind Providence should afflict him with both a smug youth of the nobility *and* a murderous Puritan maiden. Of the two, he could not decide which he disliked more--but at least he had some authority over the girl--he hoped.

"Where's your father?"

She regarded him scornfully, still alight with her dramatic role, and lifted a defiant chin.

"From that, I gather that he's not here." The major was reasserting the dignity suitable to his rank, from which he had been briefly and embarrassingly parted. "Which, as he's an officer in the Roundhead army--"

"Parliament army," she corrected him. "Our heads are no rounder than yours."

"--means he's away on duty with his regiment. Where?" And he stamped forward in the menacing lunge that always caused his men to flinch.

His men had never lived with Aunt Huldah. Verity had; so, even though he had already struck her once, she did not so much as blink. This earned her a brief, awed, almost respectful silence--even though thrashings were normal training for the young. (After all, Original Sin must be beaten from the young. Especially young females.) Everyone there--including Verity--mistook fearlessness for courage. Sergeant Sowerbutts's prominent light-blue eyes rounded. Verity's chin, encouraged, inched up in a way that would have warned anyone who knew her.

"*Audendo magnus tegitur timur,*" observed Peregrine offhandedly. Verity fixed him with a brooding blue stare before turning back to Rawlins.

"You should all think shame," she said sternly. "God is watching, you know. Aren't you, God?" She glanced confidently at the high oak-beamed ceiling, as if expecting an answering thunderbolt. Actually, she merely hoped a bit--God being on the whole averse to suggestions from her sex. Still, she felt that the expectation might help her status with these enemies. "I'm sure You don't approve bullying a helpless young maiden--" (some one snorted) "--and taking away her weapons, do You? Besides taking Your name in vain," she added for good measure.

Peregrine's wayward eyebrow lurched. He did hope she was not trying to look pathetic: she hadn't the face for it. It was a narrow austere face, almost pallid, made more dramatic by thick straight brows that very nearly met in the middle, gold-tipped dark lashes and those deep blue eyes. Unfortunately, her nose, which should have flaunted a proud arch, quite failed to do so. A lopped-off chin warred with sharp cheekbones and a jaw which she tried to jut accusingly at Major Rawlins. One side was not working very well.

"And you needn't think I'll tell you anything, even if you tear me limb from limb, which I know quite well you Royalists are fond of doing." Sowerbutts and young Diggory Dove looked shocked. The chin--far too aggressive for anything so short--went up yet another triumphant notch. "Well, for one thing, I couldn't tell you even if I wanted to; because I don't even know." She eyed the officer with growing confidence. "'The race is not to the swift, nor the battle to the strong'," she added virtuously. (What a mercy her voice was low and husky! Too many Bible-quoting Puritans ran to shrillness.)

Major Rawlins, who detested Bible-quoting Puritans of any voice, but who had never before actually thought of tearing one of them limb from limb, now found himself thinking of it. He regarded her even more bleakly. She gave back a disconcerting blue stare. Peregrine watched the two of them with enjoyment. They were quite well matched, for though the major had all the weapons, she had the high ground.

But Rawlins had another advantage, which not even Peregrine yet suspected. Her arms were by now hurting a great deal in the soldiers' fierce grip. Was it possible she had pushed confrontation too far--a thing Fynch had warned her about? Mistress Fynch had encouraged literary, philosophical and historical challenges (always provided she could defend her opinion against fierce logical assault) but Fynch had also told her to be careful of what she said and when and to whom. *"Cave quie dicis, quando et cui,"* was a favorite quotation of hers; it was perhaps a pity that Verity had not remembered it sooner. Jehovah, as her late and not-much-lamented Aunt Huldah had often pointed out, was not mocked, especially by females who failed to be modest and submissive as befitted daughters of the sinful Eve. (Verity had always felt this to be unjustified. *She* had not eaten of that apple. It did not seem fair to punish all women eternally for it.)

Still, God was on the whole just, wasn't He? And any just god would surely approve her using the brains and courage He had given her, wouldn't He? No doubt He was merely testing her. It was, she hoped, not to be as severe a test as Job's. Fynch's illness was bad enough. She did hope He had not decided to let her become one of His Martyrs, like the ones in Foxe's book! That was an honor she had never longed for, even a little bit.

Her arms were now hurting abominably. She would have died before saying so. Mere fearlessness began to alter into something more like true courage--or perhaps merely mulish pride.

Peregrine, eyeing her shrewdly, aimed the errant eyebrow at the major, who was still seething at them both. Not that she had not goaded him: she

6

certainly had. Still-- "Planning to take her out and execute her, then?" he inquired affably.

"Witling!" barked the major, who had in fact been thinking wistfully of something very much along those lines--for both of them. But clearly there was nothing to be had from the girl. Perhaps the servants would talk? It occurred to him that he had not seen any.

"Where are your servants, girl?"

"Gone," she managed, briskly. "Well, you don't think they'd stay around with you crashing in like that, waving your weapons around, do you?"

The major bristled. Plague take the shrewish chit! "Do you claim to be totally alone here?" He did not believe it. "Spread out; search the place," he told Sowerbutts belatedly. This brazen baggage had distracted him. "If you even suspect an ambush, shoot." Roundheads were notoriously treacherous. "And don't let the wench escape."

The hands on her arms tightened. She clenched her teeth (under carefully relaxed lips) and breathed short careful breaths, her lips quite white by now. Peregrine saw. Like a cornered cat, she was! "If you just twist her arms entirely off, then she couldn't shoot any more arrows at you, could she?"

The major looked, made a curt gesture, and the hands mercifully removed themselves. Verity refused to rub her bruised arms--even were she able to lift them, which was not altogether certain. Nor would she thank the youth, whose motive was clearly amusement rather than good will. Anyway, he was a slight, weak-looking fop, ridiculously dressed, with wide lace Van Dyck collar and cuffs, an elaborate emerald waistcoat and embroidered sash, and full breeches gathered at the knee, with tassets over scarlet leather bucket-topped boots. He also had odd eyes, the lower lids being curved and the upper ones straight across instead of the other way around. And though his eyebrows were almost red, the hair that sprang urgently from his head was tawny. And it curled to his shoulders with an even longer ringlet dangling over the left one, tied with a bow of ribbon.

Verity had never really seen any Royalists before: not close up. No wonder decent sober people tagged them with the insulting nickname of Cavaliers! To the eyes of a simply clad Protestant, even the soldiers seemed stupidly overdressed.

Overdressed--but men. All of them murderous and eager to rape, Fynch had said. Verity was not at all sure what rape was, but she knew it was dreadful. She eyed them uneasily.

"I suppose," she blurted, cheekbones well forward, "you'll burn down the house, now. With me in it." The faces all became blank, from which she

7

assumed the worst. Well, Royalists were like that, weren't they? "But God will be exceeding angry if you harm my governess: she's never done a thing to you, and she's dying."

No one believed that, an obvious plea for sympathy. The major pounced. "So you're not alone here, after all! What other lies have you told? Are the servants hiding? Where?"

"Been no servants here for weeks," Peregrine observed helpfully. "Or else they're monstrous lazy. Look around you." He indicated the state of serious neglect in the dusty room, which was being belatedly and unevenly swept by the raw winter wind rushing in. He thought of his sisters, who--each in her own way--would by now have turned Rawlins and his men into eager knights of chivalry. One supposed this was how Roundheads raised their women?

"I never lie," she retorted, rallying. "The Elect can't, you know, or perhaps you don't. I *am* alone, except for my poor old governess, and she couldn't possibly harm you; so if you burn the house with her in it, it will be murder of the innocent, which the Lord hateth unless it was His idea, like the battle of Jericho. And my father would be marvelous annoyed, as well." Her voice was steady, she was pleased to note, though it had dropped a full four notes, as always when she was wrought. "Anyway, as she's dying, I refuse to let you disturb her."

"The way you refused to let us enter?" Peregrine murmured sweetly.

The major showed his teeth. "You may choose, mistress. Lead us to this Fynch, or we shall find her ourselves, which I doubt not she'll find even more disturbing."

The unbruised side of her face flushed with new anger. Clasping her hands she stood quite still, face turned upward, ignoring him infuriatingly.

"Well?" the major barked, properly infuriated.

"Be quiet," she commanded, sparing him the slightest flicker of blue glance. "I'm asking God about it, and it's impolite to interrupt. Especially if it's God you're interrupting. I hope You've noticed his bad manners, God, besides everything else."

In the brief uneasy silence, Sowerbutts led a scatter of troopers back to say that they'd found nobbut a few poultry and two sheep, no horses, a little grain, the kitchen deserted and no fires lit, think on. Verity went on consulting God, so the exasperated major seized her arm and shook it.

It was an unfairly unexpected attack! She caught her breath and sent an angry protest to God, Who might have given her a *little* warning as easily as not, and saved her this loss of dignity. He jerked his hand back as if burned.

8

Shock, realization and finally chagrin crossed his face and he muttered something about God's nightgown. The interested Peregrine, shaking his tawny head, perceived that the major had just lost the game--and did not yet know it.

The dawn of adoration flickered behind Sowerbutts's weathered face. Pluck t' th' backbone, the little lass were!

Verity looked upward again hopefully. God did sometimes give her hints. He did so now. She felt a vague sense of rightness, lowered her gaze to look confidently at her tormentors. "He says all right," she reported, and began marching toward the wide staircase at the back of the hall. "Look to it, then, but you'd best behave yourselves and not upset Fynch." She skipped nimbly up the high staircase, Sowerbutts and the fresh-faced young Diggory Dove at her heels. Peregrine, uninvited, followed--but at a pace more comfortable to his lame leg.

Upstairs, Verity led through one cold damp chamber after another (for the notion of hallways and corridors had not yet been thought of). Presently they stood at the entrance to a bedchamber containing a small smoking fire with very little warmth, some wall-hangings, old rushes on the floor, a clothespress, a stool, a table, a chest, the usual stinking chamber pot and a large curtained four-poster bed. In it, a tiny old lady hardly raised the eiderdown. A small fluffy tortoiseshell cat who was curled up at her feet raised a head and snarled at them all impartially.

"That's Naomi; she's guarding Mistress Fynch. Fynch, *en nukti boule tois sophois gignetai.* That means," she said over her shoulder, "for her to take counsel of her pillow, which seems rather appropriate just now. Mistress Fynch, if you happened to notice a lot of noise a few minutes ago, 'twas these barbarians breaking down the front door; and here they are, though I distinctly told them not to come in, and they're not to disturb you."

The face was lined and sunken, but the pale eyes turned toward the troopers were very much alive. "Well, you've taken your time, gentlemen, haven't you?" she whispered. "I put in a request for you several days ago." Confusion spread across three faces. They looked at one another nervously. "Well, come here so I can see you."

She *was* dying! Even Diggory, without a battle to his name, could see that. And Verity, now seeing Fynch through their eyes, was shaken with the fact that her mind had known but her heart stubbornly refused to accept. Now it was forced to. This was by far the worst moment of her life. What was she to do? What was God thinking of? She clenched her teeth and held her breath, lest she distress Fynch.

Fynch looked the men over carefully, not seeming much impressed. "Mmm." Her voice was only a breath. "Well, you're not at all what I'd hoped, but you'll have to do. The best God could manage, I suppose. After all, we can't expect Him to be omniscient *and* omnipotent, can we?"

From the soldiers, shocked silence.

"Are you suggesting He isn't? demanded Major Rawlins, unable to believe such blasphemy.

"Of course He isn't! How could He be? He gave mankind free will, didn't He? Well, then! *Anagke oude theoi machontai.* Now listen carefully... because I'm dying and don't have much time... or energy left. You're to take care of Verity."

"We?" sputtered the major. "*Her?* But-- Impossible! We aren't your servants, woman. We're a royalist troop, on the king's business."

"More important than God's business?" Fynch retorted. "Verity, come here." She looked with interest at the scarlet handprint on that cheek. Major Rawlins bristled, prepared to defend his action aggressively--and was spared the need. "Well, I see you've been... annoying people, child. I did... warn you. *Cave quie dicis, quando et cui.* You'll learn hard, I fear, but it will probably..." She paused for a moment, breathing shallowly. "--improve your character. Fetch me... some of your father's malmsey wine, child. And don't disgrace yourself."

Verity, who had spent all her tears anyway, went from the room, not even caring whether she had anyone's sympathy now. Fynch was all she had; all she had ever had, for years now, ever since she was four or five. Father had always been a remote figure more interested in politics and Jehovah than daughters. Aunt Huldah had been an unloving martinet. God seemed remote and unpredictable and often ruthless. There was only Fynch: rigorous, abrasive, loving and demanding, who had sharpened Verity's mind like a whetstone. Fynch was her sword and her shield, and the rod for her back, and the rock that she stood on and sparred against, and her only companion! It was not The Almighty, she now perceived, who was her refuge and her fortress, but Fynch.

The fop had just reached the top stair, limping. He paused, regarded her curiously. Verity stood there unseeing, looking into the fearsome void of the future. Then, her face blank, she descended the stairs.

And in the bedchamber, Rawlins watched the old woman rally her energy.

"Now... you! You'll see her to safety. Try to understand... that basically she's sixteenth century, not seventeenth. Queen Bess's time, my time: when

10

women were educated and taught the value of Reason, not told to sit around... and be obedient and submissive. She isn't." The sunken eyes closed for a moment, opened. "Then, learned women were... respected and usually consulted and we had peace and prosperity on the whole. All that went out... forty years ago, when King James came to the throne and said females were too inferior to be educated. And now look! Women who can neither see nor speak common sense, nor prevent you idiot men from blundering into civil war." She breathed painfully. "'Twill be a long one; you've no notion how long and terrible."

At this foolishness (for everyone knew that though the King had somehow failed to win the war by Christmas, he would certainly do so by Easter) the Major moved to take back the command which he seemed somehow to have lost the moment he entered this wretched house.

"Woman, you ask the impossible. I'm a Royalist soldier on the king's business in a war, whether you approve it or not. I cannot, with the best will in the world, take a young female with me."

"You will," she said simply, "or I shall haunt you for the rest of your life, and don't think I can't. I can and will. Yes... and... your obstinate and unwise King Charles, as well. You!" She looked at Peregrine, who had just appeared in the doorway. "Here, lad."

He obeyed because he chose to, composure in every muscle; and looked down at her with interest. She reminded him vaguely of his *other* grandmother, Granny Val, whom he liked and loved and admired.

"I know your... hair and eyes. Who are you?"

He opened those odd-shaped greenish eyes wide. *Could* she know--? Yet, why not? She was probably older than Granny and Granfer, still-- "Peregrine Lennox," he told her obligingly. "M'grandfather's Sir Nicholas Raven. My hair's like his."

"And you get your eyes from Lady Valerie," Fynch retorted disconcertingly. "Don't leave out the distaff side, jobbernowl!" Peregrine blinked, stupid being the one thing no one had ever called him. She ignored it. "Not in the King's army? Too young?"

"Not really. There's this." He stuck out an indifferent leg. He was not in the least embarrassed by it, and it sometimes provided a convenient excuse for avoiding bloodthirsty things he'd as lief not do. Like hunting and that brutal game, football. And, especially, war, which he considered totally barbaric. "Pony fell on it when I was two, and it never set right. Army doesn't want me. Just as well: I don't really want them. Don't think much of king *or*

Parliament: both sides mistake themselves for God. Never told anybody else I think so," he added, surprised at himself.

To his surprise, she chortled weakly. "Wise lad. *Cave quie dicis*--" She closed her eyes. "Where was I? Oh yes... Where are you going with these troopers? ... Don't narrow your eyes at me; I've a right to know."

He sighed. "Going to Corfe Castle. Sir John and Lady Bankes' home. Foster exchange with their son John. He's going to Oxford for the Michaelmas term, and I'll help his mother run the Castle. John and I are to wed each other's sisters when we finish University. We're full young yet." She just looked at him. "But this maiden doesn't belong at Corfe," he explained kindly. They're Royalist: 'tis no place for her. She'd hate it. They'd hate her, too," he pointed out with accuracy.

Fynch's eyes had closed again. She did not open them, but a smile flickered somewhere near. "Very like," she breathed. "Good discipline for them... You, too, both of you: too cocky by half. Verity's... coming up now." She did hope the girl would try not to be too challenging. But she had always been that way, and Fynch had not discouraged it: only the sin of self-righteousness which so afflicted Protestants who knew themselves to be Elected to heaven. With that she had had indifferent success--still, that shining mind did at least question itself... now and then...

"Intelligence should never be wasted." she told Peregrine. "Even in a girl," she added sharply, "whatever you may think. Prop me up, now." The cat swore again as Peregrine obeyed. "Take her with you as soon as I'm buried," she ordered the fuming major, "Or Else! You'd hate being haunted, I make no doubt. Now all of you... go away and let me tell Verity... goodbye."

They obeyed meekly.

This day the pride of Mistress Verity Goodchild and the smugness of Master Peregrine Lennox had--if only briefly and slightly--been shaken.

CHAPTER TWO

DEFIANCE

"Shan't!" said Verity, dry-eyed and stubborn and feeling like a small animal trapped between savage lions and a cliff edge. Her fearlessness had unfairly vanished; nor had God, in the past three days, bothered to restore it even when she begged Him. Now she was indeed without refuge, and she was about to be torn from her fortress, and those men, rough-faced and brutal and large, seemed altogether menacing. All she could do was imitate courage and try to make that officer ashamed again. One cheek had now become a glorious livid purple edged with green, and she displayed it. "I shan't go with you, and you can't make me, no matter how often you smite me. For Jesus said 'Resist not evil; but whosoever shall smite thee on thy right cheek, turn to him the other also.' Of course, you got it wrong and smote me first on the left, but I shouldn't think that matters." She tilted the right side of her face toward him challengingly. The major reddened; rather more with anger--and perhaps temptation resisted--than shame, but he did, she noticed with satisfaction, shuffle his feet just the tiniest bit.

"Your granny-- nurse-- that old woman-- said--"

The corners of her mobile mouth pulled tight. She looked and felt altogether mulish, and her voice dropped another note. "I don't care *what* Fynch said: *she's* not the one who's being Abducted; she's safely dead."

A pale sun shone diffidently in at the tall windows. Mistress Fynch (who had died promptly and neatly as soon as she had ordered things to her satisfaction) was buried. All the livestock and food and fuel had been consumed. It was long past time for Major Rawlins to deliver his two detestable charges to their destination and continue proper army business--and now this.

"By God's pantofles, you *will* go," he said. "We *can* make you. It will be easier on everybody if you come nicely, but we can make you."

She knew it was true. She also knew that she could not stay here: not and survive: not without food or fuel or protection. But to be taken away to an unknown fate with these dreadful men seemed even worse. She felt altogether pigheaded.

"Why?" She confronted him. "'The way of the Lord is strength to the upright, but destruction shall be to the workers of iniquity,' and besides, I'm perfectly certain God doesn't have teeth or wear pantofles or nightgowns, so you're blaspheming. And I know quite well you'd hate taking me; you've said so. And I'd hate going. So I shan't."

"Don't then," he growled, goaded. "You're right; we don't want a whining female along. You'd be a great nuisance, and there's no one to chaperone you, and we don't want you crying rape. So stay." That would call her bluff.

Verity was not bluffing. Well, not entirely. Certainly, she would not back down. Her brows met. "Excellent good," she said under those sharp cheekbones. "Farewell. Shut what's left of the door when you leave." She turned to go up to her cold and lonely bedchamber, fighting despair. Well, she'd been here virtually alone before they came, hadn't she? Aunt Huldah had died last summer, and then Fynch had got sick and then the servants ran away with all the silver and horses, leaving Verity alone to tend Fynch. It would be much easier now, she assured herself, with no one but Naomi to keep fed and warm, or worry about-- And she knew she was lying. The old house loomed at her full of shadows and loneliness, and she would certainly starve and freeze. She would not for worlds have said so.

She looked at the fop, who had not moved. None of them had. They were looking disconcerted. They, she realized, had been bluffing as much as she. It seemed to be an impasse, and one she was no longer certain she wanted to win. "I shall ask God about it," she temporized.

The fop looked pained. Probably he did not even believe in God. (Actually, he did, but it had been his experience that those who kept consulting Him in public were using Him for expediency.) "Tell Him to find you a chaperone," he suggested dryly.

Verity gave him a stern look. "You shouldn't just *tell* God to do things, as if you knew better than He does," she said virtuously. It was advice she herself found it hard to follow--although ever since Fynch had made her write *"Vanitas vanitatum, et omnia vanitas"* a hundred times, she tended not to bother Him when she thought she probably knew the answer. Just now, she did not, and she badly needed one. "Anyway, I'm going to ask him about it right now," She did so, face turned upward, mind open to divine suggestion, which usually took the form of being comfortable or uncomfortable about a possibility. Somewhat, she supposed, like Socrates' daemon, who was probably really God, only the ancient Greeks had not known about Him, having many false gods instead.

Peregrine watched cynically as her forehead crinkled. She would presently announce--as Puritans always did--that God was on her side.

God surprised them both. Verity took a deep breath and opened her eyes wide in startlement, for she had never had such a direct hint before. "He says I should *let* you Abduct me!" she exclaimed. "Well!" she told the eaves very imperiously for one who has just denied dictating to God Almighty, "You had better provide a chaperone, then, or I'll know you're really Satan just pretending."

At this point Naomi sauntered casually down the stairs, staring with feline calm at the score of strangers in her hall. She was an aristocrat, was Naomi: a perfectly groomed dilute tortoise-shell, her longish coat a swirl of gray and pale peach, with one blonde eyebrow. Somehow the argument suspended itself as she descended. At the foot of the stairs she halted, tidied a bit of shoulder fur, and strolled over to Major Rawlins. While he stood torn between doubt and gratification, she sniffed his fine bucket-top boots with interest, and then wove a figure-eight around his ankles, purring loudly.

Gratification won. With the smug kindness that some males use for females and small animals, he reached down to stroke her silken head.

"She swears," Verity murmured artlessly just as Naomi did so. Loudly and luridly. Sergeant Sowerbutts, who had once served aboard ship, reckoned language like that would put the most hardened sailor in a pudder, come how. The major jerked his hand back as if bitten (which it wasn't) and did a bit of swearing, himself. Peregrine grinned, and Verity looked virtuous.

"Well, you can hardly blame her, the way you just burst into her home without so much as an invitation, all noise, and eating her food, too. Cats are civilized people, you know, and they resent that sort of thing."

Major Rawlins had had enough of the baggage. Both baggages. "Go up and pack your things," he snapped. "We shall go as soon as you're ready, and if you dawdle, I'll send some of my men up to help you."

Verity, trying not to look as relieved as she felt, mounted the stairs with dignity, and began to pack. Her Bible and Fynch's precious books went into the clothes-chest first. Then all Fynch's other treasures: comb, eyebrow tweezers, reticule, needle-case, kerchief, quills, horn spoon, her silver-and-mother-of-pearl musical box (which she had never played outside her own room because of Aunt Huldah thinking music to be sinful) and the clove-stuck oranges to ward off plague. Things to remember her by--as if Verity needed any help. One small salt tear escaped, but any others were banned. Fynch had said she was ready to join God, and that Verity was not to mourn her. Anyway, a woman had her pride! Next she stuffed the chemises and stockings and shifts and sleeves and skirts and bodices and kirtles and petticoats and fichus and caps and aprons in. Finally she rammed the unstrung bow corner-to-corner on top, and all the arrows, and closed the lid.

"I need some one to carry my chest down," she announced from the top of the stairs, "and also some one to put holes in another one for Naomi."

"Who?"

"Naomi. My cat. Well, she can hardly ride horseback, can she? Naomi washed a paw and eyed the major's boots, which hastily backed up a step.

"We're not taking any cat."

"Then," pronounced Verity flatly, "you're not taking me. What would God say about leaving one of His creatures to starve?"

"It's only an animal." He regarded her with dislike.

She lifted her chin and quoted at him. "'Inasmuch as ye have done it unto one of the least of these, my brethren, ye have done it unto me.'"

The major virtually brayed. "*Human* brethren! By God's toenails, you gooseish wench, it means humans!"

"It doesn't say humans."

"Well, it means it."

"How do you know? Are you God?"

He opened his mouth, closed it, tried for the attitude proper in addressing a mere female. "Animals." he explained with elaborate patience, "don't matter: they don't even have souls." He looked at her bellicose face. He looked at the furry creature on the herb-covered floor, now sharpening her claws in what seemed casual menace. He gritted his teeth.

Peregrine saw that Major Rawlins was doomed, one way or another, to lose this battle, too. It might or might not be a good thing: Peregrine was not sure he altogether liked cats, himself. They sometimes seemed to have an arrogance not suitable for soulless animals. Still--

"Why not take it?" he shrugged. "As we have to take her other things, what's one more chest?"

"A lot," began Major Rawlins. "If--"

No one ever knew how the argument might have ended. Excited voices rose from the cellars, one of them female. Two astonished soldiers appeared, with a stout woman covered in dust, cobwebs and querulence. Into the silence, Verity's voice rang like silver bells.

"Peggotty! Wherever have you been and whatever took you so long? Didn't you hear God calling you? We're going to Corfe Castle, and you don't have to be a scullery maid any more. God says you're to be my chaperone. You see?" she added to the amazed men before her, "God did as He promised. And He wants you to leave a note for Father to say where you've taken me;

and you're also to fix the door, because he would *not* like to find the house filled with foxes and badgers and hedgehogs and stoats. 'Poverty and shame shall be to him that refuseth instruction, but he that regardeth reproof shall be honoured.'"

Somehow, bowing to common sense, decency and possibly God, Major Rawlins found himself resentfully obeying. Verity read his expression easily.

"I do think," she observed, "that if you'd lived in the days of Jeanne d'Arc, you'd probably have approved of burning her."

"If she was anything like you," he told her earnestly, "I'd have lit the fire myself."

Verity believed him.

CHAPTER THREE

ABDUCTED

The troop wound its way southwest to Salisbury and on toward Dorset and the Isle of Purbeck (which was not an island at all, but a peninsula) and Corfe Castle. No one was filled with joy. For one thing, it was not a comfortable journey. Even in a time when good roads were nearly unknown, this road hardly deserved the name.

"They say we've never built a good road since the Romans left, a thousand years ago," observed Peregrine.

Verity said she could believe it.

Major Rawlins was disgruntled at having to escort two troublesome and arrogant young people who had neither respect for their elders, nor even gratitude. Moreover, due to the lack of horses at Goodchild manor, some of his own mounts had to do double duty. The packhorses who bore the two extra chests snorted and grumbled--particularly the one carrying the cat. For Naomi was a lady of strong opinions and a great dislike of change. She expressed that opinion with such vigor that most of the soldiers were reduced to awe. And though Peggotty, at the other extreme, was outwardly as submissive as any male (even God) could have wished, and rode pillion meekly enough behind Diggory, her face was a study in confusion and outrage. Nor was Diggory happy.

Even Sergeant Sowerbutts was nattered, partly because he had taken a gradely fancy not only to the lad and the lass, but even the cat; and he would soon be parted from all three, choose how.

Verity was perforce riding pillion behind Peregrine, that being the worst punishment the major could devise for both of them. Neither had yet decided how severe a punishment it was going to be. The fact that he openly declared it as such, tended them both to make the best of it, if only to spite him--but it was not likely to be easy. Verity's bruised arms emerged from her blue woolen cloak to clasp his waist, slender fingers laced together, uncertain whether to tighten or loosen their grasp. Peregrine could almost feel her pain and fear. Puritan upbringing was strict. Had she ever ridden pillion before? Had she ever ridden at all? Or put her arms around a man? Or been hugged by anyone? He thought not, and his heart went out to her, poor gallant little thing, deprived of affection, neglected by her father, and forced by that Fynch woman into learning a fortitude that was unnatural and unnecessary for a girl.

His anger rose: at Puritanism, at the war and the men who created it, at the price paid by the innocent.

Peregrine was partly right about Verity. Often as she had wished to see the world, this--even with God's clear approval--was rather too much change. Robbed suddenly of fortress and refuge (and also everything else but a grumpy scullery maid, a cat and six books) she could perfectly share Naomi's displeasure. Moreover, she did not in the least know what was to become of her, amidst one pack of enemy Royalists, on the way to another. Was she a prisoner? A hostage? She did not at all know.

Peregrine's horse, who bore the amusing name of Hermes, danced sideways and peered back at them with a flirtatious eye. She clutched the fop--Peregrine, his name was--more firmly. It was quite true that she had never ridden pillion, much less had her arms around a man. Except for a rare furtive caress on the shoulder by her father and the gingerly hand of the stable master who taught her archery (and of course the major's blow) she had never known so much as the touch of a male--or ever held conversation even with the stable boys or the godly men she saw in church. Aunt Huldah had frowned upon them all, and Fynch had not disagreed. Riding this way was altogether unsettling--but, she began to realize, disturbingly pleasant.

Satan's doing, no doubt. The maleness her small breasts pressed against was firm and strong and hard, and smelled of horse and herbs. Prevented--not for fear of Satan, but by her painful arms--from holding yet more tightly, she allowed the unslapped side of her face to rest against his doublet.

Peregrine was suddenly touched. Was she so terrified?

Here his sympathy was entirely misplaced, for Verity was not one to brood for long over things that were in God's hands and not hers. She must just brace herself--for only the ginger-haired sergeant and the fop had showed any signs of friendliness; and she was busily composing a new Beatitude to suit the situation. 'Blessed are they who expect the worst, for they shall not be disappointed.' It was, she felt, quite clever. Fynch would have given her the astringent smile that was like sunshine on blooming lavender. Pleased, she almost snuggled.

Peregrine frowned thoughtfully at the just-greening countryside where violets and coltsfoot celebrated the arrival of March, and wondered how best to comfort her. He knew few girls, but those few seemed to like him, even the shy ones. This one seemed far from shy. *Decipit frons prima multos.* But then, she had been defending herself, and any creature became fierce in that case. Now she was silent. He glanced back over his own green-cloaked shoulder at the blue hooded head behind him.

19

"Are you all right?" he asked so kindly that she jerked her face away from his back, her unpurpled cheek flaming with humiliation. How *dare* he pity her?

"I'm unbelievably well and happy, of course!" she said ironically, causing his eyes to widen. "Why would I not be, pray tell?"

Peregrine, blinking slightly, stared across the hills of Wiltshire. Sarcasm was never lost on him: it was simply that he never expected to find it from a frightened girl. Possibly fear was still showing itself as anger? It seemed likely. She needed soothing, then. He smiled reassuringly. "Only a few days until we're there; can you manage?"

Verity flickered startled eyes at the blunt profile half turned to her, and reconsidered. He looked rather like an affable but conceited cat, with those feline-shaped eyes of clear hazel, like green weed and brown pebbles shimmering through brook water. Until now, none of them had bothered to ask her feelings about anything. He really meant well, perhaps. *Amicus certus in re incerta cernitur?* Haply God would make it clear in His own good time. Their eyes met over his shoulder, uncertain.

"Thank you, I can," she said coolly polite. And as if listening, a cloud or two moved aside and the sun shone forth, also uncertain, but warming. Presently both of them pushed their hoods back. The mane of hair sprang from his scalp, so bewitching even with that silly lovelock that she hastily looked away. This, of course convinced him that she was indeed nervous, like the very shy girls whom he put at ease with compliments and talk of fashion. It did not seem very suitable subject matter for a Puritan, blue garments or not. Still... *Fortus fortuna aduvat.*

"That's a very pretty blue," he said. "Did you know it matches your eyes?"

"Well, yes; it's intended to," she explained kindly.

"Oh. I didn't know Puritans were allowed to wear pretty colors."

"Well, they aren't," she informed him tartly. "At least the strict Calvinists aren't, and I suppose that's what you mean by Puritan? Which is just an insult like Roundhead, I suppose you know? *Calvinists* say one mustn't enjoy anything, even beauty, because of graven images and turning their thoughts from God and Salvation. Personally, I think they believe God dislikes beauty; which is silly, because look how much of it He created. I'm surprised," she said sternly to his left ear, "that anyone who pretends to education wouldn't know that."

"I have a classical education," he said humbly. "We don't learn anything practical, you know."

She narrowed her eyes, distrusting that sudden humility--and rightly. It was altogether spurious, and he had been, in fact, studying Law. But he was just now very much enjoying himself, as well as learning something new. He never minded admitting ignorance: only God was expected to know everything. And it was true that Greek and Latin, mathematics, rhetoric and logic all ignored modern politics. Most Royalists assumed that Parliamentarian equalled Puritan equalled Roundhead equalled enemy. This was, he knew, a vast oversimplification. His brother-in-law Evan said that social classes and even religions were in fact quite well divided between king and Parliament. Perhaps in these days a study of politics and religions would have been more practical, even though everyone knew the war would be over by spring. In any case, he enjoyed hearing her opinions.

It was a good thing, for she had not finished with him. "Anyway, it's nothing to do with me, because I'm not one. A Calvinist. Not all Protestants are, you know. That's like confusing dogs and spaniels, or vegetables and cabbages."

He turned further, pretended to fend off an attack. "Help! I surrender! What is your Father, then? Besides dog-vegetable-Protestant?"

"Well, actually, he's an Independent: they want church and government not to meddle with each other, and people to interpret the Bible for themselves. But Aunt Huldah was a Presbyterian. *They* want the church to *be* the government. Theirs, of course. And to make everyone to believe what they do. But Fynch--" Her sentence faltered.

Peregrine caught the hesitation, was too shrewd to apply direct pressure. His eyebrow slanted fascinatingly. "And which are you?"

"I'm an Independent, of course." No need to mention that Fynch had encouraged her in an independence of thinking that would shock even the Independents. She encouraged Verity to challenge *every* idea offered to her (which to Aunt Huldah, would have been sure damnation), to love God's beautiful world, and to read sinful heathen dramatists like Sophocles. She could hardly say this to an enemy, even a polite one.

"I was sure of it," he nodded. "And clearly you are on good terms with God."

How like Socrates! She eyed him for signs of irony, found none. "Well, I'm Saved if that's what you mean. And I have a wondrous strong conscience."

"So of course you are a loyal Parliamentarian, as well?"

Behind his back her eyes narrowed, alert to him. How had this conversation turned Socratic? Did Satan really suppose she could be lured

21

into confiding her dangerously radical views to strangers and Royalists? Or anyone at all? Her face again became set, austere.

"What else would you expect me to be?" she countered, not lying. The Elect never lied: that was one way they knew they were Elected.

Peregrine peered back at her. What was she not-saying? Was she afeared? That Fynch woman had seemed faintly uncanny: could she have been a witch? Sowerbutts said she had known they were coming. Verity should be happy to have been rescued from her and from the danger and loneliness of a deserted house. Given a few more curves, an unpurpled cheek and a little joy, she could, he decided, be quite attractive. The first two being beyond him, he tried for a little lightness of mood.

"You didn't mention Church of England. Are we considered Protestant, too?"

She could actually smile. It was rather a wicked one, which lit her eyes and produced small white teeth and a tiny dimple just below the right corner of her mouth. "Well, of course you are! Didn't you know? Everyone is, who isn't a Papist. After all, 'twas King Henry who started the Church of England when he quarreled with the Pope about his divorce, remember. A hundred years ago. And a bit."

Peregrine stared. Not at what she said: he'd known that, himself; but because of her knowing *any* history. Educated women were very properly taught to read and write English and French, to play on the lute and the virginals, do needlework, dance, and usually to oversee a household. This was surely enough and more than enough. For females, history was not only a useless waste of time; it was harmful to their fragile minds. Take his own sisters. Sweet Cecily was the ideal maiden. Oriel had learned politics from Evan, and become judgmental and froward, and caused a great stir of trouble at Court, and nearly didn't marry at all. For as King James had said, 'to make women learned and foxes tame has the same effect: to make them more cunning.' And in his experience, it was true! He considered Oriel, both of his grandmothers, and Queen Henrietta. He sighed regretfully.

Behind him, Verity frowned in thought. And in the chest on one of the pack horses, Naomi yelled in rage.

She yelled harder when they let her out that night and she discovered that it was raining again. She hated rain. As soon as Verity retired with Peggotty to Major Rawlins' own tiny tent (which he had grumpily surrendered to her) Naomi crawled into the center of the bedding, which she proceeded to hog. At least, Verity slept warmly--despite being mercilessly groomed all night with a tongue far spikier than a cat's tongue had any right to be.

But the rain went on all next day, relentlessly. At last Peregrine challenged Verity to request God to fix it for them.

She eyed him sideways. She disliked taking God for granted or straining His kindness, lest He should take offense and fail to oblige, or even turn into the terrible Jehovah of the Old Testament; and Verity was afraid that her faith in Him might be shaken in either case. Still... It *was* very wet--

"Very well, I'll just ask Him politely." She looked up at the unfriendly clouds. "You do understand, God, it's just a humble suggestion, and not at all telling You what to do, especially considering how obliging You were about Peggotty. But You can see, can't You, that we're most fearsomely wet down here; which You up there in heaven might not entirely have noticed."

The weather improved. Of course one might say, as the major did, that it was bound to improve if only because it had used up all the water up there. Still, Peregrine was impressed.

So, to tell the truth, was Verity.

CHAPTER FOUR

CORFE

It seemed to Verity as if Dorset had somehow been left half-finished. They entered it near Fordingbridge, and now roads were hardly even vague suggestions. Villages were little more. Towns did not seem to exist at all. Here and there were one-room wattle-and-daub farmhouses with faces appearing at doors to stare round-eyed. On closer acquaintance, they became at once terrified and resentful at having food and hay simply taken from them by 'they furriners' in the King's name. It was clear that no army nor any other part of the modern world ever came this way. At a village consisting of three cottages and a mill, a combination blacksmith and miller told them that yonder t'left were Poole Harbor, so best follow t'other road. Then, staring openly, he was bold enough--possibly because of his truly impressive size--to indulge his curiosity.

"Wha be 'ee, then?"

"King's army," said Major Rawlins loftily. "Have any troopers from the Parliament army been along here lately?" Rewarded with a puzzled stare, he explained the facts of the matter.

"Parlyment and t' king *fighting?*" His eyes bulged. "Ee, then, I never knew they two had fallen out!"

It was a long cry from Homer and Ovid! Peregrine's heart sank as he wondered where--and what--on earth he was going to. He did not dream that Verity might be feeling much the same way. How should he? It was beyond conception that a mere female might actually be intelligent.

At last they reached a real village, whose populace were no happier than any at having to provide supplies. But at least one man knew local geography.

"Corfe? Aye, just go on along t'road a bit; 'ee can't miss it." The man eyed the blue scarves which Royalists were beginning to wear across their chests as opposed to the orange scarves of the Parliament army, clearly half-minded to ask about them. But then he seemed to change his mind.

Verity had no such hesitation. But when Peregrine told her that when every regiment wore its own individual colors, no one could tell friend from enemy in the thick of battle; and this way they needed only to identify blue or orange, Verity looked disgusted.

"Well, I should have thought any *child* would have figured *that* out, before they ever started fighting. But then," she added thoughtfully, "mayhap most children are cleverer than most men. Though I wouldn't actually know, because I've never really known any. Of any of them."

As a helpless Victim of Abduction, she lacked meekness.

After a very few miles, the so-called road came face to face with a high ridge of chalk hills, dithered, and began to skirt it eastward. Suddenly, with little warning, it opened like a jaw with a missing tooth, and they stood looking down at a deep cup: a gap in the long range of high hills running from east to west. The entire troop stood still, awed. Forest crept down the sides of the hills into a wide valley below, where, in the hesitant beginnings of spring, a faint green mist appeared, dotted with shrubs and trees and farmland. The bare branches of what seemed to be hazel and elder and hawthorn and budding pussy-willow marked the path of a brook that came from the hills to the southwest. And straight before them, in the middle of that gap--

"Happen that's it," murmured Sowerbutts.

Happen it was! Three or four hills rose from the valley, but one stood alone, high and conical, topped by a formidable castle with a tall keep like an erect nipple on a breast, overlooking and almost hiding a town on the far hillside. Ahead of them, the road became a bridge with two ribbed arches crossing the sizable stream which, having joined the other brook, circled the base of the castle hill and exited here. The two together made a splendid moat--as if one were needed! If ever a castle was invulnerable, Corfe was!

"God's toenails!" breathed Major Rawlins.

"I don't believe He has any," Verity pointed out, but absently; engrossed in the hugeness before her.

"They say it's never been taken," mused Peregrine for Verity's enlightenment. "I suppose that's why King John kept his prisoners in the dungeon there. It really must be impregnable."

"Not against treachery," mused Verity soberly. "I remember now. This is where Edward the Martyr was slain by his stepmother's hirelings."

Peregrine regarded her with faint surprise. "And this is where John starved the knights of Poitou," he added.

Verity shrugged. Probably he was right, but she did not know enough either to debate or concede the point, and Fynch had taught her never to argue without good evidence or at least very strong *a priori* arguments.

They had continued along the road, which, teetering briefly on the very edge of the cup, was trying its best. Soon it plunged recklessly downward into the valley, to amble alongside the stream toward the huge cone, smooth and high and steep, too enormous to comprehend. Another hill rose to the east, and presently there was no room between for even a vagrant road to lose itself; and the castle walls above loomed so high over their right ears that to look up at it stretched everyone's neck painfully. How, Verity wondered, did anyone get up there at all? Somewhere up there a silver robin's song was challenged by the boxwood flute of a blackbird's call.

Before curiosity drove her into lowering her pride by asking, they were past the summit and she could see how the hill became less steep toward the south, and high thick walls, several houses high, shoved themselves along and down, interspersed hugely with towers that were each taller, Verity reckoned, than three or four cottages piled one on another. And even the base of the wall was many houses higher than the stream flowing between hill and road.

Everyone in the party was frankly gawping except the major, whose casual loftiness suggested that he'd seen it many times before. "That'll be the lower bailey up along there," he observed, and turned his attention back to the road, which now hesitated, turned sharply to the right, rose abruptly to the village of Corfe, turned left past a market cross, and continued hopefully on its way to the sea, leaving its followers stranded in the market square.

They stood staring around, at the town hall, a stone cross and a beautiful thirteenth century church with a tall tower in which a clock chimed two. To their left, behind an elegant manor house with a fine bow window, the rest of the hill rose, scattered thinly with cottages. On their right the castle towered above the town like Naomi about to pounce on a smallish beetle. Cottages, an ale house and another manor lined the rest of the square--and all built of golden-blue-gray Purbeck stone, even to the tiled roofs. The town pump and the stocks stood beside the market cross. A few people, some soberly-clad and some in colors, were about: shopping, chatting, fetching water, going in and out of cottages and the alehouse--and in one case, stoically occupying the stocks. All turned to eye the troop of long-haired, lace-trimmed, clearly Royalist soldiers. Some wore heavier frowns than others, but none of them much cared for sojers, they didn't. Any sojers.

The newcomers halted, staring up to the right at that overwhelming crowned green cone. At least three of the party eyed it with mixed feelings. A fourth, unable to see anything from the inside of the chest, had entirely unmixed feelings, and expressed them freely. It was Diggory who (assuming everyone to know more about everything than did he) raised his eyes to the castle, lowered them to the solid row of roofs to their right, and then to the street itself. There seemed no way through.

"How do we get in?" he asked trustingly.

Major Rawlins drew himself up. He had a splendid seat on a horse, and knew it. "Ask the way to the castle entrance," he ordered Sergeant Sowerbutts.

That was quite unnecessary, of course. Since no way through or past those houses had yet appeared, an opening of some sort must, obviously, lie ahead and to the right. QED. Verity and Peregrine had seen this at once. He lifted the reins and let Hermes amble forward, just as Sowerbutts obediently tried to do as he was told.

Since Yorkshire and Dorset dialects were as mutually incomprehensible as Portuguese and Spanish, this was quite a bad idea. The good citizens of Corfe at once changed their expressions from suspicious to alarmed, and closed ranks. The soberly-clad told one another confidently that if they girt furriners weren't actually servants of Satan, them was, at the least, wicked French sent by that there Papist queen to murder us all in our beds. There was little disagreement on that score, for many Royalists also mistrusted the French queen. The trouble was, their sidelong glances confessed, no one felt in a position to do anything about it.

By that time, Hermes had reached the end of the square and the perfectly predictable street to the right. He stood there staring. Verity peered around Peregrine's arm, for his shoulder was too high for her to see over.

"Oh!" she said softly. For the road led slightly downward past a few houses, jogged a little to the right, and became a high bridge resting on tall arches leading across to the double-towered gate of the castle. The hill itself plunged precipitously down to the stream and back up to the vast wall--surely a full thirty feet high--that began at the far end of the bridge ahead and rose to encircle the crown of hill and towered keep that soared above. It was, to say the least, impressive. Hermes rolled one eye back at his riders questioningly, and tossed an eager head.

It never occurred to Peregrine that Major Rawlins might arguably have the right to go first. It would not have mattered if he had. He sat an instant longer, looking. It was probably the strongest , certainly the most beautiful castle he had ever seen. Beauty often made Peregrine want to weep; it did so now. (No one was ever allowed to guess this, of course.)

He pulled himself together, touched Hermes' flank, and they moved ahead, across the bridge, which was sensibly big enough to accommodate large wagons. High over the moat they rode, across the lowered drawbridge, and to the massive front gateway. It was flanked by two huge round towers; and a man-at-arms stood before the lowered portcullis looking mildly interested. Peregrine considered him, eyebrow askew. Impregnable or not, that gate was all but unprotected.

The guard, an elderly man with a whiffly bit of mustache, gazed at their approach round-eyed and then, inspired by Peregrine's confident air, sketched a salute and stepped back to raise the portcullis. They rode on: under the portcullis and the machicolation slot, through a wide passageway with empty guardrooms on either side and a stairway running up the back of the curtain wall, presumably to the top of the tower. Halfway through, Peregrine reined Hermes and looked severely back over his shoulder.

"What's your name, my man? Starling? Well, Starling, you should mend your ways: you're far too trusting. There are enemies all around. I could be a Roundhead spy, you know. Both of us could, and so could those troopers behind us; come to charge right past that portcullis you've just opened and take the castle and murder you all in your beds. I should think Lady Bankes would want you to be far more careful whom you admit."

Starling blinked his confusion and turned newly-suspicious eyes to Rawlins and his troop, now riding across the bridge in brisk annoyance. "Ee, then 'tes a busy day, innit? Best I lower that-there portcullis again, eh?" He did so, and then turned, all militant efficiency, to cross-examine the indignant newcomers.

Hermes and his riders idled on into the outer bailey where they sat staring for a moment, newly awed. It was a grassy rectangle large enough to hold the village square, sloping on and on and on, bright in new grass, where stables and pens and two enormous towers along the right wall were hardly noticeable in the vastness. The ground rose gradually for perhaps half its length, until it stopped dallying, dived into a great ditch running across from wall to wall, and then shot upward again. Above it were two raised banks sporting four impudent little cannons lying off their carriages. From there, the hill rose steeply until it became a rampart, and then shoved itself almost straight up to the middle wall that separated lower from the upper baileys.

On the lush pasture before them, three cows and two horses grazed placidly, and a flock of chickens fussed and pecked with plaintive croaks. A quintet of geese hissed with outstretched necks and wings, but then decided it wasn't worth it, and turned away. To their left, the wall boasted no less than four high towers. A bay mare eyed Hermes, danced her feet coyly, and rolled a merry eye at him. Then Peregrine urged Hermes on along the path, which angled toward the left wall past the towers and a large well, and up to a second bridge and drawbridge and another twin-towered gatehouse. An impudent robin watched them from the top of the nearest wall, and then, intrigued, followed them along it, singing. Behind them came the voice of a furious Major Rawlins, taking God's eyebrows in vain. Peregrine and Verity both smiled contentedly. They had found something in common.

"Besides being fretted at us going first, and having to stop for the portcullis," observed Verity in that cool dispassionate voice she had used since leaving her home, "I do think he's puzzling at how we knew the approach was there."

Peregrine let pass her use of 'we'. He shrugged. "QED," he observed offhanded, and then remembered. "That means--"

"*Quod erat demonstrandum,*" Verity interrupted casually. She seemed to be looking at the robin--or perhaps the massive gate ahead--but her attention was on Peregrine, who looked satisfyingly shocked and suddenly thoughtful.

They reached the second gatehouse, which seemed quite as invincible as the first. Again, the drawbridge that crossed a deep ditch was lowered--but this time the man standing behind the portcullis--lean, wiry, sandy-haired, in his forties--merely smiled. He seemed quite as affable as Starling--but it was a different kind of affability.

"Good day to you, sir," he said, not moving. "My name is Winkworth, and may I enquire yours?"

Hermes stopped. The mare, who had followed, leaned at him kittenishly, and Hermes turned his head with interest. The robin sang more loudly and Peregrine smiled at Winkworth. "I commend you," he said. "This is Mistress Verity Goodchild and I'm Peregrine Lennox, and Lady Bankes expects me but not Mistress Goodchild."

Winkworth narrowed his eyes briefly, nodded to himself. "Got a short leg, then?"

Peregrine displayed another approving smile and thrust the leg forward in the stirrup. "The left one. Perhaps John could come identify me: we know each other."

"No need, sir. Just being careful, you understand." Peregrine did. They both smiled. The robin flew to perch on a branch of the small sallow tree almost within reach, and cast a very interested round black eye on Peregrine's lovelock, hanging temptingly over his left shoulder.

"Want to watch that one," Winkworth advised him. "He--or maybe she-- is bold even for a robin, and just now nest-building, and very fond of hair."

The robin proved this by swooping close, treading air for a moment, and then snatching at the tempting tawny lock. It was fastened down! Peregrine jerked, the robin flew indignantly back to the sallow; and Verity--who was fond of robins but not enough to share her hair with them, hastily covered it with her hood.

Winkworth beamed at them. "Saucy little chap. He don't give up easy, neither." All three glanced back at the outer gate. Some one down there was very angry.

"We're short-staffed, you see. Now, your horse wouldn't want to come no further; why don't we just relieve him of his tackle and let him join Belle, here, in a good graze?" He raised the portcullis and came out to help Verity dismount. "Leave your saddlebags here in the gatehouse; Madam will send some one down for them later. Come through. I'll lower this portcullis again, and wait for--whoever follows you--? Aye, then. I can't leave my post to take you around, nor could I send you up the family's private staircase: Her Leddyship'll do that anon. It goes straight to the state apartments from in there." He nodded at the right tower. Hermes was already frolicking with Belle down to the grazing ground. "You'll be all right walking a bit? Just through and around to your right, there; through the west bailey, and up to the inner ward. There'll be childer or servants around, so just--" He waved his arm.

They walked, Peregrine limping, under another machicolation slot and the portcullis, along an archway, and under a third portcullis to the long flat triangle of the west bailey reaching far to the left, where the robin found and greeted them. The path now rose sharply on the right, and through a narrow gateway up to the inner ward and the keep itself, high atop the peak of that gigantic cone.

The main keep soared some eighty feet above them, solid and towered. Past it was a large kitchen, and what seemed to be a residence arranged around a courtyard or two; and beyond, another towered building. As Winkworth had promised, women and children rushed to meet them.

By then Peregrine had realized that of course Verity had simply memorized a number of common Latin phrases. He did not ask himself why this should be such a relief to him.

CHAPTER FIVE

THE CASTLE

"I cannot believe," said Major Rawlins in a strangled voice, "that you have only four men-at-arms here!"

The Great Chamber was a splendid hall, with windows all along the south wall and a blazing fireplace at once end. The oak paneled walls were hung with gilded green leather, blue silk damask, and Turkish carpets, with crimson velvet everywhere else. Lady Bankes in a chair of that velvet quite dominated the room. She shrugged plump shoulders, looked at him challengingly.

"You may count them at your leisure. Your troopers would be a very welcome addition." She pointed a long strong chin and nose at him encouragingly. Hordes of children ranged alongside her--or perhaps it was really only a dozen or so plus a fretful cradle? They stared with interest at the major, who was struggling for suitable words, and at Peregrine, Verity and Peggotty, who were being invisible near the door. Peggotty was simply and grumpily Not There. Peregrine was being quietly observant. He had delivered the letters from Oxford, and he was now wishing with little hope that the lovely girl in rose damask might be Elizabeth, his future bride. He was also dropping any notions of helping Lady Bankes run the castle. She was clearly running it very well, and probably never asked advice about anything from anyone.

Verity, again feeling very much surrounded by enemies, carefully noticed everything, careful not to look as awed as she felt. She had never seen nor even imagined such richness! A large table inlaid with--was it mother-of-pearl?--was covered with a rich Turkish carpet, and, shockingly! there was another right down on the stone floor where it was in danger of being walked on!

The children and two young ladies were like a sea of velvet and brocade, lace and ribands, in every shade of flower and jewel: lilac and jonquil; jade, ruby and sapphire. (It was a marvel if they were all hers, for childbirth was a dangerous business for both mother and child. None of Verity's siblings had lived, and in the end, neither had her mother.) She looked wide-eyed at the girls' long full damask gowns: the bright crewel-embroidery and the slashed sleeves. None but the youngest wore caps to hide the beauty of long silken ringlets hanging over their shoulders. Almost, Verity fell into the sin of envy. Then she remembered her dignity, pulled sternly upright, and studied her chief enemy.

It was a confusing face. A commanding nose and jaw bracketed a mouth that might have caused a charging bull to veer off, and which certainly made the major look uneasy. But glossy dark ringlets surrounded soft pink cheeks and large melting brown eyes like Homer's ox-eyed Hera. Verity did not know which part of the face to believe, and this made her wary.

The children clearly felt the same about her. Almost every face was staring with dark suspicion--except, possibly, for the occupant of the cradle-- and she could not be sure even of that. She did not think she would like them any better than they did her. She was indeed in a nest of vipers! She became a Foxe's Martyr again: slim and still and courageous. Major Rawlins was still explaining that he was on the King's Business and could not possibly spare any of his men; particularly, he added (contradicting himself) since four soldiers were obviously enough for such an impregnable castle.

The melting dark eyes became commanding dark eyes. "We'll discuss the King's orders to you later. You will stay here for a few days. I shall need your help putting my four small cannon on their carriages. And you'll reinforce the gates and the sallyport, and a few other details of defense. You will go get supplies, too. At the very least, you'll bring enough to replace what your men eat. After all--" Her voice was as soft and gentle as the rising tide, and the major closed his teeth on what he had been about to say. "--you do realize that this may be His Majesty's only really secure stronghold on the entire south coast? They say Sir Walter Erle is rampaging all over the south, and has taken--or may soon do so--Dorchester, Lyme, Melcombe, Weymouth, even Poole. Wareham and Corfe can not supply us with as much as we shall need, so you will go further north to Royalist-held lands. Flour, root vegetables, a great deal of smoked meat and cheese, live poultry, cattle, sheep; grain, fodder, arms, gunpowder, ale, wine: whatever else you can find."

"But--" he spluttered. Peregrine smiled quietly to himself.

"And please remember," she added, her voice dulcet and her chin ruthless, "that my husband is Sir John Bankes, the King's Lord Chief Justice. His Majesty would certainly--approve--of all the help you will surely give me, don't you think? We have vast space for all your troop and their horses. The stables are down in the outer bailey, and the soldiers' quarters are in the New Bulwark; you may go settle them and then return for dinner. That meal alone will, of course, use up much of our stores."

Silently wondering what on earth the world was coming to, and cursing the fate that had saddled him with all these forceful females, the major strode past the sulking chest holding yet another of them, and grumped himself down several steep stone flights of steps.

The cradle yelled despite being rocked by its buxom wet-nurse. The assorted eyes now focussed entirely on Peregrine and Verity. Only John, a tall slender young man of seventeen with his father's sandy hair, twinkled at Peregrine, and said not a word.

"Welcome, Peregrine Lennox," said his mother. "Who's this with you?"

A chorus of children out-yelling the cradle informed her. "'Tis a Roundhead, Mama; just look at her!" "An enemy!" "Mama, should we not put her in the dungeon where Eleanor lived?" "Send her away, Mama; she mustn't stay here."

"Of course she'll stay," said their mother briskly.

"Am I a prisoner?" demanded Verity, equally brisk.

"Well, that depends. Are you our enemy?"

Verity considered. It was true she was not a Royalist--but she would not hate people simply because of differing opinions: only for what they did. "How can I tell? I don't even know you."

The children at once started up again. "Mama, she *is* an enemy! She'll burn the keep around us!"

Their mama looked at Verity with arched brows. "Would you?"

Thanks to Fynch's training, Verity was quick-witted at debate. "I shouldn't think so," she replied thoughtfully. "Well, for one thing, I'm not stupid. The castle is all stone, so it probably wouldn't burn; and if it did, t'would burn me, as well."

A good point. But was she an enemy? They all considered in silence, eyeing her white cap and apron and fichu, and the plainness of her dress--and also her inflexible eyebrows. It was true, many Protestants favored the king; still--

"That major said your father's a rebel colonel," said a sharp-faced child in a sea-water green gown, accusingly.

A young woman in cinnamon brocade that set off her brown curls came to the heart of it. "Do you support King Charles?"

Verity's sharp cheekbones jutted, and she looked narrow-eyed at the splendid portrait on the wall before her that surely must be Queen Henrietta. "Well, if you mean do I believe that he has Divine Right to throw out Parliament and rule like God, no I don't. I think nobody but God has the right to rule like God, and sometimes I'm not so sure about Him, considering some of the things in the Bible."

That was undoubted *laese majestas*, and probably sacrilege as well. Peregrine exchanged a woeful glance with John and rolled his greenish eyes skyward. She was going to do it again, wasn't she? And with her face still bruised from last time! She was as intractable as his elder sister, now that he thought of it--save that Oriel, sweetly candid and beautiful as a cat, usually got away with it. Verity was like a stoat: lean and truculent, with more pluck than sense, scorning tact or even self-preservation. Her short chin managed to look almost as aggressive as Her Ladyship's long one. The fact that Peregrine privately agreed with Verity on that point was irrelevant; *he* had enough sense to keep it private, even among his own family. (*Especially* among his own family, who were mostly uncritical Royalists.)

The Bankes children looked confused and angry. Their mother's formidable chin rested thoughtfully upon a plump bejeweled hand. "Interesting," she said. "But consider *our* viewpoint. We see Parliament as a mob of rebels who are trying to wrest power from a divinely anointed king. Do you really approve of that?"

It almost sounded like Fynch, starting one of their intellectual debates on Vergil or Aristotle or Galileo's dispute with the Pope, in which they would presently switch sides because of Verity needing to be able to argue all points of view. This time, of course, it was real and not just practice. Nor would she, of course, mention any of her own radical ideas. Nevertheless, Verity found herself in the familiar pattern.

"It all depends," she said sagely. "on whether you believe he *was* divinely anointed."

Peregrine tried distraction. "He was certainly anointed," he drawled. "Says the sacred oil was rancid. Probably left over from Queen Bess."

As a distraction it was not very successful. John grinned, but the others just blinked and kept their attention on Verity, who clearly had not finished. "You can't argue it *a priori*," she went on, "because it's not self-evident. So it comes back to everyone reasoning perfectly logically from their own basic assumptions and coming to opposite answers. But," she finished, forgetting her cautious intent, "I personally think *Vox popula, vox Dei* is an interesting notion.*"

She had never meant to say as much. But the blank silence suggested that, surprisingly, no one understood except Peregrine and John and just possibly--a bit--the next-oldest boy. Was this what Fynch meant, then, when she said females were no longer educated?

Peregrine, was thanking heaven for it. Did the chit know she had said 'The voice of the people is the voice of God'? He doubted it. Not even she-- Just something that Fynch woman had made her learn by heart He must warn her. Not that it would do any good, of course ...

"A scholar, as well as a Parliamentarian," observed Lady Bankes dryly. "Still, I do think putting you in the dungeon would be inconvenient for everyone. We might just keep you with us and leave your status undefined? Would you run away if we leave you unchained?"

"I dare say Father would expect me to," said Verity frankly. "But I doubt whether I would. Well, for one thing God let me be brought here, and He hasn't even hinted that I should run away, so I must suppose this is where He wants me. And for another, where would I go?"

Where indeed? The children frowned. They clearly harbored a few ideas which it was perhaps better not to mention. "She could stay in the town, Mama," suggested the next oldest boy, a lad of perhaps twelve. "There are lots of Roundheads there. She could stay with any of them."

"She's gentry, Ralph," objected John. "She couldn't live with commoners."

"Well, she could stay at the alehouse. 'Tis almost an inn: you said so yourself. Soames has a fine suite he rents out. She should be with her own kind. Shouldn't she, Bess?"

He turned, not to the young woman wearing cinnamon, but the one in deep rose, with cheeks to match, mahogany curls, an air of utter sweetness, and the loveliest face Peregrine had ever seen. Bess? His future wife? He could not believe his--possible--good fortune! (Verity for her part felt instantly and strongly that she and Bess were destined never to be friends.)

"I think," said Bess with an angelic smile, "that we should treat her as a guest and ask her."

There was a brief silence. Bess's siblings frowned at her. "Oh, *Bess!*"

But before more could be said, another opinion was heard. "YOWRRRW!" raged the chest at the door.

The hostile faces became eager ones. "What is it?" "Oh, 'tis a pussycat!" "Where is it? Who--"

"You have a cat?" For the first time, Lady Bankes sounded approving. "A mouser?" Verity nodded. "We very much need one: the old tom died, and this castle is overrun."

"She's a very good mouser," said Verity. "Her name is Naomi, she's been in the chest for days and she hates it, and she doesn't much like the food she's been getting, either: she likes mice better. If we let her out--"

Everyone but the whining cradle took a step toward the chest. "Not yet," said Lady Bankes, quietly quelling. "If she's to stay, we need to keep her shut in for a while, until she understands that this is her new home. As small a room as possible; for, to a cat, small is safe." Verity blinked sudden respect-- on that point, anyway. "I'll put you both in the room at the top of the queen's tower: it has a secure door and, I'm sure, mice aplenty." (She did not say on which side the door would be secured.) "If you wish to stay as enemy-guest, that is, Mistress Goodchild. Do you?"

There was not a great deal of choice. The townsfolk had not looked very friendly. At least she knew Peregrine. She curtseyed and nodded.

"Welcome, then," said her hostess. "You will join my older daughters in training to run a household, and in needlework. We do all the mending and sewing for the entire staff, of course. The maidservants do the cleaning and cooking. And you'll learn music and French." (Verity had seldom even heard music: Aunt Huldah considered it Ungodly.) "I take it, you read and write?" Lady Bankes added blandly. Verity opened her mouth, looked at the chatelaine's face--and held her tongue, merely curtseying again. "Excellent. You may both, if you like, use my husband's library. He has a magnificent collection of books." She seemed not to notice Verity's and Peregrine's expressions, which were suitable to newly-dead souls being shown into heaven. Probably she noticed very well indeed. This was a lady who would notice everything. "And welcome, Peregrine. You'll share the other tower with the boys. John will show you. Do you want your maid with you, Verity?" She looked doubtfully at Peggotty, who did seem a most unlikely choice.

"No!" said Verity promptly. "She came as my chaperone, but--"

Peggotty roused from her dismals to make a pronouncement. "I be no shapper-thing; no, nor no lady's maid, neither. I be scullery maid, is what I be."

"Most excellent!" said Lady Bankes. "You'll be very welcome indeed! Cook will be delighted: Grissel hates it and does it badly. She's much better at general cleaning."

Verity smiled at Peregrine and tried once more to destroy certain illusions that he clearly harbored. "*Lupus pilum mutat, non mentet,*" she observed brightly.

It was wasted effort. No one can be as obtuse on occasion as the highly intelligent. He merely decided firmly that the Fynch woman had made her memorize far more quotations than could be good for a maiden. But Lady Bankes eyed her sharply. I'll take you to your chamber," she said only. "'Tis above mine. Two of the men will bring your chests anon."

36

Lady Bankes' own sitting room was a luxurious one, dominated by a wide bed and canopy of dainty white dimity delicately embroidered in black. Verity blinked. Her hostess looked amused.

"You're quite right; not my taste. Lady Hatton lived here before my husband bought it, and she was a lady of Venus rather than of Mars. Sold the main guns to buy frippery like this, the witling! Howsomever," she added, walking right across the fine Turkey carpet that was spread at her feet, "the carpeting and the use of it is mine. Feel how warm it makes the floor! I always did think it a pity to put carpets on walls, even if they do keep out the draft. Worse, to waste them on tables. I understand the Turks *intend* them to be walked on, and think we are quite mad. Come, girl; unless you intend to produce wings and fly over them, you'd best get used to it." She went to pause at the window. "Have you ever been so high? No, of course not: who in England has? Bess and Joan and Jennet sleep above me, and you'll have the chamber above them. Best find out now if it makes you giddy. Come look."

At one window, Verity looked out across some castle rooftops to the northeast, a view of water and city, and hills beyond. "Poole and Poole Harbor," said the lady with narrowed eyes, and then turned to the south window. Verity, with a mental shrug joined her.

To the south, beyond the coastal hills, she could glimpse a slab of blue. It must be the sea! She had never seen the sea. There it lay, cobalt-colored, suddenly turning gray under a sky that could not make up its mind. And then she looked down--and swallowed.

She had never imagined such a height! The wall plunged from the window straight down--and down--and *down*, before it reached even the top of the outer bailey, where it hurtled yet further down. There were the cannons, lying like toys on the ground beside their carriages, and yet another drop to the ditch, the grazing livestock like small toys, and the outer gatehouse, and the hill still descended beyond that to the moat. 'Twas unbelievable! Terrifying!

Lady Bankes was watching her closely, those deceptively soft brown eyes very watchful.

"Well?" she challenged.

Verity leveled her short chin.

"Very pretty," she said.

CHAPTER SIX

THE CHATELAINE

"Well, 'twill have to do," Lady Bankes told the major. "Slightly more than you've consumed. One more cow, three sheep, lambs, rabbits, more chickens and geese. I'd have wished more bacon and cheese and grain: they keep well; but no doubt you did your best. At least rabbits multiply well. Thank you for mounting the gun carriages. Have you checked the portcullises and drawbridges? The outer drawbridge raises flush with the wall now? Yes? Good. Now, how many men will you leave with me?"

Major Rawlins, who had been feeling lately that he truly hated all females, even his own meek wife, burst into protest. "Madam! Lady Bankes! I told you before, these are King's men, and I can't simply hand them out: I've not even enough for myself. We were at great risk getting these supplies for you, with the rebels all--" He stopped. He should not have said that! He looked at Lady Bankes' smile, which reminded him of a sword, though her voice was as pleasant as always.

"Quite," she said.

"But you don't need-- This is as impregnable as the Tower of London! You'll be perfectly safe in here!"

"Not if we starve," she pointed out. "Despite your talk of urgent duties, I'm well aware that your orders are to report back to Oxford betimes. I have three letters for you to deliver: one from Peregrine to his family, one from me to my husband, and one to His Majesty urging him to send us provisions and reinforcements at once, for we will surely be attacked sooner or later."

Peregrine listened with wonder and an angled eyebrow. Lady Bankes must surely know that King Charles was totally undependable. He dithered when he should act, and became mulish when he should negotiate. Peregrine, for one, would not be counting upon much help. Still--one could hope that King Charles might just for once listen to the always-good advice of Sir John Bankes.

"Now, again, Major Rawlins; who else will you leave for me?"

Rawlins, as always, was having trouble accepting defeat from a woman. "But--"

To everyone's surprise, Sergeant Sowerbutts spoke up. "I'd as lief stay, Sir. Happen I'd be better defending t'castle than riding horseback, choose

38

how. Getting old, tha see'st. Eh, m'rheumatics is nobbut aches." He looked forlorn. Verity and Peregrine regarded him with faint amusement. There was no gray at all in that ginger thatch, and he had seemed fine until now. Rawlins looked suspicious. Still, if he could get away with losing only Sowerbutts--it was a better outcome than he'd feared. He nodded, failed to notice a flicker of satisfaction sidle across Sowerbutts' weathered face, turned on his heel, and presently the troop had descended to the main gate, heads down in the cold driving rain.

Peregrine and the others watched them go from the southwest gatehouse, standing between the two three-story towers. The wall that separated outer bailey from west bailey ran from the inner tower up the steep hill to vanish into the wall of the keep It was both high and wide, and the stairs that Winkworth had mentioned must run inside, starting from that door at the base of the tower.

The door groaned open just then to eject Captain Bond, tanned and dour with a limp to match Peregrine's, and herding four children.

"Found 'em up th' tower," said Bond, presenting them to their mother.

"I was about to send for you," she said, immobilizing the culprits with a glance. "Will you show Peregrine and Sowerbutts all the details of the castle, and explain the routine? They can start taking duty tomorrow. Jerome, Bridget, Edward, take Charles back to the nursery; you know you're not supposed to use that staircase without permission. You've all earned a thrashing. No, go around by the west ward. And run: I expect you there before me. Verity, come with me; we have a conversation to finish."

She led up the steep stairs, which plunged directly into the second floor of the keep. From there they took a covered passageway into another building. "King John built this and called it the Gloriette," Her Ladyship observed. "Then King Edward redesigned it to make it a more comfortable dwelling. He called this the King's Hall. We usually call it the Great Chamber."

Clearly it was now a general family room. It ran along nearly the entire south side and was filled with large fireplace, woven or embroidered tapestries, and fine portraits, which Lady Bankes said proudly were mostly by Lely and Van Dyck. Since Aunt Huldah deplored ungodly artists, Verity had never heard of them, and was suitably astonished. She stared even harder at more crimson velvet, deep window seats, and embroidered cushions. The room otherwise was filled with tables, stools, toys, one armchair, a spinning wheel, and three of the children. At the sight of their mother, they all produced instant almost-visible haloes and their needlework or hornbooks. The other four had not arrived, and their mother did not look astonished.

"Joan! Charles and the Trio are running around loose. Fetch Charles back here and send the Trio to their duties: the tables want setting, and for their sins they must do't alone, *and* help with the clearing up, and for four days. Then to the kitchens with *you*. You'd wed one day and never able to supervise a household?"

Joan curtseyed, but her pretty face puckered and she murmured something about the woes of being an elder child. Lady Bankes did not argue, nor wait to see if her orders would be obeyed: they would. She just turned to Verity.

"We'll be private in my chamber," said that sweet implacable voice, and its owner led the way past that tempting library to the family chambers, and up those steep stone stairs to the master suite. They stared out the south window in silence.

"I think we did not finish our discussion about King versus Parliament. You said you do not approve of one man having sole power. But do you not think a group of, say, a hundred men having sole power to be a hundred times worse?"

Verity, who had had this discussion before, with Fynch's nephew, almost smiled. For Master Lilbourne passionately believed rule by Parliament to be mere half-measures. *All* men, he said, should vote and rule, and all law should be writ down for all to know, not at whim of any judge or ruler.

But it was not John Lilbourne beside her now, who wished all people well except tyrants like kings and aristocrats, and with whom she could safely debate. She might personally feel that a parliament out of hand was in fact only slightly less dangerous than a king out of hand--but this was the Lady Enemy in her own stronghold, and Verity did not feel inclined to give any comfort to the enemy--nor lose the debate, either. She frowned at the staggering view before her, conceded a small point.

"Well, Madam, perhaps, if all the hundred were evil, which I doubt, and if all agreed. But they never would. How could they? *Quot homines, tot sententiae--*" She stopped, glanced sidelong at the impassive face beside hers, decided that a translation would make things even worse, and changed her quotation to a Bible one. "'In the multitude of counsellors there is safety.' They have to make compromises, and that means--well, it *should* mean-- they'll not agree on anything that's too extreme. One king ruling alone--he can. He can order anything he likes without asking anyone."

Lady Bankes had turned her head and was looking at her, brown eyes keen. "Even though you're wrong, you *have* thought on it, haven't you? That surprises me. Few people do even in normal times, much less during war. How old are you?"

"Nearly seventeen." Verity met her gaze, suddenly missed Fynch horribly, turned back to the view, her throat stiff, and--since God did not deign to warn her against it--found herself again saying more than she intended.

"My governess-- I did dialectic with her a lot. And learned to--well-- dissect opinions. And argue both for and against, to see which side held up best. She said I had to train my judgment. Sometimes her nephew--well, great-nephew, I think--came to visit and brought news and we debated things. He said no one wants to give an inch. Especially the king, who says he doesn't ever have to. He says he's the sole decider, and everyone, even Parliament, must obey whatever he orders. Like slaves. So he's worse. Much worse. He's a tyrant."

Lady Bankes looked enigmatic: the brows were arched, the large round chin like steel. It would be a wonder if she did not, after all, have Verity thrown into the dungeon (which, it turned out, was under the westernmost tower, casually called Dungeon Tower, and not the keep). Still, she did not seem angry enough for that--though it was hard to tell, with all her features contradicting one another as they did. Verity decided that the role of enemy-guest was likely to prove very difficult, so she looked out the window again. She could just see, over the roofs, the market cross and the far half of the town square, where, now that the rain had eased, people went about their business.

They watched together for a moment. "Make friends in Corfe Village," commanded the lady.

Verity's head snapped around to stare at her, eyes wide and blue under brows that virtually met. "Why, Madam?" Her voice had dropped a note.

"Because I think you should. That includes Mayor Bastwick, who is, of course, also Magistrate."

She glinted her eyes. "Why? Which side is he on?"

"That, you must learn for yourself. I shall send you there to shop there for the castle, as well. What provisions our tenants can't furnish us, we buy at the markets at Corfe and elsewhere: especially fresh food, for there's little in the castle garden now. We forever need meat and poultry, oysters and fish, fruit and herbs, and so forth. Rawlins' men ate almost more than they replaced. A few of the Puritans believe it wrong to sell to Royalists. You will go into Corfe looking virtuous and disapproving as you can do so well, and especially with your plain garb and bruised cheek; and I think those people will warm to you, which would be good for all." The profiled long nose and chin turned at last. "You might find your own kind."

"Well, I must say," announced the shocked Verity, "if Starling was too trusting letting us in at once just because Peregrine acts like a royal prince, you're even more so. Trusting, I mean. You *know* I'm against the king, and you're practically inviting me to-- well, I could spy on you and tell them about everything I see or hear in the castle!"

"But would you? Tell me, girl, how strong are your loyalties to Parliament? What are you willing to do for them?"

It was an important question. She took her time about answering. "I think what you're really asking, Madam, is if I would betray your hospitality or do something to harm you. Well, no, I wouldn't. Not even if I could. How should I? The Elect simply don't behave that way! 'For I was a stranger and ye took me in,' and I've eaten your bread and salt. But if I make friends in the village--"

"The villagers," observed Lady Bankes, "are in an awkward situation. They've been friends with us ever since my husband bought the castle back in 1634, eight or nine years ago now. Any differences in religion and politics didn't matter: no one dreamed of civil war then. Now, it does matter to some, and it's an unpleasant choice: friendship or principles. If you make friends with them, you could, of course, find yourself in much the same position. It's up to you."

Verity frowned. She could almost feel her cheekbones grow even sharper. One of them was still fading purple and yellow and green. Lady Bankes was, she began to suspect, deep and subtle and more than a little sly; and Verity did not feel inclined to follow any suggestions of hers at all. On the other hand, it might be nice to meet people who were not The Enemy. She murmured something wary and noncommittal, and tested her feelings for a Godly hint. But He sent no sense either of comfort or discomfort. She scowled.

"You'll go in the next day or so," said the lady, taking the scowl for submission. "Wear your most sober gown." And Verity, for once, did not feel like arguing. She was eating their food, wasn't she? She curtseyed. But she did not have to like being used and ordered around, and she didn't.

A doorway covered with a watchet damask hanging opened to the tower landing. From up the tower stairs, a small imperious voice announced that the mice up there had unfairly run away, and Naomi was now quite ready to go find some more. She pushed her head through the hanging, left eyebrow a pale apricot, perfectly groomed as always, and sauntered into the bedroom.

Sniffed the carpet, approved, stepped onto it, studied her hostess and pushed her shoulders all the way around those mulberry velvet skirts.

"She swears," Verity warned as Lady Bankes stooped to scritch around the silken ears. "She asks for petting, and purrs and kisses, and then she swears."

"Indeed?" Pudgy fingers simply moved down to jaw and throat, which stretched out in blissful compulsion. Naomi turned her head to kiss the fingers, and then, feeling that her dignity had been weakened, stopped purring and swore. (Verity was not the only one to be a great believer in dignity.) Her ladyship failed to jerk an alarmed hand away. "Naughty poppet," she murmured, and rubbed just above that peach eyebrow.

Naomi stiffened under the impudent fingers, purred again, caught herself, snarled.

"She can swear and purr at the same time," Verity pointed out.

"Indeed." Lady Bankes began working her fingers down both sides of the cat's backbone. Naomi's tail shot skyward and she undulated. Her shoulders arched, then her spine, and finally her narrow rump rose so high that her back toes fairly lifted off the ground. Being a fair-minded cat, she kissed the fingers again, and then waited. She understood all about taking turns, did Naomi. Again, and a full-throated purr harmonized with a full-throated curse. Verity stared astonished as the ecstatic cat turned and began to groom Her Ladyship's hand lovingly. (It was a good thing animals were not expected to be governed by Divine Reason.)

"I presume she's all bark and no bite?"

"She bites if you touch her feet."

"I shall remember that," Lady Bankes promised, "but I never worry about mere verbal abuse." She withdrew her abraded hand from that spiny tongue. The outraged Naomi lashed her tail, hissed, stalked into the sitting-room, clearly thought little of it, and turned back to the stairs.

"You may leave," Lady Bankes ordered Verity. "Try to make friends with my children. If you can. They'll be in the Great Chamber. Do you remember how to get there? Down the stairs and along the passage on the left. I would suggest that calling their king a tyrant was not, perhaps, the happiest beginning."

Verity met her hard look with one of her own, chin and brows level, blue eyes unyielding. "Well, you *did* ask me," she pointed out. "And I never lie." Then she turned and went down the stairs, leaving Naomi to follow if she chose.

The Great Chamber was filled with children, together with the plump Lucy (Lady Bankes' personal maid) the fretful cradle, and the buxom young wet-nurse. They were all busy: doing needlework, reading, playing games, cuddling dolls, squabbling over toy soldiers, settling the squabbles, and rocking the cradle. Verity felt no great interest in that cradle, but just for curiosity, (she already knew what it sounded like) she crossed the room and stood looking down.

Predictably, it was a baby. Round head with a little fine hair on it. Button nose. She knew nothing of babies, and cared very little. She was about to turn away when she realized that every eye was fixed upon her, and that her future status with this family might well depend on what she did at this moment. Cock's bones! What, prithee, was she supposed to say? She looked down at it again. Baby. Pink face. Wide open mouth. Feet vigorously kicking the tight swaddling around them as if trying to be free. Again, curiosity took over.

"Is it all right? I mean, wrapping its'-- his--"

"'Tis a boy," piped a small child that could also have been either boy or girl, for they all dressed the same at that age, in long full skirts to the feet, and shoulder-length hair. Verity decided not to reveal ignorance again so soon.

"His, then," she agreed. "Is it right to wrap him all tight together like that?"

Well, how was *she* to know? She certainly could not remember her own babyhood. Still, if she had not avoided appearing ignorant, at least she had smashed the dour silence. In a chorus, they assured her that it was not only all right: 'twas necessary.

Ah, well; in for a penny, in for a sovereign. She abandoned dignity in her need to challenge. "Why?" she asked.

Blank silence was followed by a new and perplexed babble. It seemed that no one knew the reason; it was merely an Absolute Truth. Like the sun circling the earth, say, or the Divine Right of Kings. Since Verity had no faith at all in the second and was undecided about the first, she was about to push the challenge; but then paused. Lady Bankes' had told her to make friends with them. Looking around, she began for the first time to see individuals. Not too many to take in, for the older ones were not here. Only--six? No, seven, and the baby.

"Never mind," she shrugged. "What's his name, then?" She jerked her head at the cradle.

The poppet in sea-water-green damask, with pale cheeks, thick oak-brown hair falling down her back, and her mother's challenging chin, answered. "He's Will. He cries a lot. More than Arabella did. He grizzles."

44

Grizzles? Verity's eyebrows arched. At least three children chose to educate her. "Yurra-yurra-yurra," they whined in unison, sounding just like the cradle.

Oh. The green damask child tilted her head, decided that Verity understood, and pointed at a toddler with round red cheeks, fair curls and bunchy pink skirts. "That's Arabella. She's nearly three. She gets into things, and she talks a private language that no one can understand except Charles." She nodded at the other unbreeched child. "But he usually won't tell. He won't tell anything, much. He's four. He's stubborn. That's Ralph on the window seat: he's twelve, and he's clever but irr-- doesn't do his chores. And there's the Terrible Trio. Jerome's eight and Bridget's seven and Edward's just been breeched now he's six." They looked up with identical expressions of angelic purity. Jerome boasted a mop of gorgeous curls, Bridget's dark hair and innocent ox-brown eyes were much like her mother's, and Edward had sandy hair, rosy cheeks and long lashes. "They're very wicked," went on the merciless child, and casually ducked a flying fist. "Edward snoops--"

"A healthy curiosity," said Nurse Maud fondly.

"--and Bridget tells tarradiddles--"

"Such a good imagination!"

"And the one with all the curls is Jerome. He's more conceited than you can believe."

"But he's so beautiful," cooed the nurse.

Actually, Jerome had little beauty beyond his hair, for his face was oddly long for a child, and his mouth was too small for that wedge of a chin. Still, he was clearly content with himself. He preened, and gave Verity a superior glance. She returned it, unimpressed. A new challenge had just occurred to her. "Why," she asked, "do small boys always dress like girls?"

This time there was wary silence. This one asked questions no one ever thought of. They decided it was best to ignore them. The green child took a breath and continued her tally of siblings.

"John's seventeen, and he thinks he knows everything because of going to Oxford. Molly is a grown-up. She's twenty and she's to marry Sir Robert Jenkinson, but she says how could Madam Mother possibly handle us all without her? I wish Mother could. Molly's a sore scold. She's down in the kitchen now making Bess and Joan learn to manage a household. Bess doesn't want to. She wants things always to be easy and fun; and she believes everything anyone tells her! Even lies. Like Bridget's. Bess is sixteen, and Joan's fourteen, and Joan tries to be a femme fatale, and she flirts with everyone, even old Short."

Verity fixed her with a glinting blue eye. "And what of you?" she challenged.

The child met it with fierce hazel eyes, and brows not unlike Verity's. "I'm Jane and they call me Jennet, and I'm ten years old, and I'm quite horrible. When I get angry, I kick people, and I often say things best left unsaid. Like you did when you came. About the King."

Touché! Verity's hidden dimple appeared briefly, and she regarded the dreadful child with an odd twinge of fellow-feeling. She could, she felt, get to like her. A sense of wicked humor, never before encouraged, began to rise. "Your mother thinks you'll always be angry with me because I said I don't approve of him. King Charles."

They agreed instantly, in a clamor of assent.

Verity suddenly fell into the role and even the manner of Socrates--or at least of Fynch Socratically baiting a younger Verity before she had yet learned the game.

"Lackaday! You would have me lie?"

Everyone shook shocked heads except Bridget, the tarradiddle-teller, who produced her mother's sly smile.

"But did your mother not ask me what I thought of the king?"

Innocently, they all agreed except Jennet, who chewed a finger and looked wary.

"I see. But then, if I don't lie to your mother, you would have me be rude and refuse to answer her questions?" She was by now feeling exactly like Socrates. Unfortunately, it was quite wasted, for they all--even Nurse and Lucy--innocently agreed that of course she should not be rude to Madam. Verity sighed. None would understand the trap they had just fallen into, even had she explained it to them. She wished for Fynch, gave up the baiting, saw Jennet's suspiciously puckered brows, and gave her a challenging grin.

Jennet returned it with an engaging scowl. "*I* think you're laughing at us behind your face," she announced accusingly. "That's not the way for a guest to behave."

"Even an enemy guest?"

Jennet considered it. Bridget announced that Madam Mama had said Verity was to abide in the dungeon under the tower. In chains. Verity observed briskly that her tarradiddles were too silly for remark. Bridget looked shocked. Nurse said they should all try to get along, that the sky had cleared, and that it was time for Charles' and Arabella's naps.

Somehow, the air had cleared as well as the sky. They trooped down the stairs and into the courtyard between the massive keep and the kitchen--and found Naomi there ahead of them, energetically looking into some interesting holes.

The new recruits had finished their tour. Here at the high north-east corner of the inner ward, they faced a large garden. Behind them rose the gloriette and the main living quarters--including chapel, new kitchen block (the old one being over in the keep) bakery, wine cellar, two separate courtyards--and the royal apartments: king's hall, king's presence chamber, long chamber, king's chapel and queen's chamber. It was confusingly impressive.

"Tis new, the gloriette," Captain Bond had remarked casually. "Not above four hunnert years, they say. Household water comes from the upper well, here. Ye saw the one in t'lower bailey for the livestock."

They stood studying that well. There was a four-foot rim around it and a grate over the top--altogether needful with so many children. But-- Peregrine frowned. How deep was the water source? The floor of this inner ward must be some two hundred feet above the valley floor. And Castle Hill must be near-solid rock, to have held the weight of the castle for so long.

Sowerbutts peered down into the blackness, shook his ginger thatch. "Eh, lad, however didst tha dig this-here well?"

Captain Bond shrugged, his craggy face uninterested in anything not of immediate practical importance. "Don't know. 'Twasn't me. They reckons 'twas dug when the first fort were built, and that's maybe six-eight hunnert years. Any road, there's no way an enemy could get to it to stop the water or poison it, even did they know where it was. Well, ye've seen it all, now, and can start your duties tomorrow. He nodded at Peregrine. No one mentioned limps. They both had them. One made do with the body the Good Lord gave one.

The robin appeared, triumphant, and made another impressive snatch at Peregrine's lovelock. Peregrine ducked. It looked as if he would get considerable practice as this. Bond, disdaining the bird as frivolous, ignored it.

"Dare say Master John will give you his workaday clothing: 't should fit you, and him not needing it when he gets to the University. And Sowerbutts here, he'll leave off the military boots for working, and that royal sash when he goes into the village. No point fussing them few hard Puritans out there more'n needful, M'Leddy says."

"Happen I could--" began Sowerbutts

Peregrine missed the rest of it. A pair of charming English flowers had emerged from the kitchen, haloed in daffodil and pale blue taffetas, sweet smiles, dark ringlets and large baskets. The younger--Joan, was it?--eager to be recognized as a woman, batted long lashes coyly over plump cheeks. But there was no coquetry in Bess: she was simply, delightfully, happy to see him. Huge brown eyes smiled into his under perfectly arched brows and dark lashes. Her nose was short and straight, her mouth soft and full and adorable, her face a pure oval.

"Give you good day, Master Lennox. Cook sent us to see if the troopers left any cabbages or parsnips. I shouldn't think they did, really, should you? They had such splendid appetites!" Joan giggled. Bess looked at least as severe as a baby bunny. "It was very interesting having them all here, you know: we don't usually get any excitement or even news, and I'd love to hear about Oxford some day! But they did eat a lot, didn't they? All those troopers?"

Unlike the posing Joan, she was unselfconsciously enchanting. Peregrine blithely agreed that troopers ate a lot, and added that he'd be delighted to tell her all the news about Oxford and the King and Queen and the two older princes, Charles and James; and also the King's nephews Prince Rupert and Maurice, who had come from the Continent to fight in his army; and she was, please, to call him Peregrine.

Verity, arriving on the scene just then amid a bevy of small children, saw the silly smile he bestowed on Bess, and turned away. It was nothing to do with her.

CHAPTER SEVEN

THE GYPSIES

"I truly don't understand how you can look so--so--well, almost beautiful!--in such plain attire, Verity. I do think it must be a gift from God."

Verity turned suspicious eyes on Bess, who was radiant in the deep rose gown which became her so well, and also displayed to perfection that womanly figure which Verity so sadly lacked as yet. Bess, she had learned, was to marry Peregrine!

Not that Verity cared, of course: nothing to do with her. But-- It was just that-- Well, for one thing, Bess spoke no Latin, much less Greek, and would surely bore a clever husband. This was simple fact. Verity bore her no malice, for this was not permitted to the Saved, so she could not allow it. Anyway, Bess seemed quite honestly a disconcertingly sweet person, which would make it very hard to dislike her properly. In fact, she acted in all ways quite like the Elect, who showed by their behavior that they were going to heaven. Could an Anglican be Elected? God surely would not send a truly good person to hell just because her parents took her to the wrong church--would He?

Verity found herself gnawing on same old puzzle. Again. It was the fact of predestination: everyone being consigned to heaven or hell before they were even born. Oh, she quite understood that He, being omniscient, knew in advance how everyone was going to turn out-- but-- but-- She really could *not* understand how even God could *know* a person's behavior in advance without somehow *causing* it.

In which case, how could God fairly hold people responsible for their actions?

And why should anyone try to behave well if their behavior didn't matter and their fate was already determined?

What if one of the damned changed his mind and really truly wanted to be good? Or would he be unable to, because God already knew he wouldn't?

Fynch said when God gave free will to mankind and let them choose good or evil, He suspended His own omniscience. That seemed the least impossible answer, though she had never heard it mentioned in church. And she sometimes wondered if having such irreverent thoughts could make her Unelected, after all. Even if she was Predestined to think them--?

Oh, what fustian! She had always known she was Saved! The Saved, said Aunt Huldah, always knew they were Saved. One couldn't be mistaken about a thing like that! She found herself staring fiercely right through Bess, whose pretty face was puckered anxiously. "What's amiss, Verity? I haven't offended you, have I?"

"No, you haven't," Jennet announced from the doorway with a severe face. "I don't think she likes you very much," added the dreadful child.

Verity came back to earth, and glared at Jennet. Whatever God did, *she* must not be unkind, even though she might now and then wish to. For one thing, the wish was probably a temptation either from God or from Satan, and in either case, was best ignored. She frowned.

"Well, you're quite wrong, Jennet; no one could possibly not like Bess! But it isn't true that I look well in this, because we all know quite well that gray is unbecoming to me."

"Yes, especially with your lovely hair all hidden," said Bess frankly. "But if your religion allows you to wear that lovely blue, Verity, perhaps you could uncover your hair, as well? Just here in the castle? I could brush it for you. Peregrine admires it, you know. And my gowns would be too big for you, you're so--slender--" (she tactfully avoided the word bosom) "but Joan's beginning to outgrow all hers, and Jennet's much too small for them, and they might fit you."

"I-- Perhaps. Thank you," Verity managed, stunned. Jennet sniffed, kicked a stool, and said they'd better ask Joan's permission before they gave her gowns away.

Sowerbutts was waiting at the lowered drawbridge with the baskets, talking to Peregrine, who always just *happened* to be on duty when Verity went into Corfe town. It was not quite certain--even to him--whether this was chance. In any case, he told himself, since he had known her longer and in a way brought her here, he had a special duty toward her. Not that anything could happen, of course. Some of the townsfolk had quite taken her to their hearts, it seemed. Howsomever, he had noticed, her face was always straight-lipped and straight-browed when she passed this gate.

She spared him a small cool smile (for he was not merely betrothed to Bess, but clearly smitten with her) and a warmer one for Sowerbutts (whom she quite liked); and they went on through the gate. It was much better guarded these days, for Starling's duties were now always with livestock or garden or the inner wards. The robin (or his or her mate) eyed the silver-gilt hair flowing from under her demure white cap. As good a nest-liner, perhaps, as a lovelock? Somewhere a green yaffingale rat-a-tatted on a tree-trunk. Somewhere else, a hopeful cuckoo shouted invisibly for a mate: Cuck-coo, cuck-coo, cuck-coo, unceasingly. The yaffingale answered with harsh laughter.

Verity's austerity on market days was no accident. Her conscience was uneasy, and the Protestant conscience was indeed a terrible thing to live with. Not that she was committing any *real* sin, like lying. But neither had she told the complete truth--not to anyone, even her own father. They all (except possibly Peregrine) thought her a strict Calvinist and a loyal Parliamentarian. And she let them think so, though in fact, she had misgivings about both. And though Verity did not *think* that merely neglecting to explain such complexities was altogether a sin, neither was she quite sure it wasn't, and God was being of no help whatever. And so it embarrassed her to accept the careful friendship of the villagers

A few were friendly at once. Mistress Abbot, who reminded Verity of a plump hen with a brood of chicks running round in all directions, sold herbs and greens that her brood gathered from the stream banks and hillsides. Verity bought most of what she had, both for her kindness and because the castle could use it. Dandelions and cowslip in particular: to eat boiled or raw, or for conserves and tonics, and even wine, which Fynch had taught her to make without Aunt Huldah needing to know, and which Lady Bankes approved.

A thoroughly-freckled youngster with jug-handle ears, young Gaston Winterbloom, grinned toothily. Old Noah and Leah, the fishmongers, smiled at her warmly. They said Verity was like their daughter dead of plague all those years agone. "Ee, 'ere she be," said Noah. "We've good fresh lobsters today, luv; we've saved six for thee. I know 'tesn't what Quality folk mostly like; still, her leddyship allus buys 'em." Verity loved lobster in butter. She nodded enthusiasm. "Ee, then, fasten down t'basket or they'll all jump into moat."

He and Sowerbutts fussed over it, glaring mutual jealousy. Verity, who found it new and strange to be on chatting terms with any man, even Father, found their devotion very gratifying. She produced her dimple, divided it between them, and moved along to the freckled and amiable Dorcas Winterbloom for some eggs. Salamon Soames was in the stocks, she saw. Again. He was, said Dorcas, clearly Damned, for he stole all the time, even slipping into peoples' homes; and he was never penitent. Verity went over to look at him sternly. "What did you steal this time?" she asked.

He had a smooth, guileless, unused-looking face, like Will or Arabella's. Ungodly, Verity decided astutely. Truly godly people worried about virtue and sin, and it showed on their faces, but the unchastened Salamon had a totally relaxed conscience or perhaps none at all. (Had God planned that, too?)

"Only some tarts, is all," he told her, all wounded innocence.

"Well, why didn't you buy them?" she demanded. "Or get them in the taproom? You're the son of Master Soames, aren't you? Or nephew? He surely had tarts, and you surely had money."

"But I wanted those, and right away," he explained reasonably. Blatantly damned indeed, unable to understand either Good or Evil, but only his own desires. Confusingly, God had not yet seen fit to punish him much on earth-- or at least his devoted family never did, which came to the same thing. On the other hand, if he really did *not* know good from evil, like Adam and Eve before the Apple, it seemed unfair to damn him, Original Sin or no Original Sin.

Verity sighed, and brooded at Salamon's handsome brother Oliver, who was bringing the rogue some more tarts (which could not at all improve his Knowledge of Good and Evil). He also gave Verity a look which she very much disliked, as if she herself were a delectable tart. She treated him to a freezing blue glance, ignored the surly Dick Brine's suspicious frown, and went to see what herbs Enoch Powl and his young and pregnant wife Nancy had today.

They had new onions and lettuce and leeks and some of that newish herb called turnip. (Most gentry, Joan had said with her pretty nose turned up, did not eat such herbs. Her mother said tartly that she would eat what she was served or do without.) It was while Verity was bargaining hard with Enoch for enough new radishes to boil for the entire castle, that the three men rode into the square and sat looking around just as Colonel Rawlins had done.

Every head turned, every hand paused. More of they sojers? folk grumbled. What was t'world coming to? Enoch narrowed shrewd eyes, and then relaxed and began dumping radishes generously into Verity's basket. "Tes all right, poppet: they'm sojers to be sure, but our side. Look."

Verity did. They did not wear orange sashes, but their doublets and collars were severely plain, and their hair cropped short at their earlobes (which had given rise to the jeering term 'Roundheads'). Moreover, their faces wore the stern stamp of duty. She was not sure how she felt. For a moment, she had thought they might have come to rescue her, but at once knew better. Father was far too busy fighting a war, and so were his men.

"Ee could ask 'em to carry thee away home," whispered Enoch, his long face both eager and wistful. Nancy nodded shyly.

Verity gloomed at them. It did not seem at all a good idea. For one thing, she'd be a fool to trust herself to unknown soldiers. From either army. She'd been lucky before. Best not to tempt Providence. For another, she did not wish to go home. No one was there. Especially not Fynch. She was, she quite understood, much better off here, in enemy hands that had proved surprisingly kind.

She murmured something of the sort to Enoch, who nodded wisely, and they went on staring at the soldiers, who were demanding to see the mayor. Since they had halted directly in front of his house, a chin or two jerked in a manner no friendlier than Rawlins had received. Sojers was sojers.

The sojers dismounted, gave young Gaston Winterbloom a farthing to hold the horses, banged on the door, and were presently admitted. Business want on idly. Enoch said 'twas all right, poppet, she could have the radishes at no cost. Lady Bankes was allus fair to her tenants, of whom he was one; and he owed her some herbs, any road. Verity, greatly curious, gathered the nervous Sowerbutts to her and lurked her way around all the stalls, buying more than she had intended, even talking the distracted Thankful Coombes into selling her several violet plants for the garden. The buds made very nice salad, along with dandelion and turnip leaves, and they kept on budding.

At length Mayor Bastwick appeared in his doorway with the soldiers, genial, pointing to the Soames taproom and up the west road where there was a large home or two among the cottages. He was clearly no Puritan, for the fiery green velvet of doublet and knee breeches were set off by a deep lace-trimmed collar slanting from ears to shoulders. And though he did not wear those silly lovelocks, neither was his hair cropped short.

"Happen he's telling 'em where to quarter their troops, choose how," Sowerbutts muttered into her ear. "A right hirdum-durdum. We maun get shut of here, lass, an' go warn her leddyship." (He, for one, could never for an instant think of Verity as an Enemy.)

She nodded and followed him as he edged ever so casually to the western end of the square and then around the corner to the castle road. Among the trees the yaffingale was having a rest, but the robin sang his summer song and the cuckoo still called tirelessly. From somewhere else he was answered-- though whether by a possible mate or a rival, Verity was not certain. April was a busy month for cuckoos.

"Well, we're warned," said Lady Bankes. They were gathered in the large room King John had named the Long Chamber, now a second family room. (Two were certainly needed! Few couples indeed managed to have a dozen living children!) The nod she gave Sowerbutts and Verity was less of gratitude than simple acknowledgement of duty well done. "We must keep the drawbridge up at all times, and put a watch atop all the towers from now on." She glanced at Captain Bond, who nodded. The towers were monstrous high: a watcher there could see far and wide.

"At need, women and children could watch from the top windows of the keep, could they not, Madam?" Peregrine suggested. "They'd see further afield. Bess and Joan and Grissil and Lucy and Peggotty and--" He paused, not yet knowing how much old Barbary or the little ones or the Terrible Trio could be depended on, or whether Verity should be included.

Lady Bankes' nod suggested that she had already thought of that, but John nodded approvingly and smiled at him. He would, Peregrine felt, make a splendid brother-in-law.

"Good idea. What of Bridget, Madam Mother? You know how far-sighted she is. And quite sensible when she wishes to be."

Bridget at once disproved this by rushing in to announce that Edward had fallen down the well. No one looked worried. (Edward, it later turned out, had in fact been busily digging around in Verity's belongings.)

Jennet suddenly began chewing her finger worriedly. "But what happens when we *do* see them?" she demanded.

It was a good question. Lady Bankes looked positively maternal. (Verity had noticed that she did this when she was being most ruthless.) "I was coming to that. I want everyone to train for something, women and children too. From Jennet up, they can at least learn to load muskets. Emmot, you could learn to shoot one, I fancy. Peregrine, may I assume you already can? You and John can help Bond train others. The younger children will help gather stones to stockpile on the walls, and we need a good supply of fuel. Sowerbutts, can you supervise that? All of us will learn to defend the walls with stones, and bedpans of blazing coals, and even boiling water at need. Not you, I think, Verity: 'twould be unfair." (She did not say unfair to whom, and Verity did not ask.)

Bond grunted. "Dunnot want anyone wasting gunpowder: we're already short."

"They'll use little for learning. No need to shoot accurately, just to shoot! And if we're short, you should have said so sooner. Buy more. Some of our local friends might help. The Lawrences, for a need. John, can you ride over to Creech Grange tomorrow?"

"Jennet will load muskets for me to shoot," Jerome announced loftily. No one paid the least bit of notice except Jennet, who aimed a kick at him.

April was slipping by peacefully, in a warm and early spring. The cuckoo still shouted noisily from the trees. (Verity loved the call even though it was truly a wicked bird, laying its huge eggs lethally among those of hapless smaller species.) The violet plants throve, and down in the outer bailey the rabbits had already multiplied and were playing among the cows and horses. In the long narrow triangle of the west bailey, hedge sparrows displayed, and primroses shone pale yellow among the just-budding cowslips and daisies.

Since Peregrine's self-opinion was based not on family or muscle or even brains, but in his own being, he always felt secure in himself. It was just as well. Jennet came marching up to him one day, put her head to one side, and proceeded to stare.

"Why do you limp?"

"Jennet!" said her mother.

But Peregrine was not in the least disconcerted. "Because I broke my leg when I was small, and it mended all crooked."

"Oh. And why are your eyes so funny? They look upside-down. Like a shrewish cat."

The entire room focussed on the eyes. Jennet had put it well, for they did give him the look of Naomi about to swear.

"Jennet."

Jennet and Peregrine paid no attention. "Why, they just came that way," he said easily. "My gran's are the same. So was her gran before her. Do they displease you?"

She considered. "No," she decided, and turned away.

"But *you* have displeased *me*," said her mother. "You may go and do mending for an extra hour! Now!"

But though Peregrine had not minded in the least, now for the first time it occurred to him to wonder whether his betrothed was as delighted with him as he was with her. Not that he had any serious doubts, of course. Still, it was only considerate to make sure--

In a castle as unpopulated as Corfe, it was not hard to find Bess alone, in the sunshine of the west bailey with the Trio quite out of earshot. As she turned those admiring brown eyes on him, he marveled anew, and gently took her slim white hands. "Bess, are you quite happy to be betrothed to me?"

The eyes were astonished. "Of course, Peregrine! My parents would never choose any man not suitable, or too old, or cruel."

Peregrine had always been ruled firmly by Reason (the principle of divinity) rather than Passion (the source of evil). And although he naturally wished his future wife to be the same, he now found uncomfortably that he would have chosen rather more passion and less reason in this reply. He pushed the matter. "But does it worry you to be marrying a man who could never do certain things?" He pushed the crooked leg at her.

"Of course," she said simply. But before his heart could more than lurch once, she turned on him a face sorrowful with compassion. "I think about it all the time, Peregrine, and I worry whenever you walk lest it be hurting you or even just discomfortable, and lest it distresses you that you cannot play tennis or football or stooleball or ride to hounds. Does it bother you very much, Peregrine?"

How had he deserved such a maiden as this? Peregrine shook his head in wonder. "Nay, not at all, really: only that it's weaker than the other." Though, now he thought of it, he was of late using it more than ever in his scholarly life and it bothered him less. "To tell truth, Bess, I can ride perfectly well, but I mislike hunting harmless creatures for fun; nor did I ever wish to play games of mindless violence: I prefer chess, or even draughts or backgammon."

It was quite true, but Bess thought he was being brave and noble. There were tears in the lovely eyes. Amazing! (Verity, now, would merely have debated the matter of games, without any thought of melting compassion.) He blinked, and smiled at Bess.

At that point, Starling called down to the Trio from the massive Dungeon Tower, at the far point of the west bailey. "Tell her leddyship the Gypsies is back." He pointed downward. "Them as M'lord lets camp i'the valley barring they steals nowt from around here."

Jerome, Bridget and Edward merely paused in whatever bit of mischief they were plotting, and went back to it. It was Jennet who ran up to the inner ward. Presently their mother came down. "You're sure? The yellow wagon?"

"Aye, Your Leddyship. That Sammywell--"

"Psammis."

"Aye. Him. I see'st him, and his wife, too. They see'st me."

"Good. Wave them to come. I want to talk to them."

At length they arrived--very much at their leisure--at the outer gatehouse. Verity (supervised by the castle robin in full song) was in the broad pasture of the lower bailey where the livestock grazed, trying to catch a buck rabbit for tomorrow's dinner. She looked up to see a huge, half-familiar bearded man with overhanging black brows, and a queenly woman with deep dark eyes who held a little girl of perhaps eight firmly by the hand. Their once-bright clothes had faded to soft muted shades--except for the child's emerald satin kerchief, no doubt stolen quite recently. They stood in proud dignity, asking nothing. The other castle occupants began to appear, curious and wary.

56

Jennet, fascinated by the little girl, edged closer and closer. Their eyes met and held for a moment, then looked away. They were from different worlds.

"Psammis," said Lady Bankes. "Sheba. And--Willow?"

The child turned in her mother's grasp, thick hair rioting uncombed over her shoulders, huge black eyes missing nothing. She was, Verity could see, going to be a raving beauty and a spawn of Satan. Indeed, clearly, she already was. She smiled brightly. So did Lady Bankes. Neither of them meant it for a moment. "Yes, I remember Willow from last year," said the lady dryly. "'Tis well that you keep hold of her."

Willow met her gaze with artless pride. "They say I mustn't steal from you," she said regretfully. "'Tis a pity. I shall grow up to be the best thief we ever had."

"I doubt it not," said Lady Bankes. "However, if you practice here, you could lose your tribe their rights. Psammis, Sheba, I don't know how long you'll be safe here. The Parliament soldiers are like to attack us. Best to have a care of our farms down there, too, for I cannot well say how anyone feels now. And when you leave, I have letters I would ask you to carry safely away from here and start on the way to Oxford." (They had had no answers from the ones Rawlins had taken back, but this was not surprising.)

Sheba bowed her head royally. "We hear the warning. We shall take your letters as far as we can." She looked around, black eyes shrewd. "Your enemies will not break in, but they could starve you out. Before we go, we can perhaps add to your supplies."

"My thanks. Our tenants provide what they can, and we buy from here and Wareham, but I hate to send our few men too far, lest the enemy come upon them."

The Gypsies seldom wasted words. Both of them bowed again--the slight bows due to equals, Verity noticed--and turned. Psammis stopped and looked at her.

"I have seen you before."

Unexpectedly, Verity liked them--and now she recognized that massive figure and the queenly woman. She produced the furtive dimple that few but Peregrine had seen. It was a great surprise to the others.

"I remember you, too. 'Twas the only time I ever went to a fair. Near Nether Wallop. You had a yellow wagon. A boy got caught cutting a purse, but then he vanished and no one could find him." She very nearly twinkled. Psammis very nearly twinkled back. Peregrine shook an amazed head.

"That was Neco," said Willow scornfully. "He was clumsy. I *never* get caught." The hand on her wrist tightened, and she was swept out, protesting.

CHAPTER EIGHT

MAYDAY

The caravan with the yellow wagon lingered through most of April, though Lady Bankes and Peregrine had already given them the letters for Oxford.

"They will take their time, but yet do better than most," Lady Bankes said tranquilly. "Once they give their faith, they can be trusted."

Peregrine hoped so.

Everyone caught cold, and Cook needed to make a tisane for their coughs, so the children with Bess and Verity were let out of the sallyport behind Dungeon Tower, where they slid giggling all the way down the steep grassy slope to the stream that surrounded the castle hill. Both robins, fearless, hopped close, singing and chittering their friendly curiosity and eyeing all the heads of hair. On the hillside a pair of badgers were spring-cleaning their sett. An otter family sported further along the stream with soft clear flute-like sounds as they slid and dived. In the meadow beyond, a wily fox rolled around and chased his tail while a couple of unwise rabbits crept nearer and nearer in fascination until Jennet's warning yell frightened them off and cheated the fox of his dinner. He gave her a baleful glance and loped off.

Along the banks, the coltsfoot seed heads rose white and fluffy from a thick green carpet of leaves. "We'll gather as much as we can," said Bess, who managed to be unfairly beautiful even with a red nose. "Cook'll be needing a good much for the tisane, and what's left, we can dry for when we need it next." She glanced up to the octagonal bulk of Dungeon Tower (Butevant Tower was its true name) which adorned the arrow-like point of the west bailey. There, old Edward Short kept a keen watch on the western part of the valley.

Having filled the baskets, they idled for a while in the warm sunshine. The younger children romped joyously, even hampered as they were by coughs and long bunchy petticoats. Arabella came and delivered a long hoarse speech to Verity, who could not understand a single word; and Charles refused to translate. Bridget pretended she could have done so had she chosen. Jerome, who should have known better, tried to bully Jennet and received a small hard fist in the belly for his pains. Bridget at once claimed that Jennet had broken Jerome's leg and liver. Joan, who really did not much like the Trio, called her a lying scullion. No one else paid any attention.

Verity turned from Arabella and stared around. The valley and hillsides were viridescent with vivid spring foliage that seemed to shine from within itself. High before them, the West Hill rose. Over to the left, a stream joined the moat.

"That's the Wicken," said Joan, pointing southward. "See, it flows from those hills, and past the village, and that's all our land: and so is the Powl farm, and some village cottages, and the mill over there--" She jerked a chin to the right where the mill of Purbeck stone rose strong beside the stream. "--where Tom Gloys grinds everyone's grain." Her eyes became soulful. (Jennet snorted. Tom Gloys, Verity assumed, had taken Joan's romantic fancy.) Upstream to their left, one could just glimpse the tidy farm worked by Enoch Powl. The willows and elders that edged the stream, newly-leaved, reached long branches over the brook to form a watery tunnel. Soon the leaves would hide it altogether.

"Could the enemy creep up on us from here?" Verity asked, forgetting her enemy-guest role--which was, in fact, harder and harder to keep in mind. "From the town? Once all the leaves are out--and look, there's hawthorn, too: that's very dense--surely a number of men could stay well-hidden, right up to the moat."

"Mayhap. I don't think the villagers would: they're our friends. We'll ask Mama." But Bess glanced uneasily along the stream. It was indeed due soon to be a well-shaded tunnel. "Last summer before the war started, we girls, and even Molly and Nurse and Grissel--but not Mama or Lucy or Cook or Barbary or Emmot--used to come down here on hot days and cross the moat and go upstream where no one could see, and bathe. With nothing on!" (Verity felt shocked--and then oddly envious. She imagined warm sunshine on her bare skin, and liked the thought, even though God must surely disapprove.) Bess was pointing her creamy dimpled chin. "There's a clearing up there where the sun comes, but the trees and bushes hide it from the Powl farm and the mill and even the watchmen on the towers." She sighed. "Certes, 'twould be sad to cut them down!"

Jennet, who had begun to wander along the moat toward the Wicken, suddenly came rushing back. "I hear a babe crying!"

They listened. Then they all heard it: not like Will's grizzle, but a small, tired, despairing whimper that went even to Verity's unmaternal heart. In a moment they were all across the moat and wetly following the sound upstream, the younger ones held firmly by Joan, who was much firmer with them than was the idle Bess.

It was, predictably, a Gypsy toddler, sprawled half on the stream bank, legs in the water, unable to climb out. Tiny brown fists clutched at a flimsy willow branch. He wailed anew when he saw them.

"The poor babe!" Bess flew to the rescue--and just in time, too, for the grubby hands were slackening. He roared and struggled when he found himself in her arms--perhaps fearing the stream less than the strange Gorgio who had snatched him from it.

"I'll fetch Psammis," Verity offered, for it was doubtful how long Bess could hang on to the frantic child. And picking sodden blue kirtle and gown up to her knees she raced, with Jennet close behind, through the fringe of trees toward where the caravans rested. They were met halfway by most of the tribe. Presently, in a welter of confusion and alien speech (to which Arabella added her bit) the baby was placed in the arms of a large wild-eyed mother, who at once examined him all over to be sure the Gorgios had not taken anything important. This included a certain feature of male anatomy which much astonished Verity. Did all boys have this extra bit? She had never even suspected such a thing, and could not imagine what they would do with it. It looked to be both inconvenient and vulnerable, and not at all beautiful. Was it Adam's punishment for the apple? (She had always felt that Eve had an unfair share of the blame.) The Bible did not say. She did not think she could ask anyone. It probably came well within the range of Forbidden Conversations, or Fynch would surely have told her about it.

Dinki was found to be whole, and his mother nodded at them and mumbled in Romany, uncertain how to treat a Gorgio. One did not mingle with them on social terms. Sheba clutched her own babe with one firm hand, hauled Willow away from Bess's tempting silken pocket, and nodded like a queen. "We owe you," she said simply. "We will take your letters nearer Oxford than we had planned, and at once; and although we do not enter Gorgio cities, we will send them the rest of the way safely--though I do not know how long it may take."

Well, that was understood, of course. Three or four years ago, there had been no less than eight postal lines running over England, but now with the war, letters were again chancy things that could wander for months before finding their goal--if they ever did. This was a great service, and Bess produced her adorable smile. They turned to go. But Willow and Jennet were exploring each other's eyes again, and Arabella had found some one else who spoke a different language. She had thought herself the only one. She planted herself in front of Dinki's mother.

"Cammer hiff, ettle mott purvil mott daggin," she announced earnestly. The Gypsies stared, deeply impressed. Then Willow leaned forward and spoke in Romany. Arabella beamed, patted the filthy hand. "Umper ettle muck, yurra yurra yurra," she replied, and looked around at the astonished faces with satisfaction.

"What did she say?" Jennet asked Charles, but he was scowling.

"She said," Willow smirked, "that she likes our baby better than your baby, because yours always says yurra-yurra."

"Yes, he does," Jennet confirmed. The two girls flicked glances again.

Charles, bewildered at suddenly being unneeded, grumped. That ragged girl had taken his special role! Moreover, if she and Arabella could understand each other, why then could he not understand the ragged girl? Disgruntled, he turned back toward the castle, stomping, determined to throw Arabella's doll right across the nursery. But Jennet and Willow, mutually fascinated, each stared back over her own shoulder as long as the other was in sight.

In the morning the Gypsy caravan was gone.

Lady Bankes, when the coltsfoot--not too wilted--had been delivered to Cook and they had all, snuffling and coughing, drunk the tisane, agreed that it would be a pity to cut the trees. "I'll talk to Captain Bond, but I doubt 'twill be necessary. Even if our tenants didn't see invaders, our guard would, when they reached the moat, and of course that's kept clear of undergrowth. And they'd have to cross it, and then come up that steep bare slope with no protection, under fire from the towers and walls. I'm more concerned about May Day."

John suddenly sat straight. "Perdy!" he said "The stag hunt! I'd forgot!"

"I hadn't," said his mother grimly, and turned to explain to her bemused guests. "Tis an old custom. Every Mayday the mayor of Corfe and all the gentry and barons living near have permission to course a stag in this valley, beyond--"

"Last year we slew seven hundred and forty-two," interrupted Bridget, her eyes shining with candor. "Maybe eight hundred and fifty-seven," she added with artistic verisimilitude.

"--the farms. 'Tis a great occasion, with processions, and people coming from all over Purbeck and even Dorchester; and of course most are friends so 'tis wondrous fun. But now--" She shrugged, nose and chin fierce.

"'--how ill all's here about my heart,'" Verity murmured, unheard by any but Peregrine who turned a startled head and then shook it. Coincidence. No Puritan read plays--much less knew them well enough to quote them! The half-forgotten Shakespeare least of all.

"We shall still hold the hunt," Her Ladyship was saying, "but with our blessing rather than our presence, I think. After all, we've all had those terrible colds, haven't we? I may be over-suspicious--but better that than over-trust and rue it. We need to plan for emergencies. John, you and Peregrine might ride over to Creech Grange and ask Sir Edward if he can come discuss it. And--"

"Tis market day tomorrow: I'll see if I can hear anything," Verity volunteered, and then sat still in dismay. Was Satan teasing her? Or God testing? Whose side was she on, anyway?

Somewhere outside those walls, the cuckoo called derisively.

Market day seemed, on the surface, quite normal. Well, almost. Salamon Soames was not in the stocks, for a wonder. Was it her imagination that people's faces seemed tense behind their skins? Sowerbutts certainly was. He hovered, his beaky once-broken nose turning suspiciously from side to side, especially when Salamon and Oliver strolled innocently by; one looking altogether too interested in her purse, the other in her person.

Verity bought tiny new carrots and onions and sparrowgrass from Enoch, and eggs from Dorcas. Dick Brine had prunes and raisins and a few of those exotic luxuries from afar, dates. These kept forever, and Lady Bankes would very much want them--but Dick scowled when she offered to buy them all.

"Marry, why not?" she demanded. "Sell them all to me, and then you can go home and sleep for the rest of the day."

"Thee dunnot know my wife," he grumbled, but shoved them into her basket.

Noah had eels as well as winkles, but his wide mouth turned down at her. "Thee take 'em quick, and go back and tell her leddyship to stay to home," he murmured, low. "Tesn't right for folk to go make war on women and childer, I say. Go home."

But Noah's stall was up by Market Cross, and before she could get back across the town square, Mayor Bastwick had halted his portly figure in front of her. She had had no chance to get to know him or even decide anything about him. He wore lettuce-green taffetas today, and an odd expression on his round rosy face. The jovial crinkles alongside his eyes drooped.

"You're the lass they're keeping hostage at t'castle?" he murmured, eyes flicking under brows angled like rooftops. "But you seem unshackled?" His chuckle seemed to the wary Verity a little too rich, like warm butter. "My good lady would like thee to visit us for a bit and meet our little lad, an' it please you."

Sowerbutts suddenly appeared. His body was all sinew and muscle, quite lacking Mayor Bastwick's impressive portliness--and yet it looked vaguely menacing. The mayor retreated a step. Verity, reassured, shoved a finger from the depths of her full gray linsey-woolsey skirts into Sowerbutts' thigh, and curtseyed deeply. "I thank you, good sir," she began, and her voice dropped two notes. She faltered, unsure what to say. Everything suddenly felt somehow sinister. "Tis very kind of her. If I-- Some day--"

"Nay, what's wrong with now?" The mayor had his assurance back. Verity's was oozing. An avowed enemy, she could handle; but she knew nothing of tact, nor could she lie: she did not know how. His plump hand had taken hold of her arm. He was saying that her man, there, could easily deliver her purchases to the castle and tell them where she was. Lady Bankes was a friend, he said: good old Basil Bastwick and his dear wife. She did not believe it. But Lady Bankes had told Verity to get to know him. So far, she liked him very little.

She flung a silent yelp for assistance to a God she desperately hoped was in a good mood. 'Make haste to help me, oh Lord!'--and found herself once more cool in crisis. Apparently it was only the prospect of lying that 'mazed her. But she need not lie. She cast silken lashes toward her own small shoes, and clasped her hands demurely around the basket handle. "To every thing there is a season, and a time to every purpose under the sun,'" she said, low-voiced but clear to hear. "Ecclesiastes. Truly, Master Bastwick, 'tis not now the time for me to visit you--"

But he knew his Bible, too. "'A time to weep and a time to laugh,'" he added, jovial. "In sooth, hast not wept enough? Come stay with us a while and see our little son, and smile."

She trusted him no whit! Nor did Sowerbutts, lurking behind her. But she must not anger him, neither. She heard herself reciting a line that had never yet been found in any Bible. "A time to stay and a time to go." And she smiled without her dimple.

He knew, of course. His eyebrows fairly bounded. She watched with fascination. "Saucy baggage! Now what could make thee loth to come away from the castle for a day or two? You're not in love, surely? Lusting for some man there?"

Marry, she would just have to lie, then! She lifted sharp cheekbones and took a deep breath. "Well, aye," she murmured, feeling totally unconvincing. "If you must know."

He believed her! He looked shocked, disillusioned. Then he shrugged regret. Never mind; he had tried. "Your servant, Mistress," he muttered. She curtseyed deeply. He flourished his tall feathered hat and turned on his heel.

"Eh, lass," croaked a voice behind her, "but tha didst have me in a fair sweat! Coom along home!"

Verity came, deeply shaken, for she realized in dismay that she had not lied! For she *did* lust--and for another woman's betrothed! And Scripture said lust of the heart was as bad as sin of the flesh. Moreover, her conscience said naggingly, she was again forgetting where her loyalty lay.

And God, when asked about it, unfairly offered no sense either of right or wrong. It was really too bad of Him!

Mayday dawned fair and bright and early. A skylark flung himself invisibly at the sky, singing in ecstasy. The top windows of the keep became filled with humans. The robins watched with fearless interest. A song thrush, curious, perched on the west wall and gave them a concert: singing each phrase twice over before going on to a totally different one. His beady eyes were alert for any careless snail that might not have reached shelter yet. But then he flew away, annoyed, because the valley was suddenly thronged with crowds of people running after men on horseback, who in turn seemed to be hunting something else. (It was, in fact, stags--but no stag had yet been foolish enough to show up.) The hunters drifted around the base of West Hill for a bit, staring around, but never quite out of sight of the castle's towers and keeps.

After an hour or so, Bridget, staring out the keep's highest windows, became greatly excited, and almost at once a large flag was waved from the top turret toward the hunt. The hunters saw it, instantly turned and raced their horses out of the valley in all directions, leaving the crowds of commoners on foot to stare in puzzlement. Ee, then, what ailed they? But seeing the hunt abandoned, they shrugged and had begun leaving as well when a large troop of soldiers galloped over the western hills from the direction of Dorchester. As that road was no better than any other Dorset road, the troop was much scattered, their mounts slipping and shying and even rearing; so that by the time the troopers reached the floor of the valley, it was deserted. For quite a while they cantered around the emptiness in no pleasant frame of mind. They trampled crops, disturbed the songbirds and infuriated several nesting jays and the cuckoo; but found only a few bewildered tenants heading homeward, and a contemptuous fox. They conferred. They frowned at the castle. Ralph leaned out the keep window and waved at them cheekily. Jerome, who tended to be more majestic than bold in a crisis, moved out of sight, but Jennet took his place and shook a threatening small fist. She was fond of her fists, was Jennet.

They waited.

"Here they come," said Lady Bankes quietly.

Sure enough several of the troopers were heading vengefully toward the castle. The castle failed to tremble. Every tower had its guard, and John and Peregrine were atop one of the two high towers that flanked the front gate. They had watched with interest the antics in the valley, and now had a splendid view when the troopers, having splashed through the Wicken, found themselves balked by the moat. Having perforce to follow it around to the front, they found themselves balked again. There, far under the bridge and gate and still across the moat, they reined their horses, staring upward in angry frustration. They held another conference, fixed insincere smiles on grumpy faces, waved to the castle. Then they made their way under the bridge, along to the road, back up to the town and thence across the bridge, where they reined in front of the raised drawbridge. Their smiles were by now distinctly strained.

"Tis Mayday," called their leader, a bulky man with skimpy hair and yet too little forehead. "We've come to visit. Let us in."

The drawbridge stayed where it was. So, behind it, did the lowered portcullis. Atop their tower, Peregrine and John grinned at each other, unworried. Before the gate, the friendly visitors became increasingly less friendly.

"Let us in, ye muddy-mettled carbuncles!" bawled the leader at last, and the others joined in. Their wrath fell particularly upon Lady Bankes. Brazen-faced strumpet, unnatural shrew and pernicious Jezebel were the kindest epithets Peregrine heard--and the only ones he cared to repeat later. "You'll be sorry!" they yelled. "We'll come back and take this God-cursed castle, and when we do, you'll regret it. We'll have our fun with you, we will!"

Peregrine was no longer grinning. Not because he thought there was any danger, but because of the raw vitriol that seemed to pour from them. He had never felt anything like it before. He shuddered, thinking of other women who might perhaps fall foul of it. One knew, of course, what conquering armies had always done. Look at the Trojan women! But he had not supposed, somehow, that modern men could be so bad. Oh, looting baggage trains, as Prince Rupert's cavalry did once--that was fair enough (though it had turned

65

out to be a very bad idea, with the battle still going on and their infantry unprotected.) And of course both sides destroyed property; the Puritans having particular loathing for sinfully decorated Catholic churches. But those were mere *things*--

He turned as Lady Bankes came along the top of the wide wall and up to the tower.

"Churlish tempers," she said chidingly, and then as the sounds out there changed, she looked down between the crenellations. John and Peregrine joined her. Some officers had arrived, and were berating the troopers savagely, threatening to have them hanged, driving them away.

"Lackaday," murmured the lady, and there was no softness in that pointed smile nor in the large brown eyes. "In sooth, we're about to learn, 'twas all a sad mistake. The troopers simply got overexcited, out of hand, disobeyed orders: I make no doubt of it. There was never a commission to take the castle; none at all; and if we'll just let them in, they'll be happy to apologize in person."

"Hello the gate?" called a cultured voice from below. "We're heartily sorry about that! 'Twas all a mistake, you know! They got carried away--"

Lady Bankes' smile widened, but grew no whit more kindly.

CHAPTER NINE

CAT'S CRADLE

"Well?" Lady Bankes leaned back in the fine chair that had been brought down from the keep to the far western end of the west bailey, and looked at them all. Everyone was here except those actually on watch. Even Ralph, who had been trusted as lookout from atop Dungeon Tower, was hovering on the wall with clearly divided attention. The others: family, guests, maidservants and soldiers, sat rigidly or lounged, according to their natures, over the grass that had been much reduced by the addition of more vegetable gardens. Grissil kept a wary eye on the Trio, who, angel-faced, plotted wickedness. Jennet plotted spoiling their fun. The friendly robin watched with interest and then turned back to worms: the eggs were hungry. Somewhere the cuckoo tried out his three-note summer song: cuck-uck-oo. Naomi, looking like a muted apricot sunset through fluffy dark cloud, wandered in and regarded the robin without interest. Feathers were a nuisance. Mice were better: they didn't fly away. She rubbed against the pleased Sowerbutts and then went and leaned on her second-favorite human, who obligingly scritched down her spine. No one said anything. Her Ladyship gazed first at John, who was thinking intently, then Bond, who looked dour, and then at Peregrine.

"Ay, well," he said, shrugging. It was obvious, wasn't it? *"Vis comsili expers mole ruit sua."*

Lady Bankes frowned. Sowerbutts shifted his solid butt on the grass. "Happen tha means," he said cheerfully, "that they made a right muck of t'attack, eh lad?"

"Happen I do," said Peregrine amiably. His mouth curled upward. "Happen they're sure to come back and try again, too. Most heartily annoyed, they were."

"And so," said Lady Bankes, what is our next move in this military chess game?"

"Reinforcements," said Captain Bond, brusquely.

"How, Madam?" asked Peregrine from his spot extremely close to Bess, who gazed at him adoringly. "If this is the only secure Royalist hold in the southwest, who could come? And from whence? And at whose command, save the King's? Could we spare even one man to send to Oxford? Would he get through? Would His Majesty even then bother to send any soldiers to us?"

There was a shocked pause. Some had, very likely, been thinking along those lines, but no one until now had cared to say it aloud. Ralph came down from the wall to hear better. Emmot the housekeeper, an Amazon with a strongly handsome face, looked outraged, while John suddenly frowned hard at middle-distance. Bess puckered her face in charming worry. She was, Verity decided unfairly, a lovely goose, a charming gowk, an adorable witling, and it would serve Peregrine right to be bored for the rest of his life.

"You do not much admire His Majesty?" asked the witling's mother, her pointed smile ominous."

"I do not personally admire His Majesty *or* the Queen," Peregrine agreed, matching smiles with her. "Save in music and art. No more than does my grandmother Lady Raven, who told him to his face that he's an idiot--as she did his father before him."

"And was banned from Court."

"Ay. But only after she and Granfer had already had their fill of it and gone back to their home in Chiddingfold."

"A disloyal family? You are like Verity in opposing monarchy?"

"Not a whit." He grinned past her at the startled face of Verity, who had not dreamed he harbored any such thoughts. "Not all my family, nor all monarchy: only Gran and Oriel and I believe with Socrates that the greatest loyalty is to be a gadfly. 'Tis a boon seldom appreciated, I confess. Nor do I admire this Parliament, by the way. I am loyal to the king, and I support monarchy in principle, Madam. I merely think it should be--tempered?--by some limits to royal power, since kings are mortal--Divine Rights or no--and mortals can be fools. And I venture to suppose, Lady Bankes, that many Royalists think the same. Especially those like your unfortunate husband who must deal constantly with His Majesty."

She favored him with a hard smile and went back to the subject at hand. "We do still have friends and tenants who will help us," she observed. "Those who came to the hunt, for a start."

"And ran away," said Verity tartly.

"Because we warned them to do so."

More silence came and hovered. Everyone looked at John, who was still in the throes of deep thought. The song-thrush lighted on the north wall and sang to Naomi. He did that often, of late, and no one know whether it was affability or challenge. (They did know it was the same thrush, because no two sang the same songs.)

Naomi ignored him, raised her tail, and wove herself, alternately purring and swearing, around any skirts or legs that took her fancy. Otherwise she took no more heed of the discussion than little Will, who was grizzling--as usual--from his cradle. Naomi listened, sat with ears pricked, and then suddenly jumped into the cradle. There was a flurry of panic, of bodies and hands outstretched to snatch her out. Naomi turned a menacing head, showed her fangs, hissed horribly. The hands prudently withdrew, but the panic sharpened.

"Let be," said Lady Bankes tranquilly. "Look at them."

They looked. Naomi was peering affably into the small face, which peered back from its cocoony swaddling and suddenly broke into a wide gummy smile. Naomi broke into renewed purring. The wide gummy smile became a wide gummy chuckle. Swaddled feet waved. Naomi molded her slight flexible body neatly into the space beside one arm, which jerked againsther unprotesting head.

"Perhaps now he'll give us some peace," said his mother.

"But M'Lady, 'twill suck his breath away! All know that cats does that."

"Fustian," she said. "An old wives' fable. If it please you, keep an eye on her, but we need to talk plans. Peregrine, until John feels like talking, tell me what military activity was taking place when you left Oxford."

Peregrine's errant eyebrow aimed itself at the thrush, who eyed it doubtfully. It had never seen a caterpillar like that: best not to rush into anything. "When I left Oxford," Peregrine said blandly, "Prince Rupert had taken Cirencester, and the prisoners had been bought to Oxford chained and starved and half-naked in the cold." He glanced at their faces. Ralph looked confused, Sowerbutts meditative, Bond indifferent, Bess about to cry, and Verity outraged but unsurprised. (She'd always known Cavaliers behaved like that.) But he could find no expression at all on Lady Bankes' calm face. She nodded at him to continue.

"They had captured a captain who calls himself Freeborn John, and planned to hang him. He's been in the king's hair for years now. Sedition. Says all men have the right to think and govern for themselves. Which in effect would abolish the Monarchy."

Verity's face had gone quite white. Those five long hairs in Peregrine's eyebrow aimed themselves away from the thrush (who looked relieved) and toward her. She was finding it a bit hard to breathe. Could it-- It sounded like Fynch's great-nephew Master Lilbourne! She rolled her eyes skyward and had a frantic word with God, who ignored her, as He had done ever since she was Abducted. How like Him! Peregrine had his knowing eye on her. She sometimes quite hated them both.

"But the hanging was delayed." He was still watching her curiously, and now the Bankes children turned to stare, as well. "Parliament was threatening harsh reprisal. Which," he drawled, "I find wondrous amusing. 'Tis not merely the monarchy his ideas would abolish, but the House of Lords. All inherited privilege to be banned, nobles stripped of titles and estates. And all men, however humble and uneducated, to have the vote. Parliament cannot have been paying attention to his speeches!"

It *was* Master Lilbourne! It must be! Had they hanged him, then, or not? Verity hoped her expression was well-hidden among all the other shocked faces. For his theories were, he and Fynch had agreed quite cheerfully, *lèse majesté* and quite unthinkable to upper class minds--though he had great hope for the ordinary people. 'Twould take some education, though, since people always disliked to change their habits of belief...

Verity shifted her glance into the cradle where Naomi slept with her head on Will's swaddled belly. Likely people even in a hundred years would still think cats sucked a baby's breath. Just as, even after more than a hundred years, only a few intellectuals like Fynch believed Copernicus when he said that the earth encircled the sun instead of the other way around. She had made Verity read what John Donne wrote, years ago, when that upsetting idea (among others from men like Montaigne and Machiavelli) threatened the traditional world order: 'Tis all in peeces, all coherence gone; all just supply and all relation.' (Well if he felt that way *then*, whatever would he have thought *today*?)

Face-down in the long grass, Charles in his long bunchy skirts poked at a large and interesting beetle while Arabella put a rosy face almost on top of it to see better. In the cradle, Will woke and babbled, and Naomi yawned indulgently. It was to be hoped that she would not decide to groom him with that rasping tongue. Verity stared at the song-thrush, who, quite unsettled by now, flew away. Peregrine still watched her, and Her Ladyship watched them both.

"I had hoped," the chatelaine reminded him acidly, "that you might hazard a guess whether His Majesty might be planning to send troops this way?"

"All I know, Madam, is that there was talk of a campaign further west than Dorset. To support Hopton's victory in Cornwall. Send Prince Maurice to go after Essex, mayhap. But, M'lady, 'twas only talk even then, near three months since, and His Majesty--" He shrugged. How to predict a king who managed to be at once inflexible and mercurial, and to whom facts and Divine Reason were strangers?

Her Ladyship tightened her lips again and took a deep breath. "John, you were to leave in a few weeks for Oxford. You matriculate July tenth, I believe? I want you to go at once, and take your little brothers to safety with their father. Or with Alice: she lives near Oxford."

There was brief silence. Just the boys--? Yet, it made sense. Sons were heirs, and far more valuable than daughters. Every face joined John's in intense concentration. Verity could practically follow their thoughts. Ralph looked pleased at getting away and having adventures. Nurse Maud beamed, perhaps at losing two of her adored but wicked Trio? Molly's face wore-- what? Envy? Yearning? A thought occurred to Verity. She raised her face again and muttered earnestly to the sky.

"What are you doing?" Jerome demanded.

"She's praying," Peregrine told him resignedly.

"She can't be," said Joan, scandalized.

"Yes, she can, retorted Jennet. "She does it a lot."

Bridget, for a confirmed liar, was remarkably literal-minded. "No, she can't. You pray in church and kneeling at your bedside."

"I pray where I like," snapped Verity and continued to do so.

"Belike," declared Ralph, who had quite forgotten the tower from which he was supposedly watching, "she's telling God to help the Royalists."

Verity turned a very straight neck to give him a very straight look. "What an ill thing! I never would be so froward. But I have a right to ask Him what He wants of me, since He chose to have me placed here. God!" she said aloud, and with very jutting cheekbones. "Prithee tell me, because if You do not, I shall just have to decide for myself; which, You remember, is what You were so angered at Eve for doing; and 'twould be vastly unfair to blame me then if I get it wrong. I do think You owe me at least a hint, since it was You who had me Abducted and left here among enemies." She waited. The sky remained clear: no thunderbolt, not a cloud nor even a cuckoo or skylark. The song-thrush sang tentatively from a further wall, but she could not feel that to be an answer. She sighed and lowered her gaze. Everyone was looking at her. They wore very odd expressions, except for John, who winked at her.

"*I*'m not your enemy!" Jennet announced, and marched over with a swish of sprigged sarcenet skirts to stand aggressively beside her.

"Oh, no! None of us is, truly!" Bess's lovely face puckered in distress. (She still looked unfairly beautiful.) Several other voices, embarrassed, mumbled that of course they weren't. Emmot's was not among them. Old Edward Short had quietly mounted the tower to take over Ralph's forgotten watch, and his lady mother motioned Ralph with a single finger to sit down in disgrace.

Arabella, squeezing her round baby face into a determined frown, heaved her small well-padded bottom into the air, gained her feet, and lurched over to Verity. "Ot aggin hiff eddle murp!" she told her earnestly. Everyone looked at Charles, who glanced up from the interesting beetle long enough to inform them that Arabella did not wish Verity to be sad.

"I'm not sad," Verity told her, suddenly touched. "I just needed to ask His opinion, and He hasn't given me a hint, so I suppose He means me to think for myself. And this is what I think. Jennet said Molly had to postpone her marriage because she's needed here. But now the boys will be leaving, so she'll be less needed; and God has sent me here, so perhaps He intends her to go and be wedded whilst I do her duties."

They all looked at her: Molly with the dawn of delighted relief. John grinned suddenly. "Madam Mother, 'tis well thought on. And all fits. Sir Edward has been wishing to go soon, so he can be our escort. Ralph needs a proper tutor, now he's twelve, so he can stay with Father at Oriel College. And Alice was always splendid at disciplining the little ones; she should be very good for the lads--" He smiled sweetly at his youngest brothers, who looked uneasy. "--and I make no doubt at all that Robert will be pleased to see Molly. I think indeed we should go as soon as possible--if you're sure you'll be all right?" he added--but knowing his mother, not too anxiously. "And perhaps Father will let me talk to His Majesty myself, and tell him how things stand. We must be sure you've men to defend you."

His mother nodded. "Be sure we shall do so, in any case. Send help if you can, but I shall not depend on any but ourselves. Bond, I want you to triple the provisions, while keeping full guard watch." Bond looked as if she had just told him to walk on water. She studied him without mercy. "There are for the moment seven able to stand watch, counting John and Peregrine but not Ralph, who is clearly not dependable." Ralph opened his mouth to protest, flushed scarlet, closed it again. "Concentrate on defense of the inner ward and the west bailey, since only a numbskull would attack the lower bailey only to find himself little better than before. Inform me presently, who is reasonably efficient by now at loading and at aiming, and whether you find any new source of munitions. The rest of you may return to your duties-- unless you feel that you have something useful to contribute."

Peggotty, Lucy, Grissel, Old Barbary and all of the men but Bond and Sowerbutts scuttled away thankfully. Still--they had been asked for their opinions! It was a wondrous thing, Verity suddenly realized, to consult menials at all. Especially female ones. A thing Master Lilbourne might have approved--had he ever thought of it. Possibly. (His notions of universal equality and voting rights had never, as far as she knew, thought to include women.)

Bess sighed a little, clearly wishing to help. "Then d'you think, Peregrine, that there are no kings' troops nearby?" All the cleverness in the world could not create information where there was none. He shrugged. "Then I do think 'twas knavish of Major Rawlins to leave us!"

"Doubtless he had his orders." Her mother's words were kindlier than the smile. "His Majesty may still send help. In the meantime we shall turn to our neighbor friends--and our tenants, who have little choice if they wish to keep their cottages or mill." She looked maternal and quite ruthless. Verity was unsurprised. "Most will remain loyal, I warrant. Mayor Bastwick, for a start."

Verity blurted it. "Not the mayor! You mustn't trust him! For 'a man may smile and smile, and be a villain--'" She saw Peregrine's baffled face and preened a bit. For even he, with all his Latin, would never recognize a quote from that all-but-forgotten playwright Shakkspur. (She was wrong about that: he might not remember which play, but one could not mistake the author.) "--and he's not on your side."

"Nor are you," said Emmot bluntly. Her handsome high-colored face shone fiercely combative. She would never trust a Puritan, not for a moment!

Verity, silenced, felt her face grow scarlet with anger, confusion, shame. And she did not even know herself whether the charge was true or not. She sat, mute and unyielding, for she could not in either pride or honesty defend herself.

"Nor is she against us, neither," Peregrine observed lazily. "Thing is, she's not really on anyone's side. Are you?" Verity's small head snapped around to fix him with a startled gaze. Now, how had he known that? His eyes fixed on her, peaty-green, derisive, mocking. "*Inter canum et lupum,*" he added kindly, reasonably sure that she would not understand.

She did, of course, and grinned appreciatively. 'Caught between a dog and a wolf', indeed! Still, she couldn't let him have the last word. She pondered for an instant, sought another quote from Hamlet, couldn't think of one (which was just as well, she later discovered) and wickedly switched to Greek. "*Phtheirousin ethe christh' homiliai kakai!*"

There! That had shaken him! His eyes widened like a 'mazed cat's. But before they could continue the contest, Lady Bankes interrupted, as acid as Emmot. "That will be quite enough from both of you. *Concordia discors,* prithee, if you cannot maintain a true peace."

Two heads snapped around in unison, two pairs of eyes stared at her, incredulous. John grinned. Peregrine recovered his wits. "*Mea culpa,* Lady Bankes," he said, his tilted eyes rueful and merry of a sudden. "I see I must mend my speech and beliefs. But 'tis vastly unfair; for all England knows that the female mind is incapable of serious study, even of Latin, much less Greek." He shook his head in comical but genuine chagrin. "I had thought Verity to be merely reciting by rote--but now I'm confronted with two of you! I should have heeded a certain Mistress Fynch not so long ago. Now I'm quite outnumbered by learned females! Unless-- John? Ralph?"

John just grinned again. Ralph, who had so far contrived to learn as little Latin as possible, and virtually no Greek at all, shook his brown head vigorously. "Aye, marry," sighed Peregrine. "Well, I see I'm quite undone. *Concordia discors,* Verity?"

Lady Bankes felt they had wasted enough time. "Enough showing off," she said rather grimly. "Unless anyone has a better idea, which seems unlikely, Peregrine will again go with John, to ask Sir Edward and our other friends to visit me this evening or as soon as they may. Maud, start packing the little boys' things. Lucy can help Molly. I want you gone as soon as may be. And I shall visit Mayor Bastwick on the morrow. As the town seems to like Verity well enough. I shall take her. And--" She looked at her offspring speculatively.

Jerome at once stood. "I shall go with you," he announced with superb aplomb. "I'm the best and bravest and smartest." No one gave him the lie. Neither did anyone support him. Jerome, they seemed to feel, was best ignored.

"--and Jennet," said her mother. Jennet's pointed face turned quite pink with delight, and she stood a full half-inch taller. At last she was being given the recognition she had always known she merited! Not for worlds would she have shown how much it pleased her.

Jerome looked outraged. Only Sowerbutts smiled. He was going too, choose how, whether her leddyship knew it or not.

"Any dissent?" she asked with a particularly silken smile. There was, in fact, a great deal of dissent, but no one cared to voice it, not even Jerome. Not in the teeth of that benign smile. They all looked submissive (except Sowerbutts, who looked bland) and went about their various tasks.

Bond, his face pessimistic but his report cheerful, stayed to inform Her Leddyship that Peregrine was a splendid shot for a lad who did not much like hunting, and Emmot promising. Bess had a fair eye. She, Joan, Maud, Jennet and Peggotty were well enough at loading. The others-- He shrugged. Belike they'd improve, given time. Had they enough of it.

Peregrine counted quickly. That would mean six or seven shooters and five or more loaders, depending on Her Ladyship's role. A pity about Verity. Judging from that display with bow and arrow, he suspected she would make a most excellent shot. Still, best for her sake that she stay neutral. He looked over at her face, which was, he was surprised to see, white and set with hurt humiliation. He did not at all understand her!

A brief silence fell. Maud, looking as militant as a full-breasted wet-nurse could possibly be, frowned into the cradle. The robin sang cheekily. Peregrine offered Verity a wry grin, and was pleased to see her pull herself together and return it. His disbelief in female intellect had taken a terrible drubbing, but a reasonable man could recognize his errors. He held up a hand. *"Pax?"*

"Pax," agreed Verity, but she was not altogether sure how well that peace would hold. Nor was she surprised when he found her alone within the hour and stood blocking her way up the keep stairs, with an impudent eyebrow and an affable smile.

"Tell me, sweet maid, what you know of this Freeborn John?"

She denied nothing at all, which Peregrine found just faintly disconcerting. "Nay, why should I?"

He considered. *"Aude sapere?"* he suggested, still wondering just how much Latin she could really understand as opposed to quoting by heart.

"Well, I don't see anything at all wise about it," she snapped. "You'll need to do better than that."

He grinned. *"Pax!* Let us say, then, because I'm mightily curious. And," he added, suddenly grave and with quiet eyebrows, "because I would never betray a confidence, however we might differ on some things."

Verity could not but believe him. But then she remembered Bess, who was not only his betrothed, but also, infuriatingly, the perfect ideal maiden, beautiful, sweet and biddable, and with lovely full breasts as well; as no young man could possibly help noticing.

"One day, mayhap," she said, austere.

Suddenly, from nowhere, Lady Bankes had joined them, was regarding them with severity. "With all your Latin and Greek, you two, you both have much to learn. Peregrine, accept the fact that a female can be your equal in learning and intellect. Verity, accept the fact that God does not necessarily conform to your notions of divine justice. If you expect Him to forgive your sins, you might try to forgive Him for not living up to your expectations."

And she was gone, leaving both of them bemused and wordless.

CHAPTER TEN

FOUR PAWNS

Mayor Bastwick's over-decorated parlor was not too dim for Verity to see expressions. Lady Bankes looked mild and ox-eyed. The mayor's smile crinkled his rosy cheeks but not his eyes. Sowerbutts, on the other hand, wore dancing eyes in a sober face. Jennet contrived to glow almost visibly. Mistress Bastwick effaced herself. A maidservant produced shaped jellies, gingerbread florentines, dandelion wine and pommage, and then vanished.

Jennet at once began eating greedily. The mayor and Lady Bankes chatted affably about old times and hunts and friends--and loyalty. They were playing a game, Verity saw: as complex as chess, dangerous as swords, subtle as music. It had nothing to do with romance, a great deal to do, apparently, with comfortable friendship and uncomfortable politics. At a pause in it, the mayor looked at Verity, who was busy mistrusting appearances.

"So, little maid who'd not come visit my poor wife and me, is thee a Royalist, after all?"

Lady Bankes contrived not to show surprise (for Verity had never mentioned the invitation) but those large brown eyes became very thoughtful.

"Nay, not I!" Verity flared, offended. "But I'm content where I am."

"Indeed her leddyship is a wondrous hostess, but thee'd be safer here."

So, he had known all along what was planned for yesterday! She had wondered! And what else? She trusted him even less than Lady Bankes. Much. At least Lady Bankes was openly on the enemy side. Verity fixed the mayor with stern eyes. "'A man that flattereth his neighbor spreadeth a net for his feet.'"

He beamed at her. "Proverbs 29. But Proverbs 31 says 'Who can find a virtuous woman? for her price is far above rubies.'"

Verity glittered with sudden mischief. This was a game she understood well--and in three languages, too. "'*Kaloga*--'"

"Enough," said Lady Bankes.

Verity wore her self-righteous expression "But he knew!" she protested. "About the attack yesterday! Beforehand!"

"Aye, to be sure I did," he nodded, his eyes now somewhat less agreeable than his smile.

"And you never warned her!"

"Nay," he agreed. "Wherefore should I tell her not to be a doltishly trusting gowk? Had she needed such warning, she'd not have deserved it. For 'Discretion shall preserve thee, understanding shall keep thee.' I have more trust in M'lady's understanding than you, it seems."

Verity narrowed her blue eyes at the impassive face of the lady. Was there deeper friendship there than appeared? Were they playing an even subtler game than she had supposed? She decided to suspend judgment. But Jennet, remarkably astute for a child of ten, turned her sharp little face to the mayor. Her chin was much in evidence.

"Are you on our side or not?"

Mayor Bastwick beamed at her with his eyes as well as his mouth. "In truth, poppet, I try to be on both sides."

Jennet chewed a finger, thinking. "You can't be," she decided.

"And why not? Is not our Puritan friend here?"

The thick brown hair flew wide. "Nay, she's *against* both sides. Peregrine said so. That's not the same." It was not exactly what Peregrine had said--but rather nearer the truth.

"What difference is there?" asked their host.

Jennet was sure of her ground. "If you're *for* both sides, then you have to try to help both sides, and how can you?"

"As opposed to hindering both sides?" He looked at Verity. "Is that what you're doing, mistress?"

Verity stuck out her lopped-off chin. The wits sharpened by Fynch took over--along with a bit of intellectual snobbery. "Well, that's both a false premise and a *non sequitor* to start with: *Cadit quaestio*. Besides, I don't wish to hinder both sides, exactly--though perhaps I do, in a way. But--" She looked severely at Lady Bankes. "I had not supposed my politics to be the reason for our visit here."

Her Ladyship looked just as severe. "You are living with me as enemy-guest. Are your politics not pertinent?"

Verity blinked as if slapped. "Oh," she said, and sat very still. How surprising and unreasonable that she should feel so wounded by a hit from the enemy! She pulled herself up in pride, as straight as a heroine from Foxe's Book of Martyrs. "I see. I should not have come. I'll go."

"You'll not." The soft brown eyes looked remarkably hard. "And do not act the martyr with me. Did you think I brought you today for my amusement? It would seem that you know the local stall-holders and even some of my tenants rather better than I, just as I hoped. Perhaps better than

Mayor Bastwick, as well. If you will, you may help us to learn how many of my neighbors would willingly come to our aid if there's need."

"'T'isn't market day, think on." said Sowerbutts. "T'won't fadge, unless tha goes t'all their homes."

"Just what I had in mind," said Lady Bankes briskly. "Talk to their wives, as well. Come, then, Verity; we'll begin with those you know. We leave the tenants until last: they'll help, will'ee nil'ee. But what of the Winterblooms? Fletchers? Soames? Dick Brine? Ned Coombes? The others?"

Mistress Bastwick spoke. "Let Jennet stay here and talk to Miles. You have never met my little boy, Jennet; he is near the age of your younger brothers."

Jennet shook her smooth brown head. "Nay, I'll help with this. But I shall come to see him tomorrow." She did not, Verity noted, bother to ask her mother's permission, nor was she chided for it.

It took the rest of the afternoon to go around the village, and then to the west of town, down the steep track and along the Wicken to the two valley farms and the mill, And a reet sight it was, Sowerbutts observed to himself, t'see a fine leddy doing that. It was also effective, especially combined with the little Puritan, and the liveliest castle daughter. By the time they finished, quite a collection of friends, tenants, and stall-holders had agreed to come at the beat of a drum from the castle--or at least send sons--with perhaps several more when they had made up their minds. Even Noah had volunteered, and he were that plagued when Leah said he were too old!

John and Molly, satisfied that the castle was as safe as possible, and their first duty now to reach the king's ear, could hardly wait to leave. Molly, her plain face wreathed in joy at her own liberation, organized the little boys, told the outraged Trio briskly that although separation might grieve them, it might also improve their characters, and packed all her own things. John took Peregrine aside and asked him what his sister Cecily was like.

"Very like Bess," Peregrine assured him. "She's not beautiful, but she has a kitten face with eyes you could drown in. Especially when she makes an accidental *bon mot*. She sits there with huge eyes, wondering why people laughed," he added, believing it. "And she's sweet and modest and biddable, and already a splendid housekeeper." Though that betrothal was not entirely settled, John looked the way Peregrine had felt when he first realized Bess was for him. "But," Peregrine warned him, "My Madam Grandmama now has Sessy in her clutches, and intends to wed her where she will, and my father can never say her nay,"

John at once looked less delighted and more determined.

And then suddenly they were gone, and Corfe Castle was deplorably empty. No John, easy-going and kind, bringing smiles to everyone. No Ralph somehow getting everything all wrong but engagingly eager to put it right. No Jerome swanking around being Important and Wonderful, nor Edward snooping into things--nor Charles to interpret for Arabella! No one had thought of that! Arabella, distraught, trotted all over the castle calling and chattering incomprehensibly, and finally cuddled up in her mother's bed, hugging her little night-rail for comfort.

No one had realized, either, how much Molly had done. Verity had perhaps been too hasty in offering to replace her--especially with Sir John's library sitting there tempting her. Still, it was a challenge, and she was determined to meet it.

And 'twas not just housekeeping. She belatedly realized how much Molly had done with the little ones. Well, then, Verity must just learn about children. Perhaps she should start with Bridget, who was as unhappy as Arabella, for the Terrible Trio had been as close as triplets. Verity, sorry for the drooping little girl, offered to take both her and Jennet to the village for more provisions. For though there were five--no, six fewer mouths to feed, there was the future to think of.

"I've a nice haunch o' veal for 'ee, Mistress," said Dick Brine with a sour wink that caused Verity to stare in confusion. There was no love nor trust lost between them. "Enough for the fifty of ye there in t'castle."

Bridget, who knew a tarradiddle when she heard it (and no one better!) looked interested. Jennet opened her mouth, looked at Verity, and surprisingly closed it. Verity narrowed her sapphire eyes. Dick was one of the tenants who had agreed not very willingly to come at need, and he surely knew that though some thirty-five had promised help at drumbeat, none were there now. Why should he say such a thing? She squeezed Jennet's hand warningly, produced the smile without the dimple, and shared it with the dumpy form of his wife sitting silent.

"I make no doubt we can eat it all," she said from under her eyebrows. "How much?" They fell to bargaining, but all the while watching each other warily. Finally, price agreed, she looked at the haunch doubtfully. They could no longer spare Sowerbutts to come with her.

"We cannot carry that!" Jennet announced forthrightly. "Not even all three of us."

This was patently true. Verity turned to Dick's chubby and withdrawn wife with a new tact that surprised her. Stretching her non-smile a bit, she aimed it at Ruth. "Could you by your favor lend your husband to help us as far as the gate?" she asked in her meekest tones. (Fynch would have blinked, and Major Rawlins gaped.) "'Tis very heavy for young maidens."

Ruth indicated that Dick was master in their household, and needed no leave from her. Dick scowled and picked up the haunch. And once they were on the bridge and well out of Ruth's sight and hearing, she turned on him.

"Why did you say that about fifty people in the castle?"

He brooded at her. "'Tes being said in Wareham that Her Leddyship be taking in more provisions nor she need. And all that grain two days gone."

Verity, always stimulated by wit, could be silenced by unreason. She blinked.

"Well, we do need it," Jennet pronounced scornfully. "Because if all of you come to stay in the castle at need, what shall you eat if we've no food?"

Verity grinned. "You see, even a child understands the need to stock ahead."

"'Tes said she plans to hold t'castle against Parlyment." They were nearly across the bridge. She turned her head to regard him straightly. His morose face looked more so. "Ay, well. 'Tes what the talk is. T'fight Parlyment, some dunnot like that, sithee."

"Well we dunnot like it neither, and *we*'ll never go attack *them;* but if they come here and attack us, we'll fight back!" Jennet told him fiercely.

Verity pinched her. "Jennet, you and Bridget run ask Peregrine for help with this." Jennet glowered but obeyed. Verity turned to Dick, and produced her most austere smile. "My thanks," she said, leaving him to decide whether it was for the help or the hint.

"I wonder what their next move will be?" mused Lady Bankes, when told.

The answer surprised them all. It was a letter from the garrison at Poole, delivered a few mornings later by two severe troopers who clearly expected to be invited in. Winkworth, on duty, let the drawbridge down and beamed at them through the lowered portcullis.

"No need t' trouble yerselves," he said affably. "'Tis much too pleasant a day, and a sore climb to the keep. Just you set and rest on that nice grass in the sun whilst I deliver it for you." It was clear from his artless blue eyes that he was bestowing on them a rare favor. And before they could protest, he had somehow magicked the letter from their hands to his and backed away. "Or," he added from partly up the winding stairway that ran up the back of the curtain wall to the gatehouse, "there's the alehouse just yonder in the town, and rare ale to be had there."

Then even his voice was gone, and though he slipped back presently to take up his quiet post atop the tower, no amount of fuming produced him or anyone else at the portcullis until Her Leddyship was good and ready.

She read the message to a hastily-called a council-of-war in the study next the gallery. It consisted of Bond and Sowerbutts, Peregrine, Bess, the strongly beautiful Emmot, and--surprisingly--Verity.

"They accuse us of being hostile to Parliament, and of plotting to man the castle against them," she said dryly. "Quite true. They also say that our cannon have been put on their carriages--also true--and are a present and dire danger to all Purbeck, and they demand we turn them over at once."

There was a silence almost of hilarity. Four little cannon, the largest of which shot three-pound balls hardly upwards of a hundred feet?

"All of Purbeck?" breathed Sowerbutts, awed. "Think on, if we had big ones! Happen we'd have all London in a fair sweat, choose how."

Her Leddyship spared a brief smile.

"How did they know?" demanded Verity. "About the carriages?" And though she did not exactly flinch at the looks of dark suspicion suddenly bestowed on her by both Emmot and Bond, something in her gut went cold and tight. She was the obvious suspect! For who but she went daily out into the village and talked to Puritans?

Lady Bankes looked at her. She looked back, her eyes straight and hard and angry and--although she did not know it--hurt. The lady turned back to the others.

"Anyone could see as much from up the hill behind the village," she pointed out. Bond nodded reluctantly; Emmot's shapely lips thinned. "The point is, dare we give up our only defense? Dare we refuse to do so?"

At that the debate started, and raged until nearly noon. At that time Winkworth smilingly told the thwarted troopers that Her Leddyship would send her answer in writing presently--as their own captain had done. After which the gateway remained empty and the portcullis down, and the troopers had little choice but to go back to Poole.

CHAPTER ELEVEN

ATTACK OF THE SEAMEN

Verity could not sleep. The comfortable bed was no longer so, despite down pillows and quilt and fine linen. The violet-embroidered hangings could not keep out the dangerous night air--nor even dangerous feelings. Especially, dangerous feelings. She flopped over to her other side, causing the indignant Naomi to make several nasty remarks. Verity hardly noticed. For the first time in her life, she felt unsure of herself. Not the old uncertainties about the justice of God or who should rule England. Those matters were not up to her. This was worse. She was no longer sure of her own rightness. Was she truly Elected, after all? She searched her conscience, and found much to displease God.

Well, for one thing, she was still lusting after another woman's man, was she not? And able neither to stop nor even much want to stop. How had Satan corrupted her with such feelings of passion? Where had Divine Reason gone? Had she been too proud of her own virtue? 'Pride goeth before destruction, and a haughty spirit before a fall.' Self-righteousness, then, of which Fynch used to warn her? How very humiliating!

Her face flamed hot in the dark. She turned over again. Naomi swore and left the bed. Outside, a nightingale sang and soothed her a little, so that she could grasp for Reason again and try to think logically about the other problem that beset her.

If she was truly against both sides, then where did her loyalty lie--if anywhere? The world was not, after all, a simple place of good and evil as she had been led to suppose! It was twisted, with blurred edges that seemed neither one nor the other. 'So is the world's whole frame Quite out of joynt.' She knew now just how John Donne--and Hamlet, too--must have felt, for the world was indeed quite out of joint.

She was not trusted. But why should she be? She had not come here expecting to be trusted. She was the Enemy. Why *should* they trust her? Why should she be hurt that they did not? What had changed?

What had changed, it seemed, was that she now *wished* to be trusted--or at least liked. Against her will, she liked them--or at least most of them. She had never really known any young people before, nor had any friends at all; and she found it very-- well-- invigorating. Pleasant. None of the people here were wicked, not even Emmot, who truly believed herself to be right. Life, it seemed, was much more complicated than church and Aunt Huldah or even the scholarly debates with Fynch and her nephew had suggested!

It was a warm night. She parted the hangings, pulled off her night-cap, flung it across the room, and stared out at the spangled onyx sky, her eyes dry and hot. There was a hint of breeze, and she began to drift into belated slumber. The dawn chorus began, with one tentative fluting note, then another. Then Naomi, deciding that Verity needed calming--or perhaps just a good grooming--came, purring loudly, and sat on the pillow and began work on her hair. Most of it was firmly braided for the night, so Naomi, grumbling, set about loosening it, with her spiky tongue. Then she selected the fine tendrils about Verity's face, staying in one spot until it hurt. Verity half-woke and put her hands over her face; so Naomi moved purposefully downward. A good deal of very tender skin was exposed to the balmy night. The tongue set to work again...

It was like being flayed! Verity yelped awake and knocked the deeply offended cat off the bed--and it would have been hard to say which of them was more outraged. Sleep was gone, now. The dawn chorus was in full sway, led by the robin's silver-sweet song and the muted throaty music of the blackbird. Cool thin light came in at the eastern window. Verity rose, sighing, angry, more troubled than ever, and stood staring out across the hills. There was no slab of sea showing now, to south or northeast, for pale sea-mist had arisen, pearly and luminous, filling the valleys halfway to the hilltops.

But on the road from Poole, unmisted, something darker moved.

Verity came to attention, leaned forward on the sill, the frightening height forgotten. The unnatural darkness covered the road, coming steadily this way. She was not far-sighted like Bridget (who, poor child, had difficulty making out the letters in her hornbook) but her vision was very good. All uncertainly fled without trace. She whirled from the window, not stopping for robe or pantofles, rushed down the tower stairs, through the chamber below where Bess, Jennet and Joan had been sleeping with untroubled minds.

"Wha--"

"Arise!" Verity flung over her shoulder, and was down the next flight of stairs, and into Her Ladyship's bedchamber.

Lady Bankes was a light sleeper. "What?" she demanded, fully awake.

"The Poole road. Coming here. Men. Lots of them!"

The window confirmed it. They had a little time--though not enough to drum for the villagers. The sleepy-eyed girls were ordered to alert the men-at-arms sleeping in the keep, then waken Nurse and the children, and get

84

dressed. Lady Bankes, disdaining the services of Lucy, was pulling on her own clothes. "Verity, go up and get decent, and then go relieve Nurse Maud."

Instead, Verity stalked into the nursery clad only in her billowing night-gown and a sudden towering fury. Fury at men who made war on innocent families in their homes. Fury at herself for not having sooner realized the sinfulness of this, no matter who did it. Fury even at God and Peregrine and everyone else for not having given her a hint. And fury that she was treated like an enemy, untrained to help, good only for watching babies. Her fine hair, freed from both cap and braids, floated around her like demented cobwebs as she seethed, making her look like an avenging angel. Naomi came and seethed with her, so that Bridget and Arabella took one look and became exceedingly well-behaved.

By the time some forty seamen had roared through Corfe and across the castle bridge to the gap in front of the drawbridge, everyone was alert, and its lady was atop the tower. "Let us in!" they roared in voices somewhat the worse for rum. "We'm come for t'cannon! Give 'em up, whore of Satan! Ho, in there; rouse yourselves!" And they stamped on the stone bridge and fired their muskets uselessly at the raised drawbridge.

"Yes?" inquired a coldly calm voice from above, prudently invisible. "Soft you, now: wherefore so splenitive? Speak your mission calmly, one at a time."

There was disconcerted silence for a moment. Everyone--especially the lady--should still be abed up in the keep! Then a single voice. "Your cannon, Madam; you are ordered to give them up at once."

"Ordered by whom?"

"By the commissioners."

"Can you prove it?"

"We have a warrant."

"Show me."

"Let us in."

"Let one of you go down under the bridge and cross the moat to this side, and come up the hill and pass it through the gap behind the drawbridge, for ye shall not come in."

The stalemate went on for some time. Peregrine joined Lady Bankes. The other defenders gathered at the southwest gatehouse, prepared to scatter to their posts at a moment's notice. The longer the delay, the more time Cook had to fill the bedpans with hot coals, and Bond to organize the cannon. In the nursery, a terrified Lucy rushed in, clutched at Verity's night-gown and begged to be the one to stay and watch the childer. It seemed that she, the most skilled of the loaders, had fallen apart when faced with the real thing. Verity, unsympathetic, hauled her to her feet, told her not to be a witless jabbernowl, changed clothing with her, and rushed outside.

While she did so, a single baffled seaman, sodden from the moat, discovered to his chagrin that he could not, after all, push himself in behind the raised drawbridge, for it lay so close to castle wall that only his arm and shoulder would fit; and that, only barely. Nor could his musket be turned to aim through the gateway. So he finally shoved a grubby bit of parchment in, and an arm came through the lowered portcullis behind and took it. Lady Bankes and Peregrine pored over it by lantern light. It was not only grubby, but torn, crumpled, wet and all but unreadable. Still--it was parchment...

"It *could* be genuine," Peregrine admitted grudgingly.

"It could be anything, retorted the lady. "You! Out there! How d'ye expect us to read this?"

The seamen, none of whom could read at all, did not see the problem. "We'll have them cannon presently, leddy!" one shouted.

"Indeed you shall," murmured the lady, and gave orders. While the seamen debated their next move, every able-bodied person in the castle was at work on the cannon, loading and aiming the biggest one.

Captain Bond applied the match. It went off with a splendid bang. True, the ball failed to get over the thirty-foot wall, but no one realized this in the excitement. Rum or no rum, it took the sailors very little time to change their minds and rush back to Poole.

The castle tended to swagger a bit. They'd routed some forty or fifty men. (Hundreds and millions, said Bridget, angel-faced, and holding up the Trio's reputation very well on her own.)

Everyone knew by now that it was Verity who had roused and warned the castle. No one was quite sure why, so no one mentioned the matter. Not until Jennet, hurtling along the nine-foot-wide top of the western wall, nearly ran into her, stopped short, switched full skirts. "Are you on our side now?" she demanded.

Verity, with still no hint from God, considered the matter. The misplaced dimple peeped, discovered that it had not been summoned, and hastily vanished.

"Well," Verity said severely, "in a way, I am. Because I'm against men making war on innocent people in their homes who never did a thing to warrant it. People like you. *And* like me when Major Rawlins' Cavalier troop broke into my house and abducted me." And then, having made it clear that she was still no Royalist, she went on her way.

86

The sun was now well up, and Corfe villagers, hiding inside their homes until the seaman had retreated, heard the belated beat of a drum from the castle. "Ee, lass, 'tes th' signal," Enoch Powl told his dismayed wife. "We'm off t'the castle, then; all of us what said we would."

Nancy hurled herself on his chest and wept.

The volunteers began to drift in, eager or resentful or excited; dutifully armed, bringing what supplies they could. There was room and to spare, for the castle had been built to house at least a hundred. Grissil, Maud and Lucy eyed the young men with interest. So did Joan. Her leddyship, who missed little, offered dire threats to anyone caught flirting. Grissil and Lucy privately vowed not to get caught at it. Joan looked thoughtful.

So did Peregrine. "A point to us, but their serve," he observed, for he knew tennis even though he did not play it. And he wondered--as all did but the few innocent souls who fancied the game was won--from what corner of the court it would come.

If anyone (like Bess and Grissil) had still been naive enough to think their troubles were over, the illusion was short-lived. Almost at once, the threatening letters began. If Lady Bankes did not hand over the cannon at once, she would be sorry. Everyone would be sorry. Houses would burn, not to mention the wives and children in them--by name: Powl and Coombes, Winterbloom, Brine, Gloys; even Reverend Gibbon. Some one was indeed a very efficient Roundhead spy! Dark glances went Verity's way again, and it actually seemed now that some of her village friends trusted her more than did the castle.

Verity saw clearly that it was Satan's doing. Why, she demanded angrily of God, was He just sitting there doing nothing? Was He punishing Corfe for *her* sin? She had often thought, she told Him candidly and defiantly, that He tended to punish the innocent. Like the people of Jericho, and all the poor animals who got left out of the Ark. Besides, there must have been *some* good people besides Noah, and they had drowned as well. Why? 'Wherefore hidest thou thy face, and holdest me for thine enemy?'

Peregrine, who never expected Divine Interference, felt quite sorry for her. She might be annoyingly self-righteous at times, but at least she had intellectual honesty and strong feelings about justice. "*Fortus fortuna aduvat*, he murmured encouragingly, and she flashed her teeth and dimple briefly in gratitude.

The letters were, of course, also sent to the village; and the wives, as Sowerbutts said wryly, came all-a-bits. They flocked malten-hearted to the castle, where they crowded wailing, holding up the babbies, begging their husbands to come home.

Their husbands, of course, came.

Not that it mattered by then. For the Poole garrison had become active. They waylaid supplies--including the two-hundredweight of powder from Sir Edward Lawrence! They forbade Wareham and all the other the market towns to sell them anything. And they began lying in wait to seize anyone who tried to enter or leave Corfe town.

The end was inevitable. After a week, Lady Bankes agreed on a treaty: cannon for peace.

This time, not even Bess believed it.

CHAPTER TWELVE

ORANGE SASHES

"Certainly not!" said Lady Bankes. "Whatever gave you that idea?" Starling blinked. He had quite supposed-- "We've sacrificed four pawns, only," she went on, "and they were quite expendable."

Four of her audience already understood, a few more were beginning to. The rest were baffled or too young. Warm rain pounded the courtyard outside the tapestry-lined king's hall of the gloriette, which was, if not exactly crowded, well-filled with all the castle residents.

"Oh," said Bess, relieved. "In sooth, I had thought it checkmate."

"Check only. And our move next."

Old Edward Short, scowling, thought about it. "But how can we do aught, Madam? They's took all our guns away. How can us move without our guns?" He was a great believer in guns, was Short. He looked at Peregrine appealingly.

Peregrine patted his hand. "Not to worry, man. 'Strewth, what good were they except to make a noise, and fright a bunch of drunken seamen?"

Short looked skeptical.

"The ball came down *inside* the wall," Captain Bond informed him with a dark look at whoever had aimed it too low. Probably Starling. "And that was the *big* cannon."

Cook looked grumpy and restless. Cannon were nothing to her: food was. And at this rate, dinner would never be done.

"But in truth, Your Leddyship, they have beat us!" whined Lucy.

"They haven't!" said the militant Jennet.

This aroused a clamor. "Ay, they have, Madam, and they'll be back!"

"And us without cannon!"

"And they've those soldiers living in the village now, watching to see we don't bring in more supplies."

Verity could hold her tongue no longer. "Ay, the poor castle, all defeated and pigeon-livered and wailing and wauling, and no head held high!" she scorned, low-voiced, flicking a blue glance at Her Ladyship, who returned it with a glitter.

"Indeed 'tis what they believe, and that is our weapon. Let them believe it so. We shall wait. And betimes--" She leaned forward. So did everyone else but Will, happily nursing, and Naomi, who swaggered in with a mouse which

89

she proceeded to eat in its entirety, fur and all. She was the only cat anyone had ever met who could eat, swear and purr all at the same time, and with her tail erect. No one praised her. Disgruntled, she muttered darkly and stalked from the room to find a second course.

"Hark now--" said Her Leddyship.

Corfe Castle lay quiet, obviously defeated. A little smoke rose from the chimneys, the drawbridge was passively down (though so was the portcullis), and no man tried to leave for provisions or anything else. Only a great deal of grain went quietly down to the mill behind the hill and returned as flour. And two or three innocent little girls in long bunchy skirts slipped daily from the main gate with geese or sheep, to let them graze along the vast hillside, between walls and circling streams. Presently, on the new small path thus made, they brought a cow out, and the grazing moved further around the flank of the castle, out of sight of the village. And if, now and again, livestock went in that had never come out, who would possibly notice? For there were never more than two sheep or one cow visible at any time. And the troopers had better things to do than count them. They were in the village to make sure no man left the castle, and they could do that perfectly well from the alehouse. None even vaguely noticed that the people and activity in the valley were now, as Sowerbutts said, 'throng'. Nor could they see a certain sallyport hidden behind Dungeon Tower, which had also become exceeding throng of a sudden.

As for the gray-clad white-capped Puritan girl who differed from others only by the shining purity of her face, who trudged up the steep stream-bank west of Corfe from her home in the valley almost daily--well, what of her? It seemed that she was entirely too pure to consider a little dalliance or a kiss or two, and the mayor and villagers seemed very defensive of her virtue. So the attention she got was only of frustration, leaving no thought for the odd fact that instead of bringing produce to the market, she took it away.

No, Corfe Castle were finished. Them inside was quite helpless and subdued. The castle was Parliament's at any time they chose to take it. The troopers relaxed even further.

The activity from the castle grew. Sheep were led from the tenant farms on the far side of Wicken Stream around behind Castle Hill. There they grazed, placid and unseen, until humans slipped out of the sallyport above, skidded recklessly down the steep slope and through the moat, seized an unwary animal, and dragged it bleating and struggling back up the hill and into the sallyport.

It was not an easy job. It took three or four just for a single sheep. Seven for the one time they engaged a heifer, which then turned out too large for the sallyport; so it had to be left to graze on the hill until it had calmed down enough for children to bring around to the main gate.

Presently a hundred-and-a-half of powder for muskets with a large quantity of match followed the same route: down the far side of Wicken Stream behind the trees, around the shoulder of hill, across the moat and up into the sallyport. More provisions of every sort slipped in, faster and bolder as the watchers in the village grew more and more casual, sometimes hardly leaving the taproom at all. What an easy assignment, watching over a defeated handful of old men and females!

They were quite annoyed to be called back to Poole.

Verity had been finding hers an easy assignment, as well. How pleasant, at last to be more or less approved by almost everyone in both town and castle--and quite possibly God, as well. For though He had offered no approval to anything she had done since her abduction, neither had He indicated any objections, either to her actions or to her scolding of Him. The food she was bringing in by the sallyport, though she often had to have help taking it up that terrible hill, was welcomed. And she had become quite fond of most of the villagers and tenants--especially Noah and Leah, Enoch and Nancy, and Dorcas and Gaston Winterbloom, whose Uncle Soames owned the alehouse. (She was still in two minds about Mayor Bastwick: he who affably claimed to be on both sides. She suspected the only side he was on was his own. But as he accused her of being the same route only t'other way 'round, it was hard to decide.)

She had been visiting Enoch and Nancy (who was big with her first child); and was reluctant to start home. Enoch was giving her a cockerel, but it was ill-tempered, and rain was falling. She dreaded the crossing of the moat (though today she'd be just as wet beforehand) and the climb up near two hundred feet of steep slippery hill. 'Twould be nasty even without the cockerel. Much easier to go around through the village against M'lady's orders--if only it were remotely sane even to try.

So she dallied with Nancy and Enoch. When what sounded like the entire Poole garrison pounded into the town up beyond the Wicken, the three of them rushed to the farmhouse door and stared uselessly at the thick screen of trees. From the village, came sounds of angry shouts. Armies was armies, and one side hardly more welcome than t'other.

"'Thee stay here, Mistress, where 'tes safe," urged Enoch. "They Parlyments'll never find we here, nor bother with 'n"

But Verity shook her head, and for once God approved her decision with that sense of rightness. "They're my friends, too," she said, edging out the door. "They need me. You'd not have me abandon them?"

Enoch clearly would, but Nancy patted Verity on the rump. "Hurry, then, and take t'cock with thee."

And so Sowerbutts watching atop Dungeon Tower was treated to the fascinating spectacle of Verity's return, clutching a struggling, shrieking cockerel by both legs while with the other arm she tried to defend herself against its beak and spurs, and climb as well. She did not let go even when she fell full-length: once crossing the moat, and thrice more climbing the slick grass of the hill. She found herself muttering imprecations not only to the cock but to the bulky and hampering clothing that she increasingly hated. Naomi would surely have admired the passion of her invective.

"Plague take you, son of Belial!" she growled so ferociously that the cock paused a moment with its beak open to fix a beady eye on hers. Then it pecked again. "Ouch! A pox on you, then! Unnecessary zed! Carbuncle! I shall eat your liver, myself! Rantipole!" She had a few more things to say, but needed her breath for the struggle.

"Get shut of it, lass!" Sowerbutts called from above, but she shook a stubborn head. What, and let this cullionly cock win? Not she! At last, bleeding, she reached the sallyport, which was instantly closed and barricaded behind her. She then refused to give the wretched creature into any of the hands held out for it, but, still hugging it fiercely, marched into the kitchen and shoved it toward Cook.

"Dinner!" she said vengefully.

"Not yet a while," returned Cook, blinking at the state of Verity's face and hands, but intent on the most important matter. "Put it in a store room, poppet; we can catch it later. Short says they'm two or three hundred come to attack us. Help me build up the fire, and then fetch more wood and water. And when you've done that, wipe that blood off your face. You're soaked, too," she discovered. "A mercy it's warm rain. Still, best go up and change afore the fighting starts."

Verity ran up to her tower room presently, no longer even noticing the long steepness of the stairs. Peeling off the soaked gown, she stripped naked, toweled briefly with her blanket, and dragged the older gray gown over her bare body, fuming. (She still had not learned even how to reload, much less shoot.) Ignoring all undergarments: chemise, stockings, corset, petticoats, and even shoes, she stalked over to her chest and took out the bow and arrows, strung the bow, settled the quiver over her head, and went down to fight.

The second attack had begun. It was a little less all-a-bits than yon seamen, said Sowerbutts later, but a bit of a hobble, all the same. They seemed to think that any castle so cowed, and mustering only five men-at-arms, would have enough sense to leave the drawbridge down, so that two or three hundred troops could just walk in. Still, though disappointed, they produced two cannon which they placed on the hill behind the village; and they had also at great inconvenience brought five or six ladders--though no one had thought to check their length.

While some arranged the cannon (to the anger of muttering villagers who felt that enough was quite enough, but thought it wiser not to say so too loudly) the ones with the ladders debated which side of the castle to attack (not noticing that to gain the outer bailey would be virtually useless). The western hill slope was less sheer--but 'twas hard to reach, and the curve of the wall exposed it to crossfire. Better to attack from the east, where the road ran along the stream below the steeply-rising hill. This, of course, involved falling over the ladders and into the moat a number of times, and (like Verity on the western side) sliding back down that enormous rain-slick hill almost as fast as they climbed up. By the time some of them reached the foot of the thirty-foot wall and stood staring up, it was to see a number of unfriendly faces staring back down at them.

And all four of the ladders, they soon discovered, were too short.

From the wall nearest the kitchen, Lady Bankes and the children prepared rocks to greet anyone who ventured that far north. Verity, awkward with her bow, ran to the east wall and scrambled up Plukenet Tower--which just happened to contain Peregrine, with Jennet as his loader. She ranged herself beside him, wielding bow and arrows with total fearlessness and rather more skill than she had supposed she had, firing into groups rather than trying to aim at any single man, even dashing along the wide top of the wall to peer between crenellations for likely targets. She was alight with excitement: almost exalted. She should have been a man! She'd have made a splendid warrior! Compassion was not in her: she aimed recklessly into the welter of orange-sashed men below. (She still confused fearlessness with courage.) At one point she ripped her skirt all the way up, providing a stunning view of a long shapely leg. She was not aware of it, nor even of the long deep scratch down her thigh.

Peregrine, unlike Verity, was soon and unexpectedly filled with revulsion. It was not fear, exactly. It was the discovery that physical violence assaulted his soul very much as malignance did his stomach: it was sickening. Far worse than hunting! His body mercifully took over so that he did his duty, coolly and efficiently--but his heart was shamefully lily-livered. (He was in danger of confusing manliness with callousness.)

Bess, who could not for her life have attempted to injure anyone, even the enemy, discovered that she stayed calm in the face of danger--even when one bullet passed close enough to hear, and even when poor Starling was grazed by another. Joan managed to do her duty, but then fainted. Bridget, surprisingly, was very helpful to Cook. Jennet made no discoveries at all; she simply got on with loading muskets, just as she had been trained to do. And Naomi for the first time in her life found herself totally ignored. She hated it. She hated the noise worse--until a few castle mice, terrified, rushed out of their holes and skittered around in panic. She forgot her grievance and chased them delightedly.

Suddenly a cannon above the town went off. Everyone, attackers and defenders alike, flinched and ducked behind whatever was handy. Verity and Peregrine found themselves behind the same crenellation, clutching at each other and keeping Jennet low between them. (It was now that Peregrine noticed the torn skirt, and a lovely view of the first female leg he had ever seen, bare or otherwise. His body jerked to pleased attention even while he waited with held breath for the crash of the cannon ball.)

The only crash they heard was nowhere near the castle, but in the village. Eyes met, puzzled. Below the wall, there began a hurried skidding down to the road. Though certainly not a rout, it was definitely a retreat: orderly but determined.

The other cannon went off, and again everyone ducked. This time a cannonball landed unnervingly near the orderly retreat, which at once became less orderly.

"All females into the castle!" roared Bond. "Men, get well under cover. Keep an eye open for anyone coming back up the slope."

Verity, who had discovered herself to be a full fortnight older than Peregrine, refused to hide in the castle if he did not. They both stayed, waiting out the long periods of reloading between cannon shots. It started raining again, warm but heavy. A vague brightness lighted the west where the sun was still well up though it was now late afternoon. As summer sunsets were very late, and twilight very long, there was still time for rather more battle than anyone (even Verity) really fancied.

Smoke began rising from the village. "The blundering varlets have fired houses!" Peregrine observed with scorn; and Verity, thinking of her friends, for the first time felt fear along with anger.

And still they waited. It rained harder, and dusk began to fall. Both attackers and defenders had become exceedingly soggy. Four or five more shots came from the cannon, and then no more: perhaps they'd used all their ammunition. One ball had hit the wall quite near Peregrine with thunderous noise (causing worse panic amongst the mice) and ricocheted harmlessly. At least two rolled down into the moat.

A long silence, and then a tucket of trumpets, and the lagging troopers hurrying up the road to the town. Then a delegation of officers in body armor marched across the bridge, diagonal orange sashes belligerent.

"Ho the castle!" it called. "Do you surrender?"

"Don't be cacklewitted," Lady Bankes barked from the tower top, staring down at them scornfully. "Why on earth should we?"

The delegation consulted. "Because 'twill be best for you to do it now," it returned. "Else 'twill go the harder for you." Silence. The chatelaine did not deign to reply. "We shall return!" it threatened.

"Do that," said the lady, and left the tower.

When, later, the troops had departed in angry frustration, the clouds opened for a mother-of-pearl moon, which shone complacently over Dorset. It found equal complacence within the walls of Corfe castle (except among the mice). The humans, having not only won, but also nobly gone to the village and helped put out the fires in four houses (at least one probably set deliberately) were very full of themselves. With one or two exceptions, they definitely swaggered. Especially Bridget, who--even though she had been kept firmly out of danger--bragged of her own prowess in a manner that even Julius Caesar would hardly have considered excessive. She no longer much missed Edward and Jerome, who, being boys, had usually hogged the best roles.

Verity discovered her scratched leg, very much to her surprise. She was turned over to Cook for treatment, and then ordered by the scandalized Lady Bankes to go up and cover herself decently. She now appeared, limping hardly at all, demure in her old blue gown, presumably also clad in hosen, shift, corsets, chemise, bodice, and petticoats (though in fact she was not) and certainly decently covered except for her glittering hair. (She had not been able to find a single cap, she said blandly.) She had no idea that she had titillated Peregrine, or indeed showed him her leg at all.

Peregrine joined the others in checking for unnoticed damage of either castle or personnel, but his thoughts were otherwhere. He had a lot to be thoughtful about, for he had discovered some disconcerting things in the past hours about both himself and the militant and lovely-legged Verity. He eyed the area where the leg was now regrettably hidden, and reminded himself that he was betrothed to Bess. The leg was altogether unimportant. It was a well-known fact that danger often caused people to lose all Divine Reason and make passionate love. At least he had not so forgotten himself as to say or do anything unfortunate. He had merely--er--enjoyed artistic appreciation. Temporarily, of course. He now felt no interest in her at all.

The war-conference was again held in the king's hall of the Gloriette. Lady Bankes told them how wondrous brave they had all been, paused for them to appreciate themselves, and added, "Now--"

"Provisions!" they chorused.

As if in answer, Naomi emerged with a new mouse, which--since she had already eaten two and was full--she laid graciously at the feet of her second-favorite human. She was a great believer in provisions, was Naomi. And also in having her spine scritched.

Her Ladyship obliged. She did more. Those delightful fingers moved relentlessly from Naomi's spine down her side. It was too much. Swearing in outraged dignity, she flopped over sideways and then presented her belly to the fingers.

CHAPTER THIRTEEN

BLUE SASHES

"Halloo th' guard!" bawled Sowerbutts from the top northern window of queen's tower, peering through morning haze. "More troopers! From t'north again!

So soon? They had barely started laying in new supplies! The new batch of grain was not milled! Instantly the other tower lookouts leaned and peered northward, while the courtyards filled with alerted personnel. "Mebbe sixty, eighty all told," called Sowerbutts, who had much the best view. "Coomin' in a fair sweat."

"Up, Bridget," ordered her mother, appearing in the courtyard, and the child scampered importantly for the tallest tower in the keep. Joan, overexcited, pushed Jennet, who used a ready fist. Lucy wailed that the Roundheads had learned of the new provisions and would slay them all in their beds. Peregrine murmured blandly that it wouldn't be easy, with all of them out here in the courtyard.

Emmot turned upon Verity, her handsome face cold in justified rage. "'Tis she! Only she could've told them of our new provisioning! I've said all along, she's betraying us to them! She said herself she's against the King." She raised a vengeful hand toward the shocked Verity, to find it suddenly held fast and painfully by Peregrine, whose muscles had hardened remarkably since he came, and whose amiable smile was suddenly not at all amiable.

"Inasmuch as Verity has done rather more for us than you have," he observed, "I really think I have heard enough of that song. Howsomever--"

Jennet, scowling, marched up to Emmot and kicked at her inadequately through two sets of full skirts and petticoats. Verity, quite able to defend herself verbally, turned upon her tormentor. "Matthew seven, one to five," she said, pithy. "And in case you never bother to read the Bible, which belike you don't, it says 'Judge not, that ye be not judged. For with what judgment ye judge, ye shall be judged--' And-- you can learn the rest for yourself." She turned away, tight-lipped, with no sense of self-righteous justification. Only hurt, for she had been ready to fight or rejoice or even die with them. Was God now, after leaving her on her own all this time, reminding her pointedly that she was still stranger and enemy? Aye, and would always be so, even should she be held here for years and years--which, at the moment, seemed altogether likely.

But she still had her dignity--if little else. Cheekbones jutting, eyes dry, she stood still and straight, feeling rather as Ruth must have done amidst the enemy in the grain fields of Moab, uncomforted even by Jennet's alliance. She turned her head at last to meet the eyes of Peregrine, who was also standing still amid the tumult, looking at her oddly. He had defended her. Why? For pity? She stiffened, torn and sick with it all.

"'A plague a' both your houses,'" she said clearly, and left him to shake his chestnut mane in wonder.

At that point, Bridget's clear treble rang down. "Blue sashes! They have blue sashes! Does that mean they're Good?"

Yes!

--Didn't it? The cheers faded. A few of the smiles replaced themselves with furrowed brows. *Anyone* could put on a blue sash! For once, Verity and Emmot were in full agreement. All eyes turned to Lady Bankes, who pursed her lips and ordered full guard on the walls. "Lucy, take the babes to the nursery. Those not on other duty may come down to the main gate with me-- but stay out of sight. And armed."

Verity took time to fetch her bow and the arrows she had retrieved after the battle. She must, she decided, leaping up the tower stairs, find a more convenient place to keep them. And a fletcher. Arrows did not last forever.

The troop reached the village, paused, had some brisk conversation with the villagers, and came across the bridge to pause at the closed drawbridge.

"Ho the castle!" called their leader, a large muscular man with very white teeth, a riot of red-gold curls, and lashes that would have caused any girl to ache in envy. (Peregrine at once mistrusted him. He was far too handsome, and knew it.) "We've come to your rescue," he announced with brilliant smile and melodious voice. "I've brought seventy-eight men. Where's Lady Bankes?"

It was Starling who appeared between tower crenellations. He had lost all his innocent trust, had Starling, and he glowered down from pale suspicious eyes. "Who be ye, then?"

That glorious head tilted quizzically. "Don't you know me? Ask my good lady chatelaine, then, will she not let us in? We've come a goodly distance to succor her."

The lady had arrived at the top of the wall from the southwest gatehouse, followed by Verity, and was taking her time. It was a very long wall. Starling glanced around at her and proceeded with his duty. "Perdy, then, how does we know ye be what you say? We'm been assaulted here, one way or t'other, full three times now. Can you prove who ye be?"

The mustache managed to look deeply wounded. "Indeed, can you not see?" He indicated his sash.

"Any Roundhead can wear a blue sash," Starling retorted, pleased at his own cleverness.

"Lady Bankes!" The melodious voice was now somewhere between angry bellow and outraged bleat. "Prithee send for your lady, fellow! Lady Bankes!"

Verity had run ahead, was peering down at whole rows of outraged eyes. Not outraged at being thwarted or outwitted: no. They were--deeply insulted. No Calvinist could have acted that role--nor even thought of it! Play-acting was so sinful, it was out of their ken. "They're real!" she blurted aloud, and Lady Bankes appeared at her side, stared down.

"Welladay! Young Robert Lawrence!"

"Captain Lawrence now," he said, modestly proud. "Newly detached from Prince Maurice, who's on his way west to join the Cornish forces. Parted from him at Blandford, to come to your service, at request of His Majesty and Sir John. But of course, if you don't need us--?"

"Winkworth, Short." Her Ladyship called down into the lower guardrooms. "Raise the portcullis and lower the drawbridge. 'Tis Robert Lawrence. Well-come, lad, and don't be offended. Had we been over-trusting, Corfe would now be in enemy hands thrice over."

He melted at once. Displeased frown was replaced by the large smile, white-toothed. "Then we're friends again, Madam, and I shall be happy to take command of Corfe Castle for you. And I've letters, too: for you, and for a Master Peregrine Lennox. And is dinner ready? We're fair beset with hunger."

Lady Bankes started to turn away, paused to look down at the magnificent captain who sat his horse with such proud confidence. "One or two little things, Robert," she said dulcetly. "I'm the chatelaine. You and Captain Bond will jointly defend the castle *under my command*. I do hope this is quite clear. Secondly-- Have you not thought to bring provisions?"

Captain Lawrence gaped.

"Couldn't be done, Madam," he explained, after a meal that made a large dent in the store room and garden. "No commission. King's orders--but offhand, you might say. No time to get provisions. Well, no orders, actually."

Lady Bankes glanced obliquely at Peregrine. "His Majesty clearly has much on his mind. Now your first duty must be to take your men out, as far afield as needs be, and bring fuel and provisions to last us at least three months. All of your men plus our-- sixteen full-grown adults and three children and a babe. Bring more, if possible."

"But--"

"Have you ever been under siege, Captain Lawrence? I don't recommend it. We need food that will keep: dried or smoked meat, livestock, grain-- We must needs have it ground, too, for the mill is outside the walls. How much munition have you? How much ale will your men need? Did you bring your bedding? As soon as you've rested, Bond will show you the castle and fortifications, and then you may sally out. Any questions?"

"I--" Captain Lawrence looked at her. Even though he had met the chatelaine a number of times, he had somehow expected her to have become a frail and helpless little lady under duress. It was, of course, quite improper for a female to be in command...

He decided after careful thought not even to mention it.

Peregrine, down in the sunshine of the west bailey, read his letters, especially the one from his favorite sister. "Dere Perry," wrote Cecily in the individual spelling that everyone used. "John Bankes has cum, and hee told us about Mayday and asked His Majesty to sende help. Prince Charles did, too, but I think they forgott about provvissions for all those souldiers, becaws men thinke food cummes by magick. So I hope you havve enough. Charles is onely thirteen but he is verry chivvalrus and hee says hee likes Older Women like mee. Oxford is even more crowded now, and Madam Grandmama is still--" Something was crossed out. "--verry well."

Peregrine could well imagine what she had not dared to put on paper! Dear Sessy! She did not have the distressing streak of willfulness that afflicted many of the daughters in Grannie Val's line: Gran herself, her grandam, a distant great-grand-aunt called Linnet whose portrait showed Peregrine's very own wayward eyebrow-- Even their older sister Oriel had married to suit herself, to the fury of Madam Grandmama. But Cecily, like Bess, was made of soft gold rather than iron: the only perfect maidens he had ever known. They would marry as bidden: 'twas the destiny of youth. He did hope Sessy would be as lucky as he! He looked back at the rest of the letter.

"I do hope you are not too boarred there, dere Peregrine, as you always arre."

Peregrine blinked. It occurred to him for the first time that he had not had so much as one boring moment since that moment in February when he found himself ducking Verity's arrow. After that, of course, came Bess, and a great deal of work about the castle, and the urgent interest of defending from invaders...

His mind focussed on this interesting fact while his eyes regarded the robins, who in turn were alert for noisy worms. The song thrush, now a regular visitor, was watching Naomi and the feisty cockerel (still uneaten) who seemed to be--*flirting*? They rubbed against each other, the cock making throaty sounds to match the cat's purrs. Naomi, her eyes slitted, groomed his feathers while he croaked his pleasure with half-open beak and beady eyes. Afterward, he preened her fur. Then they settled down together in the sunshine, feathers and fur fluffing contentedly. Peregrine and the song thrush both eyed them with bafflement.

Verity's voice rose from around the other side of the south tower. "His name," it said firmly, "is Dinner, and he deserves to be eaten. He's a spawn of Satan. Well, look at him!"

She came in sight, towing Bess and Joan, who stared round-eyed.

"Well, we can't eat him now, can we?" said Bess, pleased. "Not if he's been named, and is friends with Naomi."

Verity grunted and muttered something oblique about a rose by any other name.

"You cannot seriously intend to let her go into town, Madam!" expostulated Captain Lawrence, staring at Verity. "When she's a confirmed anti-monarchist?"

"*Audi alteram pertem,*" said Peregrine crisply. *Damnant quod non intelligunt,* and you'll never understand much by listening solely to Emmot." He bent a hard look at her. "*Aeturnun servans sub pectore vulnuis.*"

Captain Lawrence, like all upper-class men, had a good classical education. He stared at Peregrine and then Emmot, who stood proudly defiant in the conviction of her own rightness. Then at Verity, who, refusing the indignity of defending herself, had again become a Foxe's Martyr. "*Varium et mutabile semper femina?*" he suggested.

"Fickle and changeable females, are we? Oh, well-- Vergil could be quite silly at times, couldn't he?" Verity murmured, to Captain Lawrence's open astonishment.

Peregrine grinned. "You'll get used to it," he told the captain kindly. "I shouldn't think there's more than two or three fickle or changeable females in the entire castle. Certainly not Verity--nor even Naomi over there." Naomi heard her name, looked up and rumbled at him. "Wrong-headed, mayhap, and often infuriating--but neither fickle nor changeable." He looked affably around: at Emmot, at Verity, at Lady Bankes and her daughters, at Peggotty grumping from behind an archway, and Cook. Captain Lawrence had the grace to smile ruefully. Lady Bankes put in her ha'penny worth.

"*Agenti incumbit protatio.* And that will be quite enough Latin for now." Verity clearly understood that this meant Greek as well, and closed the mouth she had opened. "And," finished Lady Bankes, "where Verity goes is *my* decision."

"Send Emmot along with me, Madam," said Verity wickedly. Jennet bristled. That was *her* privilege. "I'm sure she can make sure we don't sell any information to the Roundheads--if she can figure out who the Roundheads are. And she's as big and strong as a man, so she can carry what we buy," She finished the double insult with a sweet triumphant bare-toothed smile that showed no hint of dimple.

"Hoist with her own petard," murmured Peregrine, and enjoyed Verity's flicker of surprise.

"If Emmot stood and scowled at them like she is now," said Jennet forthrightly, "she wouldn't need to carry anything because no one would sell us anything. And we don't need her."

Captain Lawrence had opened his mouth.

"Enough," said her ladyship.

He closed it again.

CHAPTER FOURTEEN

WHEN ADAM DELVED

A turbulent May had become a tranquil June. Blissfully hot days warmed the cold stone of the castle, and warm rain fed the flourishing garden. The robins, having finished their first brood, were working on another and scolding each other and everyone else about it. The swifts had arrived to nest all over the keep, hawthorns were white froths of blossom along the Wicken where fallow deer and dancing hares could sometimes be glimpsed. The otters had four cubs, and they all played delightfully and slid down the banks of Castle Hill into the moat. The song thrush sang joyously and tunefully. At night, very sharp eyes could see the badgers, whose sett honeycombed the lower hill, lumbering about while the nightingale sang.

Arabella turned three and suddenly outgrew every garment she had, even her leather corset, so that every needle was put to work on some marigold damask from the castle stock of material. Everyone had hoped that the loss of her translator would spur her to learn English, but the only English word she had produced so far was one that brought a her a sharp smack on her well-padded behind.

Captain Lawrence, having prudently decided not to dispute the running of the castle with its chatelaine, had settled for running the defenses. Barrels and barrels of provisions now nearly filled the lower floor of King's Keep. Naomi wandered among soldiers' feet, arrogantly casual, with her best friend the still-uneaten Dinner, whose aim, it seemed, was to out-sing the tuneful song thrush. He had some way to go. The soldiers, adaptable though they were, found they two right confusing.

'Twas no less confusing being quartered in a castle with ten women--not counting Lady Bankes. They ranged from fourteen to passing elderly, and some of them delectable--and not a man daring even a quick buss on the cheek for fear of Captain Lawrence's and Madam's wrath. Especially Madam's. It were a bit of a trial, though, for the maids were right tempting--and though the three gentry maidens were far above even wishing, so much propinquity was bemusing. The plump and rosy Mistress Joan was a sweet flirt, Mistress Bess a lovely angel, and Mistress Goodchild-- Well, what was she? Some said not even pretty; some said she'd be a raving beauty given a year or two; all agreed that her tongue could be right waspish, her eyes blue daggers, and her mind all too sharp for a female. Still--given that flirtation was unthinkable, any road, 'twas certain sure she was interesting to talk to. And as reward to them as behaved, there were village lasses.

For Captain Lawrence had astutely begun bringing the best-behaved of his men in to visit the alehouse and the market, and get acquainted with the townsfolk. No telling when a friend or two out there might come in handy, he observed. For no one really believed that this blissful peace could go on forever. Hoped, perhaps, but not believed.

For her part, Verity felt suddenly freed. She had never suspected life could be so pleasant and diverting! She became so good at Molly's work that she had time for other things. She went to town at will now, not merely to get fresh food (though she did that, too) but to visit friends. Particularly Dorcas, with whom she even stayed the night once. It was vastly interesting: the family crowded all in the single room of the cottage, on pallets, looking up at bare rafters and Purbeck stone.

Dorcas lived up on the hill overlooking town and outer bailey, next door to Salamon and Oliver Soames. (Of the two, Verity much preferred Salamon, damned or not. She did not like the way Oliver kept looking at her and wetting his lips.) It must have been from one of these half-dozen cottages, Verity realized, that Someone had watched them putting the cannons back on the carriages and reported them. She shrugged. It could have been anyone--though Salamon was a likely suspect. If it were he, it was probably from impulse or a sense of experiment rather than spite--and it didn't really matter now, did it?

She visited Noah and Leah, too, and introduced Peregrine to them, and of course to Enoch Powl, whose Nancy would give birth late this summer. And even, at last, to Mayor Bastwick and Miles, his frail five-year-old boy. She sometimes sat with Miles and told him stories--though it turned out that Hamlet, The Aeneid, Sophocles and even the Bible were not much to his taste. Jennet, who had adored him since that first visit (finding him much nicer than her own tiresome younger brothers) did much better. She told wonderful fanciful tales about Dick Whittington, Babes-in-the-Wood, Mother Bunch, Bluebeard and a dozen more. Hearing them, Verity felt that her education, splendid as it was, had been in this respect seriously neglected. Miles lighted like a candle when he saw Jennet; and Verity was happy to move aside, for her visits were sore pain to her. She very much feared God might take Miles unto Himself, and she disapproved.

"The thing is," she told Him earnestly, "You take so many, I wonder if You have enough time to spend with them all, or think about the poor parents;

or at least make sure they have a new babe, which I somehow think the Bastwicks won't." Her daimon had no comment to this. She sighed. She sometimes wondered whether God, being male, paid much attention to female viewpoints.

But above all, there was Sir John's incredible library! Shelves and shelves of precious leather-bound books embossed with gold leaf! Here were Plato, Aristotle, Homer, Sophocles and Thucydides, Ovid and Seneca, Chaucer and Spenser, and modern poets like Milton (who wasted his gift writing boring political tracts for Parliament) and Suckling and Lovelace (who, said Peregrine, were friends of the King and Queen). She and Peregrine, like starving dogs, spent every free minute there, battling joyously in three languages. Bess often joined them, pleased at being with two people she liked so well. But she was quite out of her depth, and puzzled at the way they seemed to enjoy squabbling.

"Shakkspur!" Verity said, delighted. "I want to read them all! Fynch had only Hamlet and Romeo and Juliet, and bits she remembered from others."

"I did wonder why you could quote Shakespeare!"

"It's Shakkspur," she corrected him.

"Not when my grandparents knew him, it wasn't," he retorted with a wicked grin, and she whirled on him.

"They didn't! Is it true? How?"

"They ran away, both of them, when they were young, and acted in his company. It's how they met. They-- Grandfer played Romeo." (Wiser not to mention Gran's shocking behavior.)

Verity clutched Henry V in one hand and waved Twelfth Night in the other. "How many do you know? Fynch said all his tragic characters are-- well, of lesser stature than the Greeks, but more complex and human than Agamemnon or Odysseus, or even Medea. But she said the other Shakkspur ones--"

"Shakespeare."

"Shakespeare. Is it true their tragic flaw was usually Passion? Fynch said Lear embraced the passion of anger, but that Othello was really reasonable until his Understanding was corrupted by jealousy."

Bess turned adoring but puzzled eyes from Verity to Peregrine, who was deep in thought. He treated Verity almost like another boy, she had noticed, with never a compliment and seldom a smile. Well, not an admiring one, anyway. He now aimed that impudent eyebrow at her. "The Tragic Flaw *is* different," he decided. "In the Greeks 'twas mostly *hubris*, which is--"

"Yes, I *know* what it is," she said impatiently, and he slanted his brow harder. "Don't condescend! But with Oedipus, it was anger, and with Hamlet, too. He warned Laertes, remember? 'For though I am not splenitive and rash, yet have I in me something dangerous which let thy wisdom fear.' But mostly he kept his anger in leash, which Oedipus never even tried to do. And Hamlet reasonably refused to slay Claudius until he was quite quite reasonably sure he really did murder his father."

"Yes, but then he quite *un*reasonably didn't stop to find out *who* was hiding behind the arras, and stabbed Polonius instead of Claudius, and that's what destroyed him in the end."

"Speaking of behind the arras," said Verity sweetly, "do you suppose that's Polonius behind the one over there?" She pointed to a twitching tapestry of Jonah. "Shall we stab him?"

Bess looked alarmed. Jonah quivered. Peregrine exchanged glances with Verity. "'How now?'" they shouted in near-unison. "'A rat? Dead for a ducat!'"

The tapestry thrashed around in panic, heaved, and spewed forth a panicky Bridget who stared first in dismay and then anger at their laughter. What a churlish thing to do, when she was only exercising her healthy curiosity!

"A plague take you!" she blurted, and bolted from the room.

Verity grinned at Peregrine. "*Ira furor brevis est,*" she observed. He grinned back. It was a remarkably apt quote: she was as good at it as he.

But Bess was completely lost. They had been talking about the battle in mankind between Divine Reason and satanic passion, had they not? And that any behavior not controlled by Divine Reason, even anger or drunkenness, was a brief madness. She understood that: all the world did. But what were things like hamlet (if it wasn't a village) and hyu-briss, and what kind of cat was an eedi-puss? And what had it all to do with rats and ducats behind the arras? And what was so funny? Her lovely face was quite bewildered.

Peregrine saw, and turned to give her a candescent smile: one that made his blunt features quite different, somehow. Verity instantly fell into sin: lusting even harder after her friend's husband-to-be. With passion. Satan was indeed tempting her; and it was a shock, for she had never willed it. She had always thought that sin must be deliberate, for how else could it be a sin? How quick she had always been to condemn others, in her-- her-- her *hubris*? *She?* Dear God! She quite lost track of the conversation for a moment, and found it again at an unfortunate point.

"--and most Greek tragic heroes suffered from *hubris*, which is overweening pride--"

Poor Bess looked more confused than ever. "Never mind," she said kindly. "I like listening, and I don't need to understand. Please go on."

But the thread was lost. Verity sighed again, wrenched her mind around to Shakks--Shakespeare. Could she find time to read all of his plays? Would they one day be altogether lost and forgotten? Peregrine had said the poet Davenant, who claimed to be his son or godson or something, was trying to bring him back into fashion. She smiled to think of it.

Peregrine regarded her appreciatively. She was really not too bad, after all, if spiky. Not like Bess, of course, who was like lilac and apple blossom, while Verity was more like very thorny hawthorn. On the other hand, she was much more fun to talk to. Bess for a wife and Verity for a friend might be very pleasant, indeed; and one must not even think of legs.

Had Verity suspected him of any such notions, she would have been deeply shocked. It merely seemed to her only that everyone seemed nicer lately--even Emmot.

The family often sat in the Long Chamber making music, which was still a great wonder to Verity. She had never heard any except for the birds and Fynch's tortoise-shell music box. It could not, she had decided, possibly be sinful, for God Himself must love to listen.

"It sounds so thin without the boys, especially John," Bess sighed. "Verity, you must learn to play something. The virginals, perhaps? Or the rebec or viol or lute--?"

Verity, sorely tempted, said she would consult God about it. She was fairly sure what He would say: nothing. Which meant she was free to make up her own mind. Peregrine, reading her thoughts easily for once, knew exactly what she would decide. He lowered his flageolet, leaned over it, spoke into her ear.

Tell me about Freeborn John and I'll teach you music."

She lowered cornflower eyes to the sleeve of Arabella's new marigold gown, and then raised them to his, which were peaty-green, and upside-down and enchanting.

"Some day, perhaps," she said tantalizingly, and went back to the tiny orange stitches, leaving Peregrine as curious as ever, while Verity silently told Satan what she thought of him.

As her own three gowns were becoming quite worn, Verity had thankfully accepted one the color of kingfishers that Joan's burgeoning breasts had suddenly outgrown. (Joan was developing a delectable figure, rounded and cushioned to make the men sigh.) As well, Lady Bankes had given Verity a fine length of sapphire damask for another, to make once Arabella's was finished. It was a lovelier blue than her old one, and the damask pattern shimmered in the light. She kept the old blue for everyday, and the dove gray and slate gray and her white caps and aprons for town visits. And Bess fixed her hair in the current style, with soft curls around the front, while the rest was braided and coiled in a circle around the back of her head.

"Certes, 'tis lovely that way!" exclaimed Bess, so secure in her own loveliness and sweet temper that she never grudged beauty to anyone else. "Did I not say it would be? You must wear it that way always! Mustn't she, Mama!"

"Except in town, of course," said her mother. "We don't want your Puritan friends thinking you've become a Royalist, do we?"

"No, M'lady," Verity agreed absently, twisting like a newt to see the back of her head through two small hand-mirrors. (She did not really care what people thought she believed--but was very interested in figuring it out herself. Politics was settled for now: she was against the war. But religion was still a sore puzzle. And the Anglican services at the castle chapel seemed amazingly easy-going. Nothing to drive the spirit.) She curtseyed. "Now we're at peace--for the nonce, anyway--could I go to the town church one Sunday, M'lady?"

Lady Bankes fixed an interested eye on her. "Indeed. We might all of us go: it has been too long. Reverend Gibbon would be pleased. You do realize that the service is unlikely to be either Church of England or Calvinist?"

"Not Calvinist, anyway; not in a beautiful church with surplice and an organ and fine colored windows," she said gravely. "They'd deem it sinful."

They would, indeed, she realized on Sunday, listening to the sermon; and for more reason than a sinfully lovely church with sinful music. Nor was it like the pleasant sermons of the castle chapel. Though Reverend Gibbon began with the required Protestant diatribe against the Bishop of Rome and Corruptions of the Flesh, he then shifted to talk of good works and virtuous acts. He even suggested that there might be another road to Salvation besides pure Faith--even for those already damned!

Verity sat upright, eyes blazing gentian. Her very own wonderings! That Predestination might not necessarily be final? That one might indeed change his fate by his behavior in life? Fynch had always said--privately--that there *must* be free will or all was a nonsense--and oh, how angry Aunt Huldah would have been! (And where, she wondered, was Aunt Huldah now? Listening from heaven? Angry from there? Very like!)

They walked thoughtfully back to the castle afterwards. Some of them had never heard of this particular doctrine. 'It was something to think on! Lady Bankes glanced sideways at Verity, curious. She herself had no need of soul-searching. She was fiercely and implacably loyal to king, husband and the Church of England. Still, she understood that this dauntless slip of a girl was quite as fierce and implacable in searching for loyalties she had not yet found. They two were, perhaps, not altogether unlike.

"Pure Arminianism," she observed, her voice neutral.

Verity turned on her. "Is that what it is?" she demanded, excitement lighting her face.

"Yes, I think so." Her Ladyship studied her. "What did you think of it?"

Verity, as usual, took time to ponder--but not enough. "I think," she blurted, "that I am likely an Arminian as well as a Leveller."

She had not meant to say that. They stared. "What under God's earth is a Leveller?"

"Oh-- just a name Master L-- some one I knew-- called his ideas, privately. Well, his friends did, he said."

"Oh? And what are his ideas?"

It was a clear dare. Those mild brown eyes were challenging hers, and Verity had kept silence for too long. She chanted.

"'When Adam delved and Eve span,
Who was then the gentleman?'"

"God's candlesticks!" said Peregrine, more astonished than he should have been. "John Lilbourne!"

CHAPTER FIFTEEN

NO SASHES

Corfe villagers were, Verity had slowly realized, mostly related. Well, they would be, wouldn't they? She had not yet got all the cousinships straight, except that Salamon and Oliver Soames were, it seemed, nephews and not sons to John Soames of the alehouse.

"My cousins," said Dorcas Winterbloom just before dawn on a late June morning, sorting out the recently-hatched chicks that Verity was about to carry back to the castle. "Ee do go through a mort o' food over there, dunnot thee?" She nodded across to the castle. Verity had stayed the night again. This was a pleasant change from early-rising at the castle to start the day's housekeeping. The dawn chorus of birds was pulsing the air. Morning mist lay in a pearly blanket over the town below, but the castle rose above it as from the sea itself, to dominate the sky. Verity, who was freshly astonished every time she saw it, wondered if one ever got used to the sight. She asked Dorcas, who looked faintly puzzled.

"Aye," she said vaguely. "Tes allus there. Fair big, it be," she conceded.

They stared at where it towered peacefully against the sky. Today, June 23, was Jennet's birthday. Verity must be sure to get back in plenty of time for it--though that sharp-tongued little madam was unlikely to show much sweet appreciation. She seemed to be missing her brothers nearly as much as did Bridget--who was of late trying to take on the wickedness of the entire Trio. Aside from that, Corfe had now enjoyed three or four weeks of peace, and Verity had never in her life been as contented. She looked skyward for a quick murmur of appreciation to God (Who must surely get tired of receiving nothing but complaints and demands) and turned back to Dorcas.

"They're your first-cousins, then? Oliver and Salamon?"

Dorcas crinkled her broad freckled face in a grin. "Aye." She raised her voice. " Gaston, fetch some more eggs, there's a love."

Gaston produced his equally-freckled twelve-year-old face from the doorway. "How many?"

"As many as we can spare," said his sister. "And then go across and ask Uncle Matthew or Salamon can they let Verity have a broody hen or two. I'll help 'ee take it all t' castle," she offered with a wide grin. (One of Captain

Lawrence's soldiers had taken what Sowerbutts called a gradely fancy to Dorcas, and it was clear that she returned it.)

They descended with chicks and hen and eggs into the thick mist of the town square, and had reached what was just visible as the mayor's house when Verity became aware of muffled sounds. Thumping, rustling, tramping, and muted roaring seemed to come from all directions. The girls stopped, bewildered.

"Tes from the road," said Dorcas, accustomed as Verity was not to the confusing effects of heavy sea fog. As she spoke it all erupted into an army pouring into Corfe. It swirled around the girls, filling the square with harsh commands as men marched, trampled, pushed and shoved all around, invisible in the whiteness until they loomed terrifyingly over them, with no sashes to identify them as either side.

And they were between Verity and the castle!

She'd been over-quick to thank God for favors, she thought briefly. Pulling Dorcas with her onto the mayor's porch, she pounded rudely on the door. Bessie the maid opened it, fearful. The mayor's face appeared behind. Verity faced it squarely. "May we come in? 'For the great day of His wrath is come, and who shall be able to stand?'" And, impelled just then by a sudden hard elbow into her back, she proved her words by lurching against Bessie, who lurched against the mayor, who staggered but did not lose his calm.

"In sooth," he said, and accepted the hysterical hen. "'Deliver me in Thy righteousness, O God, and cause me to escape.' Psalms. Dorcas Winterbloom, is it? Do you come in, too?"

Dorcas stood still, trembling: "I want to go home," she moaned. But Mayor Bastwick pulled her inside, and he and Verity faced each other.

"Thee cannot get to the castle," he said. "Not now."

"No."

"I dare not keep thee here."

"No."

He stared briefly, perhaps puzzled that she had figured the thing out as quickly as he, and then urged them all into the large kitchen, where another maidservant had already brought to life the banked fire in the huge fireplace, and begun to heat the iron pot hanging over it. "Durst your father keep her, Dorcas? They'll be at the door any moment. Out the back way with thee, then, and God protect thee."

He shoved the muttering hen and the baskets of cheeping chicks and silent eggs back at them. The door closed firmly just as banging began on the front door. Dorcas seized the hen and one basket, and led the way on panicky legs up the hill past common fields and the occasional cottage, until they reached her home, where her parents stood fearfully staring downward.

"The Mayor asks durst we keep Mistress Goodchild, for he dursn't. Why, Verity?"

Verity allowed herself to be drawn into the cottage and stood blinking at them in the dimness. "Wherefore should 'ee be a danger?" demanded Aaron Winterbloom. "Isn't it a Parlyment army down there?"

Dorcas shrugged. There had been no orange or blue scarves.

"Their hair was short and garments plain," said Verity.

"Ay, then. And all in town know tha'rt daughter of a Parlyment colonel. So wherefore?"

"Because," she said forthrightly, "all know as well, that I've been living in the castle and am friends with them there. And if any tell, Parliament soldiers will want to know a great many things I shan't tell them." She hoped she would not. She no longer had any faith in the civilized behavior of either side. There was a stark silence. "To give me refuge might be a danger to you, and I won't do that."

She turned toward the closed door, a bit uncertainly. For where could she go? 'Twas fine weather; perhaps she could just stay out of doors, or even find her way eventually down into the valley and hide among the trees along the Wicken? For she could not endanger Enoch and Nancy, either.

The door stayed closed before her. Aaron Winterbloom stood before it. "Ee's been our guest, and brought gifts; we'll not abandon thee. Nor would any in Corfe betray--" He stopped, not altogether certain of this. None of them were. Any child might do it by accident, or Salamon for a lark; even one or two in malice. "Any road, them's not likely to come up here and search thee out," he finished less doubtfully. "Not right away, leastways. Gaston's slipped down t'see what's up; no one's safer nor a lad. Not lasses, sartin sure. Stay. At least until he's back."

They waited, peering out the open door, able to see very little below even when the mist began clearing, for the church and those stone rooftops were in the way. At last Gaston returned. "Parlyment," he confirmed. "Tes said five or six hundred. And quartering troops everywhere, even in t'church," he added disapprovingly. The church might be a bit over-decorated for some folk, but 'twas theirs, and not for sojers to be sleeping in.

"That'll turn our folk against them for starters," said his father with satisfaction and disapproval combined. "And *against* them is *for* you, Mistress Goodchild. Stay here 'tweenwhiles, lass, and we'll think on."

"If I do, you had best start calling me Verity," she said.

Peregrine withdrew his eye from a crenellation and sat back on his haunches, almost mindless with rage and dismay. That thrice-accursed army had been pounding at the walls all day with their guns, and alert guards had now settled firmly all the way around the moat, insuring that no one larger than Naomi or Dinner--and probably not even they--could get out unseen. Nor in. He began to curse quietly but inventively. His family and friends would have stared to see their bland and imperturbable Peregrine in this state! Even Naomi looked faintly shocked. He came to the conference of staff and officers with blazing eyes.

"God only knows what's happening to her!"

"Probably getting along excellent well with the soldiers," said Emmot unwisely, and came dangerously close to being slain twice: once by Peregrine's fist, and again--more fearsomely--by Lady Bankes' eye.

"If you ever again say such a thing," said Her Ladyship icily, "you will be dismissed on the instant. Peregrine, do try to calm yourself. She's at least as intelligent as you, whether you believe it or not; and she has friends there. She is probably as safe for the nonce as we. Now--" She looked at Captain Lawrence. "Have you any suggestions for improving the defense? How dangerous is that demi-cannon like to be? And the sacres? Is it Sir Walter Erle, d'you think? What do you know about him and his tactics?"

Captain Lawrence crossed one foot over the other knee, leaned an elbow on the raised knee and his chin on that hand, and pondered. "To begin with," he said, some of you were wasting ammunition. My men--and now yours-- have orders to make every shot a reasonable one. And--"

Naomi stalked into the room, confronted him, and loudly demanded the instant return of Her Verity. She was extremely rude about it. Peregrine could have cheered her.

And not even Jennet remembered that today was her birthday.

CHAPTER SIXTEEN

ASSAULT

For the next two or three days, those on the hill had quite a good view of the attack on the castle, punctuated with news from young Gaston, who adored all the excitement and danger.

"'Tes Sir Walter Erle, right enow; they calls him Old Wat." He chuckled and then had to explain to Verity that Old Wat was a country name for the timid hare. "Howsomever, some say he's sent by Parlyment, but others say he's not, for they don't wear orange sashes. He's quartered his officers at t'alehouse, but hisself wi' Mayor Bastwick, and Uncle Soames be fair pushed to serve all at t'taproom. They'm quartering sojers at most houses, and taking provisions from the rest, and they'll surelye come here, so us had best hide everything hideable, sithee."

The entire hill was quick to do so--and just in time. Troopers swarmed up the hill explaining--when they bothered to explain at all--that as they were doing the town a service, the town must feed them. When old Mistress Coombes grumped that she could do very well wi'out their service, she was backhanded to the ground, and went around for days bragging that that she were t'only true man i'the place.

Alas, chickens could not be well hidden. All of them including the broody hens were whisked off, and the Winterblooms were thankful to be left with the baby chicks (who at least would grow into another flock) and all the grain and cheese and smoked meat and even the eggs they had hastily buried under the floorboards. Those with cattle or sheep fared far worse. The pigeons had flown away but might be back--some day. And, God be praised, the troopers scorned all garden produce: sparrowgrass, endive, radishes, leeks, onions, peas, carrots, spinach and beans, even strawberries and gooseberries, as unfit for proper men to eat.

"We must plant more," said Dorcas eagerly.

Her father was looking thoughtful. "Them at t'castle never seized our food will'ee nil'ee," he pointed out. "Nay, nor they Royalist sojers, neither. Her Leddyship takes what's fair from t'tenants, and buys what we'm willing t'sell. I'm mindful that t'town'll be more than ever against these sojers and *for* thee, Mistress--er--Verity." (Dorcas' parents had trouble being so familiar with a maiden of the gentry. Their children did not.)

"I hope so," murmured Verity, but her eyes and mind were on the castle. A demi-cannon, a culverin and two sacres had been aimed wherever the castle might seem weakest, and she felt a little sick. They couldn't do it, of course-- could they? But some cannonballs were going over the wall. They might hit someone. Would God let such a thing happen?

Well, yes. Certainly. He often had. Look at all the women and children He had told the Israelites to butcher. Why should *her* friends be favored? And what could one frail girl do even if she had her bow and arrows? She pointed her eyebrows at each other, and had earnest words with Almighty God; and the guns went on pounding at the walls for hours--or until the things got too hot to handle and a rest was called. As far as Verity could see, no impression had been made--but how long would this last? She became glum, and some of Gaston's reports were hardly encouraging.

"That there Old Wat and his captains, they'm binding t'sojers to Christian resolutions, that if Her Leddyship dunnot yield, they'm all to be slaughtered, and that there's rich booty inside, and they's to have double pay and all t'women and girls." He looked at Verity, who was thinking with horror of Jericho, and hurried with the better news. "But I heared t'sojers talk amongst theyselves. They says how *can* they have all t'women after they be slaughtered? And afore they came here, he told them t'castle were on level ground wi' low weak walls and only five old men and the rest women, ready to give up at once. But 'twas all lies; so they'm not believing what he says now. And another thing. They'm shooting notes tied on arrows over t'wall trying t'bribe folk inside to betray Her Leddyship, and 'tis said that Old Wat be ranting mad when they just tosses em back."

It was somewhat cheering--she supposed.

It was two days later that Oliver came with a message. "Uncle Soames; he has to have more help in t'taproom. Dolly and Peg has left and run home, too feared o' they sojers. Old Sir Wat, he says he wants service, he don't care how. Oliver and Salamon and me, we has to go be servers, but Uncle wants Dorcas, too."

Dorcas shrank fearfully. Gaston volunteered his services. Everyone argued. In the end, Verity, escorted importantly by Gaston, went down to the mayor's back door and confronted him. "Are any soldiers here?"

He shook his head, glanced at the door. "We must talk," he murmured, and led the way into the big, low, stone-flagged kitchen, now empty. A large table with a scrubbed top held an array of plates, spoons and knives, and at the far wall was the huge fireplace. A great iron pot hung above the fire of peat and wood, and the one chair in the room stood beside it. He handed his wife to that chair, smoothed down his sober goose-turd green waistcoat, and gestured Verity to a stool, while Gaston sat shyly on another.

I do feel we must each know more of where the other stands, Mistress. I assume you have some loyalty to Lady Bankes despite her Royalist leanings. Are you, then, still against both sides but not wishing to hinder either?"

She scowled at the irrelevance. "I said before, I'm against all men who make war on harmless civilians! And I'd hinder all of them gladly, no matter if they do say the Lord is on their side. Even if He really is," she added darkly, and leveled that flat chin at him. "And you, sir? Are you really for both sides?"

Both the crinkles and the bouncing eyebrows were still and grave. "In truth, I am on whichever side will best serve my Miles, Mistress. I will say or do whatever is needful to protect my wife and son, whomever else it might harm. You may not know: he is our seventh child and the only one to live even so long. There's naught I would not do to preserve him, did it sacrifice all the world and damn me to hellfire."

"Oh," said Verity, shocked. She had never even imagined such a dilemma, much less what she would do in like case--if, say, it were P-- Fynch at risk, or-- Nor could she guess what God would say about it. If anything. But, she realized, it was now in some sense her own case, too. Everything that she truly loved--her friends, even her cat--were in that castle. Indeed, they were now her own people, more than anyone but Fynch had ever been. Much more! And what sins, in reality, would she be not willing to commit for them?

The very thought, she realized, probably showed that she was not of the Elect, after all! Her eyes in the candlelight looked cobalt blue as she surveyed the self that was being gradually revealed to her, and she turned her former question on its tail. Could those predestined to heaven change and sin and become damned? Ot would God have known that, too, ahead of time? Probably. Even so, shouldn't it be possible to be Saved again by virtuous acts? But what *was* a virtuous act? Slaughtering God's enemies? To save loved ones at any cost--was that a sin or a virtue? And if she had the choice now--

The mayor poured glasses of cowslip wine. Verity came out of her whirling thoughts. They looked at one another, drank. "Do you blame me, then?" he asked.

"I think I would say the same, sir, but that's not why I came. 'Tis the serving maids at the alehouse: you know they left. Master Soames needs more servers, for all those soldiers. Besides Salamon and Oliver and Gaston, he wants Dorcas, and she's feared of the soldiers, and with good cause. Can you speak to this Sir Walter Erle? Tell him if all the customers are to be served, it needs women to help, so he must make his men behave."

The mayor and his wife stared, visibly astonished. Verity did not see why. A vivid discussion took place. That evening the mayor spoke to Sir Wat, who growled and passed orders to his captains, Sydenham, Jervis, and Skuts. They in turn told the troopers that any who laid a finger on a serving-maid would be hanged first and then denied access to the taproom. The first threat might not have worried them much; the second did.

Verity was not quite sure how it happened that she agreed to go serve along with Dorcas. It probably was not at all a good idea to be so much in the public eye. But Dorcas--apparently crediting Verity with divine protection--pleaded with her. So did her parents. And Oliver urged it, promising to protect her against any man. That was a promise Verity heeded not at all, but she was no proof against Dorcas--and she was also bored, and eager to see if there was anything she might learn or do that might be useful to the castle. So it happened that the five of them went down to help at the inn.

"Two tankards of ale over there," Innkeeper Soames breathed at Verity over his stout shoulder, and she hurried to obey.

There had been no trouble with the soldiers. Until now. A drunken and stinking fellow lurched to his feet as Verity was passing, pinned her against a wall and tried to thrust a disgusting tongue into her mouth. Revolted, she bit it. He yelled and raised a massive fist.

Suddenly the taproom was filled with noise and violence. While she stood scouring her insulted mouth, rigid with what she refused to admit as fear, every soldier in the taproom--altogether horrified at the thought of losing their ale--set upon the culprit. They beat him, threw him out into the square, and promised to kill him if he ever returned. Verity, so sickened and angry that her bones felt melted, was comforted, covered with apologies, seated on the best stool and fed something rather stronger than ale. A shaggy giant of a man stood over her with maternal devotion, cooing and cuckling like the broody hen which the troopers had stolen.

"Eh, lass, dunnot fidget thysen; we'll see that April gowk never comes nigh thee again."

Verity heeded the dialect, stiffened her melted bones, raised an alert head, looked at the giant, and chose her words carefully. "Nay, I'm not malten-hearted, choose how," she said in Sowerbutts' best accents, "Nobbut fatched. Happen tha'r't from t'north?" And from that moment she became as safe as a shaggy giant named Gideon and his friends could make her.

CHAPTER SEVENTEEN

THE SIEGE

Peregrine and Sowerbutts paced the eastern wall. This was not their assigned position. Lawrence's troopers were spread thinly along most of the lengthy defenses, while Lady Bankes and her people were responsible for the northeast area: the keep, queen's tower, gloriette and garden. The wall there was at the highest and steepest part of the vast cone: over two hundred feet of hill and thirty more of wall. On the inside, the projecting bay and its flight of stone steps to the top made easy climbing for women and children. Large stones were piled along there; and it was close to a constant supply of hot coals from the kitchen. But both Peregrine and Sowerbutts kept a sharp eye all along this wall southward, agreeing with no words needed that one had the brains and the other the experience to see whatever needed to be seen.

Peregrine now peered cautiously between crenellations at a sudden and suspicious activity on the road below. Then, seeing a musket turned his way, he ducked quickly. They had been very active down there today, harassed by that officer. Probably Sir Walter Erle, who usually stayed safely out of range. Captain Lawrence said he was known for that: 'twas how he got his nickname of Old Wat. In any case, the muskets were--so far--more to be feared than the cannon and culverin. Those, though they might possibly breach the walls given enough time, were doing no real damage. True, Corfe was not built to withstand modern warfare--but its defendants felt that even modern warfare might find Corfe more than it could handle.

Shots at and over the wall were something else again. There had been two minor wounds among the troopers, and one serious one; and a lamb had been killed outright. Not, alas, the plump ram destined for the table, but the little ewe lamb the children had named Dolly and treated as a pet. There was deep mourning about that, and when it was duly served up as dinner (for they could not afford to waste food) no one from Bess down would touch it. Especially, for some reason, the supposedly tough-minded little Bridget.

Peregrine did not bother his head about Bridget; he was having enough trouble figuring out his own feelings. Who would have thought he would miss Verity so atrociously that his adored Bess was almost out of his thoughts? Was it just that shapely leg that had roused Peregrine's passion? Ridiculous! He had always prided himself on his reasonable mind! He was, he decided disgustedly, as bad as Naomi, who was in a terrible sulk, guarding the tower room savagely, and even swearing at her friends Dinner, Lady Bankes and Sowerbutts.

Having crept invisibly along several crenellations, he raised a cautious head and peered down again. They were building something down on the road. Boards were being raised, fastened together in--what? Shields? Siege engines? He lowered his head again.

"They'll catch cold at that," observed Sowerbutts, appearing at Peregrine's side. A number of interested eyes were now cautiously watching as the structure began to take form under the direction of either Sir Wat or one of his captains. Two structures, actually. "A sow and a boar," added Sowerbutts, and the unmilitary Peregrine was not sure whether this was a common name for such things or not. In any case, the building of them took time and attention from shooting at the castle, and everyone relaxed a trifle.

Not that they were in serious crisis. There was enough food for at least three months: more if they were careful. They squandered neither that nor ammunition. Spirits were quite good. In fact, the arrows over the wall urging the defenders to treachery were funny rather than tempting. As if they'd change Captain Lawrence and Her Leddyship for Old Wat and Parlyment! Not even if they believed his offers for a moment, which they didn't.

One such message caused joy rather than derision, for it brought news of Verity. "Virty bee wel an gradely," it read. "Us is washing out fer shee. Gideon."

The note was read aloud to all who could fit into the great keep dining hall. "Verity," said Arabella clearly, and looked around. "Verity Verity Verity sum hoorish bor aiggin Dinner?" Naomi rushed into the room expectantly, looked around, failed to see her very own Human, swore luridly and stalked out again. Captain Lawrence, who had not yet got used to her, looked startled.

The sow and boar seemed to be finished. A row of heads peering over the castle wall watched with deep interest as what seemed to be woolen lining was inserted along the front walls of these wooden shed-like affairs, and they slowly came upright. Lady Bankes eyed them, and called on her own troops not to lower their guard at the inner ward, just in case this silly affair was merely a ruse. Peregrine at once felt as chagrined as Sowerbutts looked--but they stayed where they were. The Lady would not appreciate their presence now.

The boar, too, was now upright, but it was the sow that took the lead. Some dozen men pushed into the structure from the back, lifted it, and started walking blindly, twenty or so legs visibly tripping over one another beneath, toward the castle where the defenders watched, relaxed and amused.

"Eh, they're fair caper-witted," said Sowerbutts in disbelief. "Happen they're too throng to notice the moat."

Happen they were. They reached it. The front legs dithered while the rear ones tried to keep going. The sow fell over. A great discussion went on, punctuated by furious yells from Old Wat. Then everyone crawled out, the sow was towed with difficulty across the moat, erected again, filled once more with invisible bodies on visible legs, and started climbing the steep slope.

The castle shook its collective head almost pityingly. Not pityingly enough to resist temptation, though. They waited for the climbers to come nearer, and to make its legs more visible. And they fired on--and above--them. They were all quite accurate shots by now.

As the Royalist paper *Mercurius Rusticanus* subsequently wrote, 'not being musket-proof, the sow cast nine of the eleven of her farrow.' It was true enough. Two Roundheads limped and rolled back down the hill as fast as their punctured legs could carry them. Nine lay still in the wreckage of the sow. As for the boar, it was having none of it. Despite yells from the officers, it stayed firmly where it was, unmanned and unmoving. The troopers carried their wounded back up to the town, and for a few days peace reigned around Corfe Hill.

Not so, Corfe town. Soames and his servers found themselves suddenly idle as all the soldiers were called urgently away. Presently horrific banging brought them to the alehouse door, to see the church being assaulted as if it were the castle itself.

"'Tes, in a way," reflected Master Soames wryly as broken organ pipes were hauled out and turned into cases for powder and shot. The doors were being ripped off to serve as cover for the soldiers, the churchyard was being used as a battery for the siege guns, and it was clear that all the beauty within was being righteously destroyed.

Verity was, she found, surprised only that it had not happened sooner; for any strict God-fearing Calvinist would see it as a religious duty to destroy this satanic church of music and paintings and stained-glass windows. Aunt Huldah would certainly have thought so--though Fynch would not. (After all, had Fynch not given her Shakespeare and Sophocles to read?) Verity was not sure about her father, for she knew him very little. Still, she was sorry about the organ. Music was, she had decided, altogether godly. (She once asked

God--challengingly--whether He had not, in fact, actually created music Himself, and was almost sure she received that comfortable sense of approval.)

The destruction of the church went on whilst they watched. Soldiers cut off all the lead they could find and rolled it up for bullets without even trying to cast it into a mould. Verity eyed it with mixed hope and fear. With any luck it would stick in the barrels and not fire. On the other hand, if it did fly over the walls, it would make a vicious wound on any it hit. The surplice was born out triumphantly. Two soldiers appeared to be trying to make it into shirts. The watching town said nothing aloud--but it seemed to Verity that few now would pray for Parlyment--including herself.

She turned back into the alehouse. Oliver followed, smiled engagingly and put his arm around her. Verity stiffened and treated him to a pair of arctic blue daggers. He was opening himself to reprisal from his uncle as well as Old Wat's officers, and for good measure, Gideon. She was too proud and fearless to mention this; just regarded him with contempt. Unfortunately, he quite misinterpreted the situation.

"Just a little buss," he said, and tightened his grip. She trod heavily on his toe, and then when he merely yelped, tightened his hold, and lowered his shapely nose purposefully toward her, she slammed the heel of her hand up against it with all her might. She had no idea that this was a virtually-lethal attack: his nose was merely the nearest target, her hand the likeliest weapon, and the upward angle the only one available to her. She was quite astonished when he let go and fell back against the wall with anguished if muffled wails--nor was she in the least sorry. Bess would have been, but Verity was a strong believer in hard justice instantly applied. She watched with clinical and unpitying interest while, in response to his yells, he was tended and borne off home. And she hoped it would be some time before he could get around again, for it was quite certain to her that Oliver was a vengeful young man.

And the days passed, and half of July was gone. Sir Walter Erle, in angry frustration, pressed his men harder and harder to storm the walls, ignoring his captains' advice and exposing himself to gunfire--until one day he came rushing into the square and the mayor's house like a dismayed hare, leaving soldiers and civilians staring curiously after him. He couldn't be wounded, they agreed regretfully. Ran too sprightly for that, look 'ee.

It was Gideon who enlightened them, coming up from the road with a grin splitting his hairy face.

"Got in range, choose how," he told them cheerily. "Chance it happened t'bullet went plumb through his coat, and when he saw it, he came all-a-bits, the cabby gowk."

It was not merely the townsfolk who hid grins, Verity noted. No soldier likes to be under the command of a muddy-mettled wagtail.

The castle had witnessed the abrupt departure of Sir Wat from the danger area with bright interest. "Think we got him?" the musketeers asked one another, hopeful. They considered it. They shook regretful heads. "Ran away too sprightly," they decided.

For whatever reason, the shooting almost stopped for a day or two. Bridget, blatantly disobedient, dared to climb the wall and peer through the crenellations. Her whoop scared them all silly. "There's a big animal out there! A bear, I think! Right out there with the enemy!"

They rushed to look. Indeed, it did seem to be a bear, on all fours, creeping along the slope between bridge and town. Baffled, they peered. Jennet, feeling herself superior to her sister in intelligence if not far-sightedness, strutted up to look, and turned to them.

"'Tis no animal at all, 'tis that Sir Wat. All wrapped in a fur, being doltish."

Bridget frowned, puzzled. "Will all that fur keep bullets from hitting him? Because then why didn't it keep them from hitting our Dolly?"

CHAPTER EIGHTEEN

DURANCE VILE

Verity hardly had time to properly enjoy the matter of the bearskin before Sir Wat recovered and became his old self. So, alas, did Oliver. Almost at once she found herself arrested and haled without gentleness before the bear himself--shed of his skin and glowering from the one armchair in Mayor Bastwick's sitting room. The mayor stood near the back wall, inscrutable. He had warned her. She could expect no help there, nor could she blame him. Oliver, chest out, nose still purple and grossly swollen, and eyes baleful, was well to the fore.

"This man tells me you were a guest in the castle."

It was not exactly true, but quibbling would have been both useless and undignified. She glanced casually at Oliver and back at Sir Walter. "Does he?" she asked, dispassionate. "He seems fair angered at me, doesn't he? Has he told you what happened to his nose? And why?"

Rawlins would have been deflected--but then, Rawlins was clay in the right hands. This man was more like twisted granite. He was, she perceived, infinitely dangerous, clearly ruled by his passions--*Ira furor brevis est*--and she feared him! She perceived that she had never before been truly afraid of anyone. The humiliation of so losing her fearlessness swept her mind and then left it clear for true courage and her wits.

"Well? What have you to say? Do you deny it?"

What was called for? Defiance? Meekness? Reason? None would do. Nor anything else she could think of--except possibly Peregrine's ineffably courteous and impervious arrogance? How she wished he were beside her! She chose her words carefully--and truthfully.

"I was snatched from my home by Royalist soldiers led by a Major Rawlins, and bought here as hostage."

The pale gray eyes stared, petulant fury ready to unleash. "What? Who did you say? From where? Why? Who are you, girl?"

Her curtsey was barely civil: the absolute least required from her father's daughter. "I'm Verity Goodchild, daughter of Colonel Nathan Goodchild of Essex's army. And I wish to know why you should believe this vengeful varlet, and before ever hearing my words on the matter."

Her arrogance was subtle but impressive. Mayor Bastwick almost smiled. The petulant fury aimed itself at Oliver, who was looking shocked. Had he indeed not known who she was? Verity had thought the whole of Corfe did. But Reason seemed crowded out of his mind by rage. *Ira furor brevis est*, indeed! How might she use this? Oliver was virtually stuttering, groping for words.

Sir Wat turned to Mayor Bastwick. "Is this true, what she says?"

The mayor nodded gravely. "Why, yes. All know it."

Sir Walter looked baffled. Oliver still seemed speechless. Verity, in frantic hope, forgot to breathe. Almost, the tall clock stopped. Then Verity breathed again, and became the slim Foxe's martyr. Lifting her short chin to gaze austerely upward, she began chanting the 91st Psalm. "He shall cover thee with his feathers, and under his wings shalt thou trust: his truth shall be thy shield and buckler... Only with thine eyes shalt thou behold and see the reward of the wicked... Thou shalt tread upon the lion and adder; the young lion and the dragon shalt thou trample under feet."

She finished amidst uneasy silence, thinking for a moment that God (or Passion) had indeed stayed the wits of both men. But Oliver's malevolence came through.

"She were living in t'castle all that time, and friends with the Lady, but she never come to tell you aught to help you. 'Twere when I told her to," he finished with mendacious inspiration, "that her attacked me."

Indeed. Now it had been pointed out to him, Sir Walter saw how she had almost fooled him. His anger surged. "Why? Even if you're who you say you are--which I take leave to doubt--your silence was treachery. You will now tell me everything about the castle and the Royalist whore that runs it, or 'twill the the worse for you. Speak."

So this was true fear! Long training held, so that she kept her cheekbones jutted and her eyes level. "Well, no; I can't do that."

This appearance of cool indifference was quite infuriating to a man like Sir Walter Erle. His large hands gripped the oaken arms of the chair. She thought he might have killed her instantly except that he did not wish her dead--yet. She was afraid the pounding of her heart would show through her bodice, but she still kept her chin up, her eyes on his.

And then Mayor Bastwick spoke. "Betimes the stubborn can soften greatly if left to reflect overnight," he suggested diffidently. Verity flickered a fearful blue gaze at him, unsure whether he was trying to help or just distance himself; or even whether she herself would welcome a dreadful night of wondering what they might do to her in the morning. It never remotely occurred to her, of course, to give aid against her friends. Nor did it--yet--occur to her that she might be forced to do so. Her bones knew that she had a stubborn courage, or perhaps pride, that would not easily surrender. Her mind being less sure, she only wished desperately that she could stop being afraid.

Mayor Bastwick prudently did not offer to keep her in his home. Instead they took her, with head high and lips tight, back to the alehouse. Through the taproom she was marched, where Dick Brine narrowed inimical eyes, but at least three people froze at the sight: Salamon, in the act of serving Captain Sydenham, Gaston at the scullery door, and Gideon with a tankard halfway to his lips. They looked up as she was led past: looked up and through her, with blank unseeing eyes and no flicker of expression--and yet she was vaguely comforted. At least Gideon knew she was a prisoner, even if he was helpless to aid her...

There were of course no spare bedchambers in the alehouse, nor in the whole town. They contrived a jail for her in a small storeroom at the back: actually in the cellar, yet because of the down-sloping hill, with a small high window that admitted some air and light, at any rate. There was a pallet on the floor and a chamber-pot and a bucket of water--for which she felt duly grateful--and an occasional meal of sorts. The first night was the worst, for she did not yet know what lengths they might go to. As it is harder to face the unknown than the known; she lay in wrenching fear. And as she still thought courage to be absence of fear, she feared her fear, as well.

Several days later, she still was not sure what she faced. They questioned her grimly, Old Wat and his captains, together and separately. Sir Walter was the only one she truly feared, for his face had the dreadful look of some one who knew no reason at all. But he came seldom. Captain Sydenham, sour, avoided any challenge her eyes might offer. Captain Jervis was so threatening that she stopped believing his threats. Captain Skuts was friendly and sympathetic and anxious to spare her pain--and he always came just after Jervis and his threats. Verity had never heard of the stick and the carrot, but she had no trouble at all figuring it out. Her eyes were lifted to heaven, her face pure, noble and unyielding--and her answers were generally Bible verses. They were always appropriate verses, too; and she never ran out, nor ever resorted to Latin or Greek or Sophocles or Shakespeare--which would have quite spoiled the impression she was trying to make. For how could good Calvinists object to her quoting Scripture? Even when it hovered on the brink of insult? And there was an almost unlimited supply of verses ideal for her situation.

"'Whoso sheddeth man's blood, by man shall his blood be shed,'" she replied when Jervis threatened to give her a sound beating. "And I'm quite sure God means 'man' to include woman, too. Don't you, God?" she asked the ceiling disconcertingly.

Jervis, acting the role he had been given--and with rather more feeling than was strictly necessary--raised a hand and poised it. Verity simply thought of Aunt Huldah and looked at it with clear steady eyes, for she had not lost her physical courage, it seemed; only her fearlessness. "'For he that endureth to the end shall be saved,'" she observed, hoping she sounded more confident than she felt. God was quite possibly--and justifiably--annoyed with her for challenging His actions so often, so she felt that she could not really count on His aid with total confidence.

Once Sydenham, dropping his taciturnity, tried to respond in kind. "'Unstable as water, thou shalt not excel,'" he scolded.

She eyed him with pity. "Well, I should think a Bible-reading man could do better than that: it's quite inappropriate. For one thing, you *want* me to be unstable and give in to you, and you're angry because I won't. And for another, that's what Jacob said to Reuben, and do you remember the rest of it? '--because thou wentest up to thy father's bed; then defilest thou it:' and although I'm not at all sure what that means, do you think it's a proper thing to say to a young maiden?"

Sydenham fell at once into bleak silence. The others pushed her harder.

"It's a falsehood, isn't it, that Colonel Goodchild is your father?" thundered Jervis. "No one believes it. Tell the truth. You'll be beaten for lying, you know."

"Well, it's not my fault if you don't believe truth when you hear it, and beating me won't make it any less true, but I do think that Father will be very angry when he learns how you've been treating me, and so will General Essex, not to mention Almighty God, Who already knows it, don't you, God?"

"Almighty God is on our side," he snapped. "And with His help we'll destroy that castle as David destroyed Goliath."

She was at once sidetracked. "That's always bothered me," she told him disconcertingly. "Personally, I think David was a coward. Here was poor Goliath prepared for hand-to-hand combat, and David stood safely out of reach and hurled missiles, which was cheating; and he kept on cheating afterwards with Uriah's wife; and I can't see how God would approve that sort of thing."

If she had expected any kind of rational discussion, she was disappointed. Jervis stalked out, apparently beyond any speech at all, and was presently replaced by the Carrot.

"You say you know nothing that would help Sir Walter," wheedled Skuts. "Then why not save yourself his terrible punishment by telling us these useless little things?"

"No," she said simply, going straight to the point.

Since nothing dreadful had been done so far, Verity began almost to look forward to the questioning as the interesting part of her day. Not that she was totally bored in those lonely hours: solitude did not bother her. There was much thinking to be done, about religion and politics--and Peregrine--and friendship--and loyalty--and Peregrine--and how lucky Bess was--and how his kiss might feel; and much to be said to God about all of these things. She had done no adultery: was she really in sin for thoughts she could not help? Should Divine Reason enable her to ban them?

For welcome change she could recite to herself most of Hamlet and Romeo and Juliet and quite a lot of Vergil and Sophocles and Homer. It all helped a great deal to keep the fear at bay--but fear was there all the time, gnawing at the heart of her. Not just what they might do to her--but what if they thought to send threats to Lady Bankes? Threaten to kill Verity unless the castle surrendered? Lady Bankes would not--could not--give in, of course; but it would be a terrible decision and hurt to all of them. For, she realized, they liked her as she did them.

And the questions went on. "Be a good maiden, and be set free with every comfort and kindness."

"Wide is the gate and broad is the way that leadeth to destruction, and many there be that go in thereat."

She lost count of the days. She had no idea what was happening outside, with the siege; for though her questioners sometimes told her things, they could not be believed. And still she was obdurate.

"Speak, or you'll have the back of my hand, wretched jade!"

"God shall smite thee, thou whited wall."

Eventually they did beat her, but not very badly. For one thing, she was protected by the discomfortable but now-appreciated leather corset. For another, they were unnerved by the possibility that she might indeed be daughter to Colonel Goodchild--and as favored by God as she pretended.

"As a man soweth, that also shall he reap," she said when it was over. "God, have You been watching?"

After that, no one came near except for the water shoved through the door, and when two days passed with no questioners, and nearly two with no food, she felt a new fear. What if they didn't shed her blood at all, but just starved her to death? She was quite sure God would consider this as sinful a murder as a knife in the breast, but what good was that to her, if He never raised a Finger to prevent it? On the other hand, why should He bother with her when He let so many others, much more devout, suffer even more? Staring at the patch of blue sky out the window, she told Him she quite understood, but at least He might give her her courage back, so she could face whatever happened with dignity. (He might have felt her remarks to be--as usual--lacking in Christian Resignation, but He surely could not doubt their sincerity.)

It was far into the night when she heard a furtive key in the massive lock, and stiffened. What now? Worse questioning? Silent death? Sitting upright, she smoothed the ragged and dirty folds of the gown she had been wearing for all these days, asked God again to return the bravery He had so unfairly taken from her, and waited. Outside, a nightjar creaked and an out-of-season tawny owl hooted. In the dimness, she saw the door crack open. There was no candlelight, just a shaggy blur peering around the door, and the faintest of murmurs. "Lass?"

Incredulous, she breathed back. "Gideon?"

"Coom," he said only, and, silent, she came. A massive arm drew her into the main cellar, a slight form silently closed the door and locked it.

"I can put the key back wi'out waking Uncle," said Gaston's voice.

"Nay: that won't fadge: you'd queer him to explain it. Throw it away. Let them think they flay-boggards did it--and worry is she in there dead. Coom," he repeated, and they wafted silent as ghosts through the cellars to the back door, where other dark shapes waited.

"Verity?" It was Dorcas! Verity found she was weak from relief--and also hunger--and Gideon's strong arm held her up.

"Now, Gaston lad, take thysen home; tha'st done champion. Can tha manage, lass? Help her, Salamon. We'm going out, t'four of us, full of gig, holding one another up and-all. Can tha laugh?"

Verity found that she could. But the stars were going around in a strange way, and Gideon's arm was altogether necessary as they meandered giggling and murmuring across the castle road, westward past uninterested sentries, on to the westward edge of town; and then down the steep path and along the Wicken to the valley. Strangely, she could walk no more. She felt herself lifted in strong arms, pressed once more against a man's body, smelling the maleness of him--albeit somewhat riper than Peregrine had been, she mused dazedly. If only it were Peregrine--even for a moment! The rustling and muttering of a siege at night fell behind them, and the dark looming shape of a cottage or two, and then presently the soft sound of fingers on door, and a door opening, and the voice of Enoch Powl.

"Did'st get her? Is she harmed?" Then a softness of a straw mattress, the murmur of women's voices, the touch of Gideon's fingers on her cheek, and his voice saying farewell it might almost be tearfully. She hardly knew. The world was slipping away from her.

CHAPTER NINETEEN

RETURN

She awoke to warmth and daylight through a small window that she knew--if only she could remember. She shut her eyes and scowled behind her eyelids, and opened them to see Dorcas and Nancy and Enoch staring down at her, concerned.

"Art all right?" She nodded uncertainly. "Here, drink this."

Verity found a bowl of white liquid--milk?--pressed against her lips. She closed them. Dorcas, who was suddenly wearing all the airs and authority of the famous Dr. Harvey himself, pressed again. "I know 'tesn't for humans, milk, but in truth 'twill do thee good, weak as thee is. Look how the babby calves and lambs and kids thrives. Look, I've put some sops of bread in't for more strength, and soon, so you can get back in t'castle."

Too weak to refuse, she drank, finding it strangely thick and bland and sweet--but not unpleasant once she'd got used to it. "Back into the castle?" she echoed. "Is the siege over, then?"

They all brooded over her, even Nancy, so big with child that she could scarce stand. No no, they said, but she could get in the same way them cattle did.

Verity clearly was weaker than she'd thought, for nothing made any sense. "What cattle? What are you talking about?"

"When them came out of t'castle and brought back eight cows and a bull inside, just to show they could. You was jailed up when it happened. But if they could bring cows back in, 'twill be easy to bring you."

Verity laughed. "Who said that? Nay, you can't possibly believe such tarradiddles!"

"Tes true!" they said, hurt. "All the town knows it. And another time five boys sallied out of t'castle and brought back four cows, and some sojers on the hill called 'Shoot, Anthony,' but no one did. So all we has to do is find where they went in."

Verity finished her laugh and the milk, and pushed up to her elbows. "Enoch!" she challenged. "Think! How would they get them in? Front gate? Right past the whole army and the drawbridge? Sallyport? You and Nancy watched me struggle up there with that wretched cockerel. And it took several of us even to get a sheep up there. In daylight, with no enemy surrounding the castle. And remember how even that heifer was too big to get through? Do four cows and a bull sound likely? And what 'five boys', pray? The boys are all gone to Oxford except for Baby Will. Not that Jennet and Bridget wouldn't be the first to volunteer, of course, but... Oh, well, I did need a good laugh," she sighed, lying down again

The others regarded her with dismay. They had truly believed it. (So, later, did Mercurius Rusticanicus, where it was printed in the report on Corfe Castle.)

"Then what will we do?" fretted Enoch. "They'll search everywhere, once they discover thee missing, mayhap even now."

This was true. Someone would notice at once that the key was missing. They might not dare leave her to starve as King John had done to his prisoners here--but Old Wat was a man driven by Satan. She did hope no suspicion fell on those who helped her! "What of Gaston and Salamon and Gideon: will they be in trouble? And will your parents worry about you?" she belatedly thought to ask Dorcas.

"Nay; 'twas all planned, and they three and Uncle not suspicioned. And Gaston will tell all I'm come to be midwife to Nancy," Dorcas said easily. "Who's to know if I'm early betimes?"

Verity relaxed a trifle, but her Puritan conscience was nagging at her for putting friends in any danger--even if 'twas slight, and she had not demanded it. What might happen to them-- She shivered. So did Nancy. Verity took a sharp look at her and rolled hastily off the bed. "Nancy!"

They all looked. Nancy moaned slightly. There was no doubt even to Verity that she was going to give birth, and presently. The fear that had so hounded her of late hit her again. Childbirth was a very dangerous business! And Dorcas seemed full young for a midwife...

"Not to worry," said Dorcas briskly, pushing both Verity and the dithering Enoch aside. "Nell Coombes trained me. Verity, put on t'kettle and you can help betimes. Enoch, take yourself out o' the way. And if any come to the door hunting Verity," she said briskly over her shoulder, "jes' you tell them there's birthing going on, and that'll chase 'em off. Verity, be you on good terms wi' God? You might just have a word with Him. Now, Nancy, love, just you sit right here..."

God had apparently been in good temper with them that day. For soldiers had indeed come hunting Verity, just as Nancy was yelling lustily; and they indeed hurried away at the sound. And the birth was easy, said Dorcas (though it had seemed quite appalling to Verity), and the tiny boy was now swaddled and lying in his mother's arms. Suddenly, humiliatingly, Verity felt ready to collapse, when it was Nancy and Dorcas had done all the work. And a day or two not eating was hardly a good reason. She had fasted before, and been beaten, as well. (It did not occur to her that stress and fear and anger could be as exhausting as hunger.)

The sun shone golden across the cottage doorway, blissfully tempting to someone who loved warmth. She peered out. There was not a soul in sight, for the Wicken ran between cottage and Corfe, from the hill west of the town, northeast to join the moat below the second tower--which was on this side of Dungeon Tower where they had gathered coltsfoot so long ago. All the trees along the stream--hawthorn, elder, willow--were in full leaf, making a thick screen. There was no reason for sentries to come here where there was no view of moat or lower hill. She leaned back against the doorjamb and closed her eyes. Somewhere near a strange robin chittered at her: probably telling her not to scare the eggs.

"Here," said Dorcas briskly above her. "More milk, for you and Nancy both. 'Twill do thee good." She watched as Verily obediently drained the bowl (which tasted better than the first) and wiped the back of her hand across her milky mouth. Dorcas unexpectedly curtseyed. "Prithee, Verity-- I mean, Mistress--" Her square capable fingers laced nervously, and her manner was diffident.

Verity glanced up, saw the hands and the diffidence, and wondered. "What's to do, then?"

"I-- 'Tes another thing I heard all t'town saying. Two things, but--"

"Well, then, what--" Verity suddenly understood. ('Whosoever shall say Thou fool, shall be in danger of hell fire'). "Oh! Was I unkind? Forgive me, Dorcas. Tell me the other thing, and I promise to listen and not laugh." She rested her head again. Dorcas, encouraged, stood straighter.

"Tes said they's emptying all t'prisons around Poole and Swanage, sending murderers and all to help attack here."

Verity took a deep breath and then relaxed a little. Not even murderers could get over those walls. But-- "What's the other thing, then?"

"Parlyment ships is at Studland, and t'master of them is to send help against t'castle," Dorcas ventured humbly, "and--"

Verity sat bolt upright, eyes blazing sapphire, and Dorcas startled backward. Rare unexpectable, she were! A body never knowed what'd confound her, or what make her laugh!

"What? Where-- Where is Studland?" Dorcas pointed eastward. "When did the ships come? Who's 'the master'?" Dorcas shook her head, alarmed at the success of her news, and Verity pushed fist and short chin together, thinking hard. Had she not heard words--names--herself, while in captivity? After her beating, when she was not as sharp-witted as she should have been--

"*Mea culpa!*" she muttered, "Dorcas, did you hear the word 'admiral'? Or the name 'Earl of Warwick'?"

But Dorcas, confused, said it mought have been, but she were not sure.

"Ask Enoch if he can leave Nancy for a moment."

But Enoch was already in the doorway, long lugubrious face brooding down at her. "Aye," he said. "'Tes what I heared."

"Then I must get into the castle and warn them." He looked at her, and she looked back. No, not by mythical boys or magical entries, but-- She pictured the setting. On this side there had been less attacking, for the long arm of the west bailey opened attackers to crossfire. Besides, the east side was conveniently there by the Wareham road. True, there were sentries posted all around the moat, but-- She wrinkled her forehead. "Enoch, do they ever post sentries this side of the Wicken?"

"Nay, what be the point? 'Tes only where it reaches t'moat, sithee. They be none so alert," he added warily.

Indeed. They had been exceeding casual last night, certainly, despite the story of the boys and the cows. Likely the besiegers knew 'twas a tarradiddle. If a message could be got over the walls-- But no bow ever invented could send an arrow that far and that high from the moat. Those of Erle's men had shot from just under the walls, and most of them, she had heard, failed to get over. She abandoned that train of thought.

"How close together are the sentries?"

He gleamed at her. "Near enough to see each other, but they move together by nights, fearing bogles and devils. If you--"

Indeed. "Last night-- Is't the dark of the moon now, Enoch?"

"Aye, he said sadly. "I'd much hate for 'ee to be shot by thine own friends seeing a dark shape from t'walls."

"So would I!" said Verity. And the four of them spent the rest of the day planning and reconnoitering the banks of the Wicken.

It was long past midnight when a slender dark shape shadowed from the Powl cottage, divested not only of bedraggled white cap, apron and fichu but of all undergarments.

"They'd just hamper me," Verity had told the shocked women, shoving at them a pile of stockings, chemise, petticoats, corset, shift and even shoes. "I'd sink with all that on! You keep them with my thanks for your aid. And I promise to fly something blue from the keep when I'm safely in. And I've explained to God how particularly He needs to bless the four of you and protect you from everything dangerous." And she ghosted into the shrubbery of the Wicken.

It was quiet sentry-go here on the west side of the castle, where nothing ever happened. Off-duty soldiers could be heard carousing in the town, and the sentries were both wistful and bored. The castle crouched above: dark, silent, watchful. There was naught of interest to see or hear but the usual snuffling of a hedgehog, the hollow call of the owls. The stocky badgers, and the slender graceful fox and vixen and cubs, all crept from their holes. A slim figure slipped into the moat from the Wicken and silently moved along in midstream with only a nose and a bit of head protruding. If it seemed an odd shape for either fox or badger, no human eye marked it.

Under the castle bridge, the head cautiously rose. Above, the high narrow bridge had a gap where the drawbridge had been raised to make a barrier against the gated arch. Behind and above was a machicolation slot for dropping unpleasant welcome upon unwelcome visitors, and behind that, the portcullis and the gate itself. Only a fool would attack there--but it would be, she fervently hoped, still guarded.

Verity slithered up the bank face down, like an otter; and on up the hillside under the loom of the bridge in the same way. It was steep, but the grass had grown high now the livestock no longer came out to crop it, and it offered both cover and strong roots to grasp. Now she was under the gap of the drawbridge, but no moonlight shone through to betray her. Presently she stood cautiously, listened to the song of frogs and crickets in the blackness, reached the drawbridge itself, and pressed herself against the end of it.

("Nay," Enoch had objected, "'No man could get twixt bridge and wall!"

"Nay, no man," Verity had agreed. "But I'm no man, and my head is so small Fynch used to wonder where I kept my brains. And where my head will fit, so will the rest of me.")

She had hoped 'twas true! Now, facing the tiny gap, she stood in dismay. It was tight, too tight: nearly flush against the wall! Even Naomi would find it a squeeze!

"God!" she shouted silently. "You've left it all to me, and I'm doing my best, and now You need to help me!" Silence. A wren signaled the start of the dawn chorus. Verity looked up. The drawbridge, against the wall here, leaned outward the tiniest bit as it rose. Was it enough? Could she get that high? Girls did not learn to climb. She jutted her cheekbones, had one more stern word with God, shoved the side of one foot between drawbridge and wall, then the other, higher. There was little but the wide edge itself to hold on to. The drawbridge was harsh and splintery, the wall harsh and rough. She could never do it! She *would* do it. Her mulish obstinacy was much in evidence.

A warbler and a chiffchaff joined the chorus. Verity bit her lip, wedged a foot higher, and inched upwards, finding it easier as the space widened. Finally, chin turned over her right shoulder, she began sidling into the narrow slot. There was only an arm length or two to the gateway, but she found at once that she was in danger of being wedged immobile. She flexed her feet and painfully pressed her toes against the wall and heels against the drawbridge. One ear rubbed near raw against the stone of the wall, the other collected splinters from the portcullis. Even her cheekbones were in danger. It was a mercy she lacked Bess's womanly breasts! Inch by inch--only a few more to go--and then it happened. Her toes lost their grip. She slipped three inches: enough to cruelly jam her pelvis and rump between the sides--and there she stuck. Her feet were now in a narrower part, so she couldn't flex them or bend her knees to raise herself. If God did not help her now, she could starve here!

The thought spurred her. She shoved her upper body sideways, now scraping face as well as ears in the narrow space. She felt the back of her gown tear. The drawbridge virtually flayed the skin from her already-bruised back. She hardly noticed. Just to move her head a little further--past the edge of the gateway, where it opened to the lowered portcullis--and of course the heavily-barred gate.

She twisted her neck to look up despairingly at the machicolation slot and the arrow loops above. "Ho, the castle!" she called with what seemed the last of her strength. Someone was certainly on guard; she hoped they had good ears, for her voice was thin and strangely high. "Hark! Let me in! 'Tis Verity come to warn you! Help!"

The dawn chorus was joined by robins, finches and yellowhammers, singing joyously and heartlessly. The eastern sky grayed. "Help!" she called again. "Ho the castle! Peregrine!"

But it was Sowerbutts on duty: doleful and uncomforted during her long absence, who finally heard her. He practically fell down the twisted tower stairs, edged through the gate, raised a lantern, stared in shock at the head and shoulder emerging from nowhere, and bellowed up through the machicolation slot. And then, mercifully, the portcullis was raised, and the drawbridge released just enough for her to slither out and sprawl to the ground. Sowerbutts was bawling for Lady Bankes and Peregrine, and--as an afterthought--Captain Lawrence, to be fetched.

Verity, dazed with relief, at once thanked God loudly, and rallied. Yes, she could walk; she was all right; she was exalted above pain. She and Sowerbutts were halfway to the southwest gatehouse when the Bankeses, mother and daughters, with half the watch, came racing down to meet her in the dim gray light, several leaps behind Peregrine. And so there were a great many witnesses when those two hurtled fiercely into each others arms in a way no one at all could suppose was dictated by Divine Reason.

Peregrine, with her thin arms nearly hugging the breath from his ribs, tucked that sodden silver-gilt head comfortably under his chin with never a thgought for his intended bride and mother-in-law. (It was, perhaps, just as well that he could not make out their expressions.) For the first time, he began to understand the unreasoned behavior of Romeo and Juliet--and it was no comfort to recall what their end had been.

Just as his hands felt her bleeding back and he realized that something was badly amiss, Verity moved. Remembering her urgent message, she pushed herself away from the lovely maleness of him, turned to to the shapes of those watching, held her protesting body erect.

"M'lady! Madam! Dorcas heard there's a fleet at a place called Studland, and the town thinks Old Wat has called on them for aid; and Enoch thinks 'tis mayhap the Earl of Warwick. And 'tis said they've emptied the prisons to set the criminals on us." There was shocked silence, then voices. But Verity, having held herself in one piece long enough to complete her mission, stopped caring or trying, and permitted herself to become a boneless heap in an unfocussed place where, she fancied, she was being scolded by everyone-- including, oddly, Naomi and the abrasive Fynch.

CHAPTER TWENTY

FULL ATTACK!

It was indeed Naomi, sitting on her chest, flexing never-trimmed claws on her breast, grooming her hair, scolding and purring at once. The abrasive Fynch turned out to the the abrasive Lady Bankes--and it was odd that Verity had never before noticed the similarity. Behind closed eyes, she decided that everyone, in fact, was scolding everyone else. Lady Bankes snapped that Cook wasn't doing the mulled wine right, and Cook retorted that she knew perfectly well how to mull wine. Captain Lawrence was demanding that some one or other give him more information at once, and Maud scolded him, and Sowerbutts told him to hold his gab. Someone sent Bridget (who still carried the Trio's banner nicely) from the room in disgrace. Jennet defied a similar order. Grissil and Lucy wept, and Emmot threatened to send them out as well. Dinner was squawking. She did not hear Peregrine. Had Lady Bankes sent him away? Put him in the dungeon under Butavant Tower?

She instantly opened anxious eyes, and found she was in the warm kitchen, lying on something soft on a bench, with the kitchen fire blazing and sunlight out in the courtyard and virtually everyone gathered around. Peregrine's face--distraught as she had never imagined it could be--was before her. The errant eyebrow was perfectly flat. Bess was not scolding at all. Far from it. Her concerned face bent a loving look upon her--and Verity closed her eyes again in disbelief. Bess? Loving? After what she had surely seen?

The chaos went on.

"The fleet! That means proper seamen with scaling ladders and grapples!"

"Bring the candle: it's monstrous dim in here!"

"They'll kill us in our beds!"

"Perdy, look at her poor raw ears and cheeks!"

"Did she say Studland?"

'Here, there's great slivers to remove."

"Only Satan would think to send hardened murderers against women and children!"

"Think you 'twill leave scars, Madam?"

At the moment, Verity did not much care. In any case, she had not Bess's beauty to worry about ruining. Only--would she be cast out before she was strong enough? Into the arms of Oliver and Old Wat? What of Peregrine?

"Verity!" It was male and urgent. "Open your eyes, girl! Art all right?" Verity indicated untruthfully that she was. "Indeed? Then tell us what more you heard."

"Don't harass her!" It was Peregrine. "She's come at great cost to tell us; why d'you think she'd hold back?"

"No more," Verity mumbled. "I told you all I heard."

"Surely not." Captain Lawrence's large head loomed. Sharp eyes fixed her. "Where did you hear it? Who? The mayor, the innkeeper, the--"

"I tell you, I heard no more!" Verity snapped. Every bit of her body, relieved from all that valor, had begun to hurt atrociously. She began to feel wretchedly unappreciated. "I was locked up; how could I hear anything? But," she remembered, "I was to hang something blue from the top keep window to let Enoch know I got in safely. Please? They'll be fair worried!"

Into the silence, "Her poor face," mourned Bess.

Emmot's handsome head now appeared. "Here. Wine. Can you sit? I'll help you." But the arm pressing against her mutilated back was too much for Verity. To her eternal shame, she whimpered. And then chaos broke out again.

"All you men, out!" commanded Lady Bankes. "Yes, Peregrine, you too. Maud, take the young ones to the nursery. Jennet, you may stay if Emmot can use you. Emmot, take charge: I must talk to Robert. Robert, we'll take the information she's brought and be grateful."

And Emmot did indeed take charge, with surprising kindness. "You look like a hedgehog, girl; can you walk as far as the courtyard? We need more light to get the slivers out. Bess, you can help me, but first fetch tweezers. Warm water, Cook. Joan, make a tisane for soothing and sleep. Jennet, fetch-- let's see--I'll want yarrow, comfrey, St. John's wort, oil of lavender--and calendula, I think, for she's bruised as well as torn. Are all the men from the court? Come, then." Silence, while Verity proved that she could indeed walk. Then: "Bess, help me with her gown, and then take it to the ragbag-- 'Strewth, girl, you're naked as a frog underneath! Jennet, go find something decent to cover her."

And for a soothing but uncomfortable time, her torn fingers and ears and cheekbones and back and feet were bathed in warm water and wine (which hurt amazingly, but would help prevent infection) followed by the stickiness of honey. Deep bruises began to appear on pelvis and rump. At last she was liberally anointed with a salve of herbs, wrapped in a soft robe belonging to Lady Bankes herself and taken to a down bed in a small room nearby.

She slept for most of the day, awoke sore but refreshed, and stretched experimentally. Naomi and Dinner strutted through the room, followed by a deeply interested Arabella who planted herself solidly at the bedside, fair curls tousled. "Verity," she said clearly. "Inkle ot aigin cor Dinner ap simm."

"She says," reported Bridget, standing by the door, "that you are not to eat Dinner, because now he's a pet."

"Quite good," said Verity. "At least you're getting more believable."

Bridget stamped a red shoe. "'Tis true!" she stormed, and Verity looked at her curiously, half inclined to believe it. Bridget never resented having her *lies* challenged.

Presently Lady Bankes came and looked under the bandages. "You'll be all right anon," she said bracingly. "Had you broken bones, you'd not have been able to run as you did." There was no perceptible sarcasm in her voice. "Think you'll be fit to help us man the walls?"

Verity nodded. She would certainly hurt for some days, but pain was a fact of life, and little could be done for it; so people simply lived with it as best they could, without unnecessary fuss.

"Of course," added Lady Bankes, "had you been wearing your sound leather corset, you wouldn't be lying here with an abraded back."

"Had I been wearing my sound leather corset," retorted Verity, "I probably wouldn't be here at all."

And still no word at all had been said about her and Peregrine! Nor was it said soon. There were more urgent matters at hand.

Much of what happened next, they learned later, in bits, from villagers. Much they saw for themselves. By God's mercy, Admiral the Earl of Warwick was sent off to relieve Exeter, and could spare only one hundred and fifty mariners for Corfe.

Only? It looked like thousands!

"And they do have scaling ladders and grapnels," Captain Lawrence verified gloomily, as they watched the procession march along the road to Corfe. "And they could be carrying wildfire."

"What will they do to the villagers?" murmured Verity. The others (except for Jennet, whose eyes fretted about Miles) were busy wondering what they would do to the castle.

"Happen yon's the gaolbirds?" Sowerbutts jerked his bent nose at a ruffianly group of men being herded by watchful mariners. The ex-prisoners were divided on the benefits of this development. Those sentenced to hang, approved. The others reckoned that at least in gaol they was safe, and not cannon-fodder. But all were agreed that a quick escape to other parts was the best solution of all. There was little to be seen once the reinforcements had entered town. (That little, depressed Verity a great deal.)

"Ready yourselves," said Captain Lawrence. "Men, you know where you go. Ladies--"

"As do we," Lady Bankes interrupted. "We've a great store of stones atop the walls. Cook, keep the fires up. Are all the bedpans ready? Water on the boil? Lucy, take the little ones to the nursery and keep them there. Maud and Emmot have muskets, and Verity--"

I've my bow and arrows as long as they last," said Verity, managing not to wince as she produced them. At last no one was denying her the right to help. "Then I'll use stones and coals."

They waited. The song thrush looked at the situation and decided to sing somewhere else. Naomi, remembering last time, stationed herself hopefully at the nearest mouse hole, with an interested Dinner beside her.

In Corfe, they later learned, God was arranging another bit of divine mercy. The gaolbirds, as scummy, unsavory and brutal a lot as Sir Wat had ever seen, would have been just what they wanted for that whore inside--but that they lacked enthusiasm. 'Twarn't their war, they pointed out. Why, they demanded, should they lead the attack?

"Because," said Sir Wat, after a short conversation with the head mariner, "there's profit in it for you. Twenty Pounds for the first man over the wall, nineteen for the second, and so forth."

It was a stunning sum for ordinary men, who might with a good deal of luck make that much in a lifetime. The gaolbirds gaped, frowned, found a problem. Who, they asked, was to see or know in the thick of battle who was over the wall first or second? Or prove it? Moreover, they pointed out as the thing began to dawn on them, the first few over was like to be soon dead, and what use was twenty Pounds to a corpse?

In the end, they had to be primed with bribes and a great deal of drink. In particular, the potent, triple-distilled cider called scrumpy, without which no West Country seaman would willingly sail.

This turned out to be a bad idea. To start with, all the navy mariners, free from the stern discipline of the admiral, demanded scrumpy, too. After that, to leave out Sir Wat's men would have risked mutiny. As a result--as Mercurius Rusticanus later jeered-- "Old Sir Wat was the only man that came sober to the assault."

It was near enough true. They came staggering down the road from Corfe and paused. The castle walls were lined with defenders, who looked entirely dangerous. They hesitated. Old Wat, like a shepherd trying to herd hysterical sheep with no dog, kept shouting and waving his arms (from a prudent distance) and pointing around to the north side of Castle Hill. Peregrine, watching, spared a wry grin. Sir Wat at least had the sense to ignore the possible trap of the outer bailey. He had divided his men into two forces, and was directing them around below the inner ward and the west bailey--where Lawrence had concentrated the defense. It was now seven or eight hundred against their eighty-odd. This was only two hundred or so more than Sir Wat's original force--but the scaling ladders and grapnels and possible wildfire made an enormous difference, even though most of the approaching assailants still acted more like reluctant sheep.

Above, the defenders were braced by fury. Verity, at her position near the stairs at the northeast curve of wall, watched Sir Wat with disappointment. If not a figure of stature, neither was he today a figure of fun. A pity! She felt exceeding vengeful.

He finally chivvied his army around the hill and across the moat They aimed the assault ladders--and hesitated. The thing looked far higher and more dangerous than they had been led to expect, scrumpy or no scrumpy. Nor did they at all like the look of they defenders. The frustrated shepherd harangued and threatened from behind. Then he waved his arms, apparently offering to lead from the front--and did so.

The castle braced itself.

On they came--most of them. Well, many of them, at least. And it could now be seen that some were indeed carrying something that Captain Lawrence recognized as wildfire. Jennet and Bridget were sent running around the wide wall-top with the warning. "Don't let them get far up their ladders. They have things to throw."

And the attackers reached the walls. And for a while no one knew anything but here and now. Peregrine hated it as much as ever--and acted as efficiently. Verity, manning the north wall, between him and Lady Bankes, forgot her injuries and was again possessed by battle-madness--but no exaltation, this time: only angry determination. Her face was that of an avenging angel. Peregrine spared an awed glance. How could he have fallen in love with such a vixen?

She used all her arrows and then began seizing the copper bedpans as fast as anyone could pass them to her. "Don't waste ammunition!" shouted someone. She didn't. It took considerable nerve to wait until a savage face mounted halfway up a ladder, wild-eyed, sometimes bracing to throw his wildfire, before she dumped the hot coals accurately on to that savage face. It took considerable callousness to watch a squalling victim tumble to the ground and lie writhing and yelling--and then to do it again to the next savage face, unpitying. Verity and Lady Bankes were quite up to it, Peregrine noted with faint shock. Females were supposed to be tender-hearted.

Bess, who actually was, could not bear even to hurl rocks. She let Peggotty, who had been loading for Emmot, change places with her, and then watched with wide eyes. Peggotty, it turned out, was a born warrior.

The supply of coals ended, so they used boiling water. When that ended, there were just stones and three muskets left to defend the inner ward. Verity hefted a couple of stones. Peering through the crenellation for her next target, she saw that some of the attackers around the hill to the left were wilting under the hail of bullets from the west bailey. There were bodies lying all over the slope. The replacements faltered, the line fell back on itself--and a panic started.

Encouraged, the castle cheered, hurled curses as well as missiles, fired as fast as their reloaders could manage. Peregrine, suddenly inspired, leaned over his bit of wall and bellowed. "Ho, look yonder! The king's army! A full regiment!"

And the panic became a rout. They threw down their ladders and weapons, leaving their wounded and dead, headed at full tilt for the town--or beyond it. Sir Wat, to his credit, was the last to leave the field ... but he left it.

CHAPTER TWENTY-ONE

THE VICTORS

"Howsomever," said Corporal Fulke Sidebottom, tucking Dorcas more firmly in the curve of his brawny arm with a smile for Nancy, who sat on the doorstep nursing her son, "we did capture a few of they Roundheads, and put 'em to burying their own dead. Nigh on a hundred, Cap'n says, or at least seventy-eighty, and us had only two killed. And after, we'll let the prisoners go. Well," he added apologetically, "we dunnot want they around, does we? And Her Leddyship says she won't have them in her nice clean dungeon."

Dorcas snuggled comfortably, grinned over his arm at Verity and Peregrine and lifted her freckled face to the early August sun. They planned to wed almost at once, church or no church, as soon as Reverend Gibbon could pull himself together. One of the robins came and sang his--or her?--glittering autumn song. A song thrush--not the castle one, for this had a different repertoire--proved that he could sing louder. A squirrel leaped to the ground, pointed its red tufted ears at them, decided prudence was in order, and leaped back to the tree.

Had it been merely a day since the enemy had departed? First thing this morning the castle had sallied out to start repairs to the battered town, and help and feed and tend all who needed it, and bring the homeless to live in the castle until their houses were rebuilt. This included Mistress Bastwick with little Miles, who was now frailer than ever, and whom Jennet mothered tenderly. She would, she said, rather have him than either Charles or Edward. Much.

Captain Lawrence--whose family home was over at Creech Grange--was in charge of it all. Verity was still much bandaged and hurting quite a bit, and unwilling even to think yet about certain matters. But she had insisted on coming as soon as possible to Enoch's cottage, where she found Nancy and the babe doing well, and Dorcas and Fulke there, too.

Peregrine had come along, because he could not bear just now to be either away from Verity (from whom he surely would soon be parted forever) nor with his poor little betrayed betrothed and her mother. Bess was silent, with downcast eyes that did not meet his, nor could he meet hers. Lady Bankes, even more unnervingly, had clearly chosen to ignore the subject until there was time for it.

Peregrine had never in his life before felt deep guilt: now he was stricken with it. But then, he had never before had his Divine Reason drowned by passion, either. Worse, though he could never forgive himself for so hurting Bess--neither could he honestly regret loving Verity. Nor could he explain the love--though it must have horribly clear to poor Bess. He tried not to think about Hamlet's conflict, which was unlike his, of course--but a line kept coming to haunt him. "It is not nor it cannot come to good, but break my heart, for I must hold my tongue."

He sighed and glanced over at Verity, who was looking lovely in Joan's outgrown kingfisher-blue gown. Her eyes had changed color to match it. Had she ever before been beautiful? Was it only his besotted eyes? He concentrated on Reason, and caught up with Dorcas' story the second time she told it.

"We reckons he didn't believe it, at first, Old Wat. What Master Peregrine called out about the king's troops coming. And then he reckoned 'twere true. Uncle Soames said t'army had all run off or crowded into what's left of t'church, and Cap'n Sydenham came into the alehouse and said he'd best eat whilst he could, so he ordered a nice veal glew followed by goose pie. But just as Uncle Soames was setting it on the table, Old Wat rushed into the inn, saying king's troops was really comin' and he had to go off immediate to complain to Parlyment, and for Cap'n Sydenham to bring off all th' army and supplies to safety."

"Which he did by rushing off to Poole without his ordnance or ammunition or even his dinner, and leaving all hundred horses behind," Verity recited with relish, temporarily cheered. It was lovely to witness Divine Vengeance falling on two of those she most disliked (though it would be less nice when it fell upon her, presently). "'He that diggeth a pit shall fall into it.' I do think it was very clever of You, God, and we're all very grateful, even though we did manage a good deal of it ourselves. Could I see your babe again, Nancy?"

He was the second baby she had over seen properly. Round red face, blob of a nose, seeking mouth, and fists waving energetically when released from the swaddling. Still, not so bad. She thought she could possibly grow to like them--but only if they were Peregrine's too. She was quite sure she could never like the process of birthing them, and quite resented God for arranging things that way. (She had almost given up trying to avoid sinful thoughts. For one thing, they came anyway; and for another, why worry now? If she had ever been Saved, she surely was no longer so.)

She sat in the warm silken gold of late sunlight, and let the talk flow over her. What would her punishment be? And Peregrine's? She felt she could be quite happy if they were punished together, but this was hardly likely. Not even in hell, she assumed, since then 'twould hardly be hell, would it? And on this world--would he be sent back to Oxford? Or would he be wedded as planned, but never forgiven? He was still a good match, for his father was Lord Heath. And young men were expected to sow their wild oats before marriage, and no blame to them; so perhaps he would be forgiven. But would he ever forgive her? Would anyone? Where would they send her? Where could she go, at all? Quite accidentally her desolate blue eyes met his--and shocked dismay suddenly possessed his face. She stared, not understanding why he sat there looking at her as if the end of the world had just come.

In a way, it had. How had he not realized? Been so cruelly, selfishly blind? He had compromised Verity and left her disgraced and vulnerable to all the world, and with no refuge! He crossed his arms on his knees, rested his forehead on them, and devoutly wished he had never been born. Another line from Hamlet struck him. He almost wished he had not so avidly reread the thing. "Give me that man that is not passion's slave and I will wear him in my heart's core; yea in my heart of hearts as I do thee," he muttered.

Verity looked at him blankly. That should have been her line--except that she *preferred* him to be passion's slave.

They went back to the noisy castle, now filled with homeless villagers, in bleak silence; each knowing what was meant by the sword of Damocles! Nothing could be worse than to live under it, waiting for it to fall: for the falling would almost be welcome relief.

But it was not to be yet, for amidst all the hubbub of rejoicing and organizing, a messenger came from Creech Grange with the shocking news that Old Wat had taken upon himself a little side errand and sent a plundering party there! Lady Lawrence had had to save herself by fleeing into the woods and hiding there whilst her home was so savaged and plundered that only the walls were relatively undamaged. Hubbub! If only they had captured the cullionly carbuncle! Men roared vengeful but doltish plans to go after him now. Instead, Robert Lawrence took a good guard and went to Creech Grange to see to things.

For Peregrine and Verity, it seemed all a dream, muffled and unreal as a sea fog. They sat stricken and extinguished. Jennet, who had always seen Verity as filled with sparkly light like stars and Peregrine with a clear steady one like moonlight, stared in dismay. What was wrong with the two people whom she secretly adored? Others assumed that it was just that Verity still had unhealed hurts (and her ears likely to be scarred always) and that Peregrine must have stressed his short leg far more than usual. Jennet knew better, and went into a state of anger, kicking freely. Naomi knew too. Deserting the croaking Dinner, she began to groom Verity, determinedly trying to get under the bandages--for she quite understood that these were the parts that needed healing. And Arabella, planting herself in front of Peregrine, delivered a long speech which no one even tried to translate.

At last when things had settled a little, Lady Bankes rose one evening, silently put Emmot in charge of the household and jerked that long chin. "Bess. Verity. Peregrine. To my chambers. Now." And in silence, they went up to the rich sitting-room next her bedchamber. Their judge seated herself on the one chair, nodded at a stool next to her. "Bess. Here. You two, in front of me." And then, with Bess seated meekly beside her, pleating her flowered sarcenet kirtle as if it were she who was on trial, Lady Bankes turned to the culprits. "Well?"

For a moment silence lay on them thickly. Then they spoke in unison. "'Twas all my fault--"

"Indeed," said the lady. "Let us take that as read, then: dual *mea culpa*. And now what?" They dared look briefly each at the other's face, and both found wild despair. "Come. Bess and I need to know. Was that just a moment of madness? Or lasting passion?"

They could not answer. They should, of course, try to retrieve what they could of Bess's pride, their own futures. They could not, neither of them.

"Mmm. I see. Well, I do have eyes in my head, so it does not surprise me." How could she have known, Peregrine wondered wildly, what he had not known, himself? "So, then, either of you: what do you propose to do now?"

Verity shook her head. She had no idea. Who could put time back and undo what was done, save God? And as far as she knew, even He had never done any such thing: not though He had once caused the sun to stand still. She had nothing to say to Him, either.

"I think," said Peregrine steadily, "that I must do whatever you say." Forever and ever? He writhed.

"Bess? Will you still wed him?"

Bess looked up, her eyes wide and anxious. "Of course, Mother, if you and Father wish me to."

"Forget Mother and Father now. Would you choose to wed him now?"

146

Anxiety became alarm. Bess never wished to make decisions, even smallish ones. But her mother clearly meant it, so she blinked bravely. Her face was sweetly grave, deeply and generously concerned.

"Oh, yes. Gladly. If-- But, Madam Mother, I don't think I-- we-- should. I doubt I'm worthy of him. I think they should marry each other, for they're so alike, I think God made them to rejoice in each other. But," she added, ever the beautiful and dutiful daughter, "I shall do whatever you and father think best, of course."

Felicity and Peregrine simply gaped, shocked almost to outrage. No one could be so self-sacrificing, generous, forgiving, altogether perfect! It was unnatural: it defied human nature. It was--unfair!

Lady Bankes was not yet satisfied. She tapped long fingers upon her daughter's nearest shoulder. "That's not altogether what I meant. Aside from everything else, had you never been betrothed, if Verity did not exist, if you were given free choice, would you choose to wed with Peregrine rather than another?"

It was a slanted question of course, Verity saw clearly. Who would not choose to wed with Peregrine? To her surprise, Bess looked down and pleated at her kirtle so hard she was like to ruin the delicate sarcenet. "I--" Her mother waited. Bess looked up, her lovely face puckered with distress. "Mother, how can I say, in front of him?"

"You will say in front of him, because I order you to."

The pleating began again, the eyes lifted pleadingly. She should never have to decide such a thing. But her mother's face was merciless.

"I-- Well-- He frightens me a little, you see; I mean, he's very kind, but he's so very clever; and I can never understand the half of what he says, and nothing at all of what he thinks amusing; and I'm sure that must fret him as it does me, and I don't really think I could bear to try to keep up with him all my life. I need a husband who will--cherish me and admire me, not challenge me. But Verity laughs and matches him, and that's why I think..." She trailed off miserably. The sarcenet had very nearly perished.

"Of course you do," said her mother, dry and fond and altogether unastonished. "And I think you have the right of it: they do deserve each other." It did not seem to be an accolade. She looked at the speechless Peregrine. "And you deserved that, young man. Those with hubris seldom realize it, I think. Well, we need do nothing for the nonce but write letters to Oxford. Now we're out of siege, it's time Bess's father made a visit home, in any event. And yours should come as well, Peregrine. As to yours, Verity--" She shook her head. "Who knows where he is? Could we write in care of

Parliament? I don't think, somehow, 'twould be wise to call their attention to us just now. Perhaps some other route...? You will of course remain here until he finds you, or this wretched war is won. Now shall we go join the others?"

Peregrine sat still. He? Hubris? He could not believe it!

CHAPTER TWENTY-TWO

THE SWORD OF DAMOCLES

Except for a splendid thunderstorm or two and some drenching downpours, the rest of August was peaceful. The enemy had, for the moment, lost interest in an impregnable castle that was no threat to them. The castle, together with a village considerably disillusioned about they Parlyments, worked to repair the considerable damage to the town. The church was almost destroyed. The alehouse and most of the property around the town square (including Mayor Bastwick's home) were much damaged. So were many cottages further up the road. Captain Lawrence, having found Lady Lawrence safe, badly shaken, and furious, brought her home to the castle and changed his mind about releasing the prisoners of war. Instead, he set them to hard labor at rebuilding both Creech Grange and Corfe.

When Verity saw Gideon among them, she pushed arrogantly past the guards to clasp his hand in both of hers.

"Why are you here? I feared never to see you again! Who did this? I *told*-- Wait right here!" she ordered unnecessarily, and quickly confronted Captain Lawrence. "How dare you!" she raged for all to hear. "He's the one who saved me!: I *told* you that! Let him go at once! Well, I probably would have been dead when Oliver and Sir Wat and his evil captains finished beating and starving me, if Gideon and Salamon and Dorcas and Gaston hadn't risked their lives to free me. 'For God shall bring every work into judgment with every secret thing, whether it be good or whether it be evil.'" She paused to look darkly at the hurriedly-retreating form of Oliver.

Captain Lawrence said he need not listen to a whippety young rebel. Fuming, she fetched Sowerbutts, who spoke to Lady Bankes, who, implacably fair-minded, gave orders to Lawrence. It pleased Verity greatly when, presently, she saw Oliver take Gideon's place among the prisoners at hard labor. It pleased her even more when Gideon, freed, went on helping. He had had, he said, his fill of Sir Wat in particular and making war in general, and was minded to settle down now. Here, for a choice, where he could help repair what he had helped do.

Elsewhere the Earl of Warwick and his navy were busy relieving Exeter, the Poole garrison were sulking, and Sir Wat was in London scolding

Parliament for his humiliating failure. Parliament was not best pleased. Nor were they pleased at the furious peace marches in London, which had been the backbone of Parliament. And angry Londoners were a force to reckon with. Sir Harry Vane was hastily sent to arrange a Solemn League and Covenant with the Kirk of Scotland, which was sure to bring victory-- eventually.

Peregrine looked grim at that, for he knew something of the Scottish Presbyters.

"That's incredibly stupid," he told Lady Bankes for Verity's benefit. "Even Cromwell's New Model Army are like fluffy white bunnies compared to the Covenanters. Their God would eat that of any English church for breakfast."

Verity, shocked, wondered whether this included her Aunt Huldah. Lady Bankes looked hard at Peregrine, but all she said was "Mmm."

Still, both sides had stopped expecting to win by Michaelmas or even Christmas. The King besieged the city of Gloucester, and it seemed rather likely that the Earl of Essex would take his army--with, presumably, Colonel Goodchild--to relieve it.

Corfe knew only that no enemy forces seemed interested in them just now. They breathed again, relaxed but alert--and worked out plans for mutual warning if so much as a hedgehog approached unannounced.

They thanked the Good Lord for their deliverance. Peregrine--who had already discovered that a limp was less of a handicap than he had always supposed--was doing a man's work in the village, and making friends. It helped to keep his mind off other things like a long slender leg, and fine honey-gilt curls tucked under his chin.

He bent unforgiving looks upon Oliver Soames whenever he saw him, feeling that his punishment was not nearly enough. Nor was he alone. Most of the castle and fully half the village snubbed him. Noah and Leah refused to sell him any fish, Mistress Abbot's brood harassed him with catcalls and stones. And after Gideon, Enoch and Fulke had each had a private--er-- interview with him, Oliver took off for other parts. For the good of his health, it seemed.

Verity, much gratified, showed her furtive dimple briefly. She tried to focus on helping to run a household of a hundred or more--but she kept remembering that brief moment when Peregrine's arms were wrapped around her. This did not give restful nights. (Nor did Naomi, who groomed Verity so relentlessly that she was banned from the bedroom, and went down to complain to M'lady.)

Verity often joined Jennet in helping to care for the frail and fretful Miles, who had slept badly since the invasion. Some one had to be with him always, at his bedside, coaxing him to eat, telling him stories, watching while he dozed.

"D'you think he's going to die?" Jennet whispered to her one evening. Verity, who could not lie, set her lips and said nothing, which Jennet correctly interpreted. She stalked up to the nursery without a sound, but with tears pouring down her sallow cheeks.

And so August drifted past. The wildlife that had fled the noise and violence began to return to the valley. Otter and fox and badger cubs, nearly grown now, played again. The castle robins, having raised two broods, began getting ready to set up independent territories for the winter. It involved much quarreling and scolding. Dinner--by now undoubtedly the most spoiled cockerel in the whole of England--scolded everyone except his friend Naomi.

Will graduated from swaddling clothes into long bunchy skirts. Delighted, he spent most of the time happily kicking his feet or trying to crawl--and stopped grizzling.

Arabella learned to say 'no' in English, and the entire castle wished she had not.

Things between Peregrine, Verity, Bess and her mother, were as far as anyone else could see, quite as always. Bess--truly relieved at the idea of not marrying the awesome Peregrine--innocently assumed that all was nicely settled to the joy of everyone. But for Peregrine and Verity, torn with uncertainty, guilt and fear, it was a time of deep misery. Nor could they even discuss it together. For one thing, neither knew what to say. For another, they were both kept very busy--and well apart. Lady Bankes had put them under quiet but firm chaperonage, and they were simply not allowed to be alone together. (Bridget, for once encouraged to spy, was greatly pleased until she realized that wickedness was no fun if not forbidden.) It seemed quite unfair that Fulke and Dorcas were quite unchaperoned, and--judging by their bemused expressions--making the most of it. Their wedding was hastily performed, even without a church to have it in.

Just once, when Bridget was looking around for some more satisfying wickedness, the culprits managed to meet briefly, in full sight of everyone, on the top of the western wall, carefully at arms length. Verity did have something to say, and thought she had best get it over. She looked down at her sapphire-blue gown. She was lovely in it, Peregrine noticed, and with those fine kiss-me-quick tendrils around her face instead of the severe cap-- He crushed his thoughts.

"I'm sorry," she said, as humbly as was in her nature. "I've spoilt your life."

Peregrine, who never allowed anyone but himself to spoil his life, not even Madam Grandmama, simply gawped. Verity could not remember seeing the self-assured youth lose his composure since she first assaulted him with Latin and Greek. Her dimple appeared briefly and fled. "What?" he babbled brilliantly. "You? Mine? Nonsense."

"Well, I did, and you know it. You were besotted with Bess, and if not for me you'd have married her."

"Yes," he said, much struck by this fact.

"And been happy all your life."

"No."

"What?"

"No. I'd have been bored all my life. I might not have noticed it--" He paused to consider this. "--for a while. Thing is, I was always bored before you walked into my life."

Verity stiffened and her blackbird voice dropped a tone. "'Twas you who walked into my life," she retorted tartly. "Right behind Major Rawlins."

For an instant things were as they had been. They grinned at each other appreciatively. Quotations gathered themselves like eager blackbirds around a berry patch. Then gloom fell again, despite the song thrush who, recognizing friends, perched on the crenellation and sang to them.

"What will they do to us, think you?"

He shrugged. It did not much matter, since they would certainly not be allowed to marry, whatever happened. Nor was there anything they could do about it, for every authority of law, society, church, family and politics loomed towering against them. If only Lord Heath had been on the side of Parliament, or Colonel Goodchild in the king's army! Social class might not have mattered so much: Oriel, after all, had married a mere squire's son. But she had done so when she and Father were safely distant from the dictates of Madam Grandmama the Dowager Dragon, who ruled the family, and who thought the daughter of Lord Chief Justice Bankes only barely good enough for her grandson. (Even a lame and disregarded one was good for breeding.)

Verity had been following his thoughts. "They'll find you another wife," she mused, facing it. "But--" But her own marriage would be entirely up to her father, who was busy and uncaring. Some day when the war was over, he'd probably find her a good Calvinist officer of advanced years. She contemplated it. Her body yearned for Peregrine, was revolted by the thought of anyone else. Especially an elderly someone else with a flabby body. "I won't," she said, low. "I won't wed anyone. I'll be a spinster. But--" She looked at him, and all virtue left her. "Peregrine-- If we could manage-- I would come to your bed anyway."

For a moment she thought in anguish that he was repulsed by her froward and sinful thoughts. His face was blank, and an odd bulge appeared just in the front of his breeches. A strong instinct told Verity it was something not to be asked about nor even noticed--but that perhaps it was not revulsion, either? She carefully looked at the song thrush while Peregrine struggled with some froward and sinful thoughts of his own.

"Verity-- You must be mad!" She nodded, understanding now in her own body that passion was indeed a temporary madness. He seemed furious. "You'd ruin yourself for me?"

"Don't be a rantipole," she snapped. "Not for you; for me! Do you think if I didn't want--" She glowered at the song thrush, who hopped a little further away, unnerved. He had thought her his friend.

Anger came to Peregrine, too. "Cock's bones, minx; 'tis you who's being a jabbernowl! That sort of thing's all right for men, but if you think I'd let you-- however much--"

Bridget raced along the wall, alive with curiosity, hoping to learn exactly what wickedness she was supposed to watch for. It couldn't be quarreling, because they always did that, anyway. "Mama says you're to come down at once and go your ways. And," she added with wide candid eyes, "Dinner has just gobbled up Naomi."

September came. Gold and purple wildflowers spread over the land: poppies and mullein, corn marigolds, scabious and toadflax. Bees were busy, and blackberries ripened, and chaffinches swooped in flocks. Came the common blue butterfly--but not as blue as Verity's eyes, reflected Peregrine, wondering if they would ever again be allowed to flash at him in argument. The ripening hawthorn and elderberries attracted clouds of fieldfares. The song thrush and a horde of young blackbirds gorged on the mountain ash berries. Peregrine spent as much time as he could in the library. It was not nearly as enjoyable without her to argue with him.

Near the Ides of September, the green woodpeckers warned loudly of wild equinox storms that presently hurled themselves across England, howling, like those that had, seventeen centuries ago, wrecked Julius Caesar's fleets two years running. And Miles died, quietly in his sleep, hands held by grieving parents, while rain battered the castle.

Jennet, dry-eyed and furious, spoke to no one. Nor did Mayor Bastwick. Nor did Verity, for that matter: not even to God. What was there to say? She stalked silent through the castle, glowering at the maidservants who--even Emmot--forgave her. Peregrine, though grieved, was more philosophical. Children died. Often. It was a fact of life. He himself had seen four little brothers die--two around Miles' age--in the nine years between Cecily's birth and Lark's. But unlike Verity, he did not take God to task for it. "Suffer the little ones to come unto me," he remembered. And--having so recently reread Hamlet, he thought to ease her grief with another passage that seemed very true and apt.

"'Thou knowest all that livest must die, passing through nature to eternity'," he murmured to her and Jennet when he found them sewing together. "'Why seems it so particular with thee?'"

He had meant to give comfort, and was quite hurt when Jennet kicked his shin viciously and Verity treated him to an arctic stare.

It rained and rained. Sodden birds huddled wherever they could find a little shelter. The European skylarks came to join the locals--but not to sing. Not yet. Not in the rain. Siskins arrived to feed on alder and birch seeds; and woodcocks came, and the pied wagtail, and Sir John Bankes.

The town-castle watch system was working well, so that when a small and soggy group of riders came in sight on the Wareham road, it was watched from tower to tower until, directly below the castle, the chief among them was seen through the rain and under heavy cloaks to be portly, richly dressed and sandy-bearded. As he entered Corfe, Madam Chatelaine was sent for. When he appeared in the village square, he was surrounded by smiling villagers. Old Short at the tower watch shouted, someone was sent racing along the wall to the keep, where Lady Bankes was already hurrying down without even a mantle; and the drawbridge had trundled down and the portcullis up and the gate open almost before he reached them. No Calvinist he, he embraced his wife heartily and wetly in front of all, even while his horse and those of his escort were being stabled. Then he allowed himself and his escort to be hurried under shelter.

"You wrote a fine urgent letter, my dear; enough to rouse His Majesty's interest and sympathy. And since you have never before sent for me, and since you've been in sore straits here, the King permits me to come and stay until he convenes his new Parliament at Oxford in January. Is this Mistress Goodchild? I give you good den. And greetings, Peregrine. Now let me come to my children at once."

"Indeed," said his wife, falling into step, "and what of Lord Heath?"

"He cannot be spared, but he has asked me to write at once when I have the matter straight. And he says he knows his son would never do anything dishonorable."

Peregrine winced. Father, it was clear, did not fully understand about Passion.

The broad face face was jovial, the eyes merry all through a fine dinner; but when the five of them assembled in the library that evening, it was the Lord Chief Justice of England who faced the three young people.

Peregrine eyed him warily. He had met him only a few times. He knew that he was well-liked, and among both sides of the civil war, too--but he was not, it seemed, meek nor waffling nor apt to let decisions be made for him.

"How now?" he frowned when he had heard the whole tale. "And do children now presume to dictate to their fathers whom they shall marry?"

"Hardly," said his wife, crisp. "But mothers also have a right to opinions in such matters." She challenged him with that ox-eyed look. He knew it well, and moved one corner of his mouth just slightly. (They were, Verity decided, just such a pair as she and Peregrine might have become, given the time they would never have.) "And I myself think that Bess has the right of it: she and Peregrine would not suit. Nor am I lief to make her unhappy when it's not needful. If you're still minded to tie with Lord Heath, isn't it enough if John wed his daughter Cecily?"

"Welladay." He looked at Bess, who, undismayed by his stern expression, wrapped loving arms about him. "And whom would you wed, then, minx?

"I don't know, father: whomever you wish." She was again the beautiful dutiful daughter.

"Even an old man like me?"

"Oh, yes, dear Father, just like you! You always make me feel so safe and comfortable!"

Defeated, he looked at his wife and murmured something about writing at once to Lord Heath. Then for the first time, he gave full attention to Verity, beetling full sandy eyebrows in her direction. "And you, Mistress Goodchild, daughter of--who? A Colonel. What's he when not in the army? A knight? A squire? Not a viscount or baron, I think, nor even a baronet."

Courage rose high in Verity. Her short chin and level gentian eyes met his. "A knight, merely."

"You aim high, then. You would marry Lord Heath's son?"

"I would wed Peregrine," she said. She was about to add that she agreed with John Lilbourne about abolishing inherited rank or class, when she noted darkly warning looks coming from both Peregrine and Lady Bankes. So she closed her mouth, refusing to undignify herself by saying she'd have him were he a mere yoeman--even though it was true. Instead, she looked fiercely at the vaulted ceiling and began a long, silent, and for once useful conversation with God.

"Hmmmph," Sir John grunted. "Well, you're not under my authority. Nor is Peregrine, directly. Either he must go back to Oxford, or his father must come here. Preferably the latter. Oxford is overcrowded with His Majesty's Court and army. I shall write at once, and Captain Lawrence can send one of his men with it." He stood. The discussion was over.

But it was not, it seemed. Verity stood, as well: alight again, as she had been when Major Rawlins came crashing through her father's front door.

"I've something to say," she said, cheekbones much in evidence. "All Peregrine and I have done wrong is to sin in our hearts. And I'm not sure that's even a serious moral sin, for we never willed it; it just happened to us. But--" And she looked straightly at the Lord Chief Justice of England, "that's not a crime--is it? In law? I've asked God about it, and He said *Non culpabilis,* didn't You, God? So why should we feel covered in guilt and never allowed to speak together, as if we were criminals?"

Those very challenging Viking eyes demanded an answer. Sir John, who had never met the old pre-passion Verity, stared at her in considerable surprise.

"Mmm," he said, and raised his eyebrows at his wife. "Do you truly not trust them to talk or work together?"

She glanced in turn at Peregrine. "*Amantes amentes.* Do you trust yourselves?"

He looked at the culprits, who looked back. It was a long look. "Yes," they said, but it was a very difficult yes, and Verity said it only because she knew Peregrine would not agree to bed her unwed.

Lord and Lady Bankes nodded. But if Sir John had made any other decision, he did not inform them of it. The sword of Damocles still hung there.

Peregrine, for one, was getting very tired of it. This did him no good. The letters were written, and they must simply wait.

But Verity waited now with some slight comfort. For she and God were on good terms again. He had finally answered her with that strong sense of rightness; and He seemed to say--just a trifle impatiently, perhaps--that there was no need to nag so much: she was, on the whole, doing fairly well and He was not displeased with her.

CHAPTER TWENTY-THREE

THE SWORD DROPPED

October. It became brilliantly sunny and cold. The fallow deer mated, and elegant toadstools rose from among the gold-brown of fallen leaves. Kestrels from the northwest arrived with their calls of 'kee kee kee'; and mornings saw cobwebs spread, jeweled in crystal, on the long grasses and across every bush and tree. Hazelnuts swelled like brown satin, and chestnuts snuggled, ripening, inside yellow spiky cases that reminded everyone of Naomi's tongue.

Verity and Peregrine now spoke together at will--but there was little to say that would not sear their hearts. Nor did either of them have much free time. Still, when they were able to meet--in the library, of course--they argued enjoyably about books and philosophy, religion and politics, all too aware of how short this time might be. Bess, relieved from the burden of trying to be clever, no longer joined them. But Jennet sometimes did, scowling when things were above her head, and then sallying out to see if all was well about the castle and with Naomi and Dinner. Captain Lawrence came striding into the gloriette one day looking for Sir John, with Jennet trailing furiously and noisily after him.

"There's a tribe of Gypsies camped out in your valley. I've given orders to run them off, but this--child--"

"They're ours!" yelled Jennet. "He won't listen to me! It's Psammis and Sheba and Willow, and he--" she aimed a furious kick in his direction--" is chasing them away."

"How now, child: mend your manners." Amazing how a few words from the right mouth could quell any child. But then the mouth turned to Lawrence. "As for you, Robert, you should be able to tell Jennet from Bridget by now. Jennet doesn't lie. If she says those particular Gypsies are friends of ours, they are. Very well, Jennet, you may run and signal for them to come up. Robert, tell your men to be polite. These are friends, indeed." He rose, turned toward the study "Mary--? Psammis is here."

Jennet flew. Presently when they came up, Sheba again held Willow firmly by the hand, while Sir John and Lady Mary stood exchanging news. Willow and Jennet spent the entire conversation staring at each other wordlessly. It was a friendship, mercifully, that was highly unlikely ever to be.

The answer from Oxford came a day or two later. A packet arrived containing letters: one for Sir John from Lord Heath, and four for Peregrine, from his father, mother, Cecily--and also, he saw wryly, a short one from Madam Grandmama, the Dowager Dragon, a lady of many pungent words. He looked at it warily, and handed it to Lady Bankes.

There were enough words in the others. Cecily wrote to Peregrine merely that if hee wisht to wedd a clevver girl named Verrity he shoud do so eeven were shee a Purritan thrice over unless she was like Uncle Jeremiah, the which shee doubted, or deare Perry wouldn't wishe to wedd her. And mayhap they coud all go livve neare Hazelmere or Chiddingfold or Hinde Head away from the war...

His father (who tended to be as wordy on paper as he was reticent in his speech) wrote to Sir John that he very much disapproved the younger generation taking things into their own hands this way, and he really did not know what the world was coming to; but since Sir John seemed inclined to let the betrothal be broken, he felt he could not object. As to marriage with this Goodchild girl, he had looked into her heritage and found her father to be a knight, and gentry if not aristocracy; and since Oriel had married a mere squire, and the lines between classes were become very blurred, Lord Heath did not see that he was entitled to deny Peregrine, who, after all, was not the heir. And even though Colonel Goodchild was fighting on the wrong side, once the Royalists had won--probably by Christmas--His Majesty would surely be gracious. In fact, he himself would speak for Colonel Goodchild. Howsomever, he did not at all understand the need for hurry if they had both kept their virtue. Peregrine was far too young to marry. Moreover, he had not finished his law degree, and could not even continue it until after this miserable war was won. Still, if Sir John really felt that an early wedding was advisable, he gave permission.

So simple? Peregrine, stunned, looked over at Verity, who looked very much as he felt. They did not dare grasp joy yet. It must be a mistake: it seemed too good to be possible...

In fact, it was. They thought of it in the same instant. Joy retreated quietly.

"Of course," added Sir John, "that may have been the easy part. There is the matter of Colonel Goodchild."

Indeed! And Verity knew it better than any of them. Joy slipped out of the room altogether.

Lady Bankes finished reading the letter from the Dowager Madam Dragon and handed it back to Peregrine, who took it as if it were an adder. "Well, don't you want to know what it says?"

"Not really. Not at all, actually. But I suppose I must."

"Mmm, yes. Well, it's very simple. If you marry this lowborn maiden, she will disinherit you, forbid you her house, and never again have any communication with you."

"Lovely!" said Peregrine, much relieved. Then something occurred to him. "With the betrothal broken, perhaps you would wish me to leave here?"

"The fosterage is not broken," Her Ladyship pointed out. "You are our surrogate son, and we would regret your leaving. Would you wish to?"

"No!" said Peregrine explosively, and no more was said.

No more was said, either, of Colonel Goodchild. Indeed, what was there to say? For he was with General Essex, recently in London but now off again to Reading or elsewhere; and unlikely to approve this match, in any case. Peregrine and Verity (unlike the fortunate Fulke and Dorcas, already expecting a babe) had to be content with frustration undiluted with much hope at all. Once the village had been restored, Lady Bankes, who know skill when she saw it, promptly brought both Gideon and Dorcas into the castle for maintenance and repairs. (It might or might not have been partly for Verity, who had never before had a friend of her own age and sex.)

The clear cold weather continued. A series of hard frosts turned the leaves to flame and gold. Migrants from northern Europe flew in to feed avidly on berries. Above, wild geese in uncrowded precision followed an invisible but implacable path across deep blue skyways.

When an army officer openly wearing an orange sash diagonally across his chest, with no escort at all, approached early one morning along the Wareham road, all warning signals went into operation. When he rode alongside the castle and up to the village, everyone was quite ready for anything. When, after a longish pause, he came clattering over the bridge with half the village clustering suspiciously at the far end, the drawbridge had been firmly raised.

He seemed no whit upset, but paused at the edge of the gap and looked up at the heads along the top of the guardian towers. "Ho, the castle!" he shouted, stern-faced. "I am told that Sir Walter Erle failed to take this castle: that it is still held by Sir John Bankes. Yes? I wish, then, to speak with him."

The heads consulted urgently. Then one of them gabbled a question.

"Tell him I am Colonel Nathan Goodchild. I have reason to think he holds my daughter." Then he sat unmoving on his horse, imperially waiting. His daughter was not the only one in that family to be a great believer in dignity--nor the only one with implacable courage, either, Peregrine reflected, coming to stare down from the tower. It took temerity to ride across England and confront a hostile castle and village alone.

Colonel Goodchild stared back at those peaty-green eyes, unaware that they could hold any significance in his life; merely struck by their odd shape. He was uncomfortably aware that his heart was behaving as before a battle. If any harm had come to his Verity--

He had not realized his feelings toward this little-known daughter until he had taken leave from General Essex to stop by his home for a rare visit to her, expecting to find a well-run household with Mistress Fynch securely in charge. He had found instead a looted and deserted shell of a manor filled with dust and leaves and detritus; and it was clearly only the merciful will of God Almighty that had finally revealed to him the crumpled and almost illegible bit of parchment blown into a corner. Now he waited, braced for the worst.

It was a matter of great surprise when the drawbridge and portcullis lowered themselves courteously to his horse. He was escorted in as an honored guest rather than a prisoner of war, and brought at last--not even blindfolded!--into the richly-hung living quarters of the castle. This was not the behavior one expected from the ungodly Royalists! (He showed no hint of his feelings, of course.)

Presently he found himself ushered into a long room filled with crimson velvet and gilded green leather. He paused, still beset by uncertainty at being welcomed so easily by an enemy still unexpectedly in control of the castle. Sir John Bankes offered him a seat, and Lady Bankes, refreshment. Adults and children clad in scandalously rich colors and laces and ribands gathered to stare at him. Among them stood a slim young woman with his dead wife's very blue eyes and silver-gold hair. It curled, capless, glittering in the morning sun that poured diagonally through the southern window. He also recognized his own cheekbones and eyebrows. He pushed the latter together and jutted the former. So did she. He remembered that lopped-off chin, too--but not the disconcerting stare, which he found unseemly. She had not learned that from her mother--nor Huldah, either! He would not acknowledge how relieved he was to see her safe: it made him unwontedly stringent

"Verity!" She was wearing neither apron nor fichu, and that lustrous blue gown was very far from plain homespun poplin or fustian. "Have you been corrupted to Royalism, Daughter?"

There were one or two muffled snorts, which he disregarded. Verity jutted the chin as well as the cheekbones, abdicating nothing of her dignity. Lady Bankes spoke dryly, very bold for a female.

"If you can ask that, sir, you don't know your daughter very well."

This was true. He had seldom seen and never known or understood her-- nor seen the need. A daughter was a creature God in His wisdom chose to bestow on a man instead of a son. A father's duty was to raise her in rectitude and fear of God; hers was to provide him with grandsons. He realized that the former had always been out of his hands, for he had never had time for it, leaving it to his sister Huldah and Mistress Fynch. As for the latter--

He looked at her. Somehow the skinny pale child had become a woman whose eyes met his with an appraising candor more suitable to a man. He did not know what to do about her.

Verity had no suspicion of this, saw only her father, face as stonily severe as always. Her heart was quite thudding behind her small breasts, with panic and hope and despair all mixed with the forlorn wish to love him and be loved. She longed for Peregrine's hand in hers, but thought that would not be wise under the circumstances. And so, on impulse, she stepped forward and tentatively took the square hard hand of her father, instead.

This was, it turned out, a stroke of genius. Colonel Goodchild blinked as he felt that slight hand slip into his, which was not a thing quite proper--but it was pleasant, so he left it there. He was, he discovered, really quite fond of her.

"You are well?" he asked gruffly and belatedly. "Do you pray, Daughter?"

The sunny head lowered as she dipped in an equally belated curtsey. "Yes, Sir," she said, raising it again rather too quickly for proper humility. "A great deal."

This was verified at once by the richly-clad children. "She prays all the time," said one. "She scolds God," observed another, and added improbably that God scolded her back so all could hear. A third gripped his plain military jerkin with fat starfish hands and gabbled nonsense.

"Children!" said Sir John, and they all subsided at once except for the girl with oaken hair who took a position of protective defiance at Verity's side. A baby babbled, crawling exuberantly across a rich Turkish carpet, while a cockerel strutted across it virtually arm-in-arm with a cat whom Colonel Goodchild might or might not recognize.

"I think," said Lady Bankes with a comprehensive look around the large crowded room, "that we should retire to the library. We have much to discuss. Joan, tell Cook we have an honored guest for dinner, and to bring mulled wine and refreshments. Jennet, ask Emmot to have a the yellow bedchamber prepared and a fire lit. Verity, Peregrine, we shall send for you presently."

In fact, they had to wait upon the morning, for Colonel Goodchild found that even the bare essentials formed an amazing amount of information to take in. His Verity wished to marry! Some one she had--unfilially!--chosen for herself! At her age! And a Royalist! And, most amazing, Lord Heath's second son. Well! Unlike Lilbourne, Nathan Goodchild had no objection at all to aristocracy as such-- However--

"Lord Heath?" he asked discontentedly. A Malignant in both religion and politics, with an older son, he believed, in the cavalry of that devil's cub Prince Rupert. Surely God would not approve!

On the other hand, could the Almighty have had some purpose in placing her here--and preserving that bit of parchment--? He needed, he decided, more time: to see and assess the young man and all these strange people--including his surprising offspring, who, it had turned out, was rather more like him than her sweet and biddable mother. So he joined them at a modest midday dinner of a haunch of venison, roast goose, a shield of brawn with mustard, partridge, sallets, custards, carbonadoes, quince pie, florentines and tarts, with Bordeaux and Gascoigne wine from what was clearly a fine cellar. He spent the afternoon as a guest, glancing sideways at this stranger who was his daughter, but saying little. And the day ended with an evening of talk and sinful music (which he had never personally found very sinful, at all, though he had never cared to mention this to Huldah). Verity had, it turned out, a very sweet singing voice! And he went to a fine soft bed of feather mattress and down quilt and pillow such as he had seldom indulged in before, and which were wasted on him, for he had other things on his mind. And since that mind was indeed the father of his daughter's, he thought very clearly and practically.

Things were not going as well with the Parliament armies as he could have wished. The Colonel was one of the few who had ever considered the possibility that God might not, after all, give them victory. Having a foot in each camp might be a very desirable thing: perhaps precisely what God had had in mind when He arranged for Verity to be brought here. The lad was personable and intelligent, his class far higher than a mere knight might normally expect for his daughter. The short leg was no matter: it might even keep him safe. And with things as they were, it was quite possible that the older son would die in one of those outrageous cavalry charges, leaving this one as heir.

Moreover-- He brightened. Once Verity was safely married, he need no longer feel that faint nagging sense of neglected responsibility.

Not that he often had, of course.

Next morning when they returned to the extremely comfortable library filled with sinfully pagan books, he had almost decided. He would make the best marriage he could for her, and although this was not what he would have chosen--yet it did seem indeed to be God's Will... He looked across that carpeted expanse at the two of them.

They stood with eyes alight in grave faces, filled with incredulous hope; hardly daring to look at each other, but thinking each almost in the other's mind. They must be very careful. A mistake could yet lose them all. How could they predict this stranger? Peregrine glanced at Verity for guidance, but she had none to give. Father or not, she knew him scarcely better than did any of the others. Still, God had been quite gracious lately, so it might be a good idea to depend on Him now. She curtseyed, raised a vivid blue gaze toward the high ceiling, and her voice was low and seemly and sincere.

"'In thee, O Lord, do I put my trust: let me never be put to confusion.'"

Her father suppressed a spurt of amusement: her mother used to quote Scripture just so, to soften him up. They were not so unlike, after all. His face matched his daughter's, austerity for austerity. He spoke to Sir John.

"I cannot see why you say the marriage with Mistress Elizabeth would have been a bad match, Sir," he observed. "Those two share religion, politics and class: they seem perfectly matched."

"But not in mind or nature," said Sir John gravely, and met Colonel Goodchild's astonished frown. Matching mind or nature was the last thing anyone ever thought of: it was wealth, land, name, class. Frowning at a tapestry that did at least seem to be a Bible scene, Goodchild pursued the matter doggedly.

"Peregrine is son of a viscount, he's a Royalist, and presumably Church of England, if not papist; whilst my Verity is merely daughter of a knight, and a Parliamentarian and Congregationalist. There's unmatched if you like!" He looked at the two of them sternly.

"Not entirely, Sir," said Peregrine, and glanced at his host, whom he was about to shock greatly. "To tell the truth, sir, I have long shared Verity's reservation about the Divine Right of kings. It seems to us altogether a bad idea." He glanced again. His host seemed singularly unastonished and not particularly disapproving. (He had to work with this king a great deal.)

"And nor am I altogether a Calvinist, sir," confessed Verity, with heart crowding her ribs. This truth might destroy everything for them--and yet, they had agreed together, they could not marry on a lie, even were Verity able to tell one. She looked anxiously at her father's cheekbones. They jutted.

"And what are you, then?" Had she turned to Anglicism? Even worse, papacy?

"I think--I'm almost sure--I'm an Arminian."

The cheekbones relaxed, relieved. Oh. Well, then. Arminianism, he had sometimes secretly felt, had some small merit. So he frowned even more ferociously at them. They were by now shamelessly holding hands, and facing him with insouciant eyes. Incredibly, they were going to win, and they knew it. Joy had flown back, and was lighting their faces like May sunshine.

But victory was not to be given so easily. That stern narrow face fixed upon Peregrine, with a challenging stare not unlike his daughter's. "And you, Master Peregrine?" Have you no quotation from Scriptures to persuade me?"

Verity swallowed. This was something they had not foreseen! She did not think that Homer or Sophocles or Vergil or Shakkspur--Shakespeare-- would please her father. Not at all! She flicked a panicky blue glance at Peregrine, who smiled back and squeezed her hand gently.

"'Entreat me not to leave thee, or to return from following after thee; for whither thou goest, I will go; and where thou lodgest I will lodge; thy people shall be my people and thy God my god; where thou diest, I will die, and there will I be buried; the lord do so to me, and more also, should ought but death part thee and me.'"

Colonel Goodchild sighed, not at all discontented.

EPILOGUE

MAY, 1653

The little road still wandered along the stream between the two massive hills, with no room between for even a vagrant road to lose itself. On one steep hillside a throaty blackbird sang his heart out. On the other, a cuckoo called. Cuck-coo!

The little party of travelers were dressed somberly--at least compared to ten years ago--in rich shades of russet, jade, gentian and wine-in-sops: the men with the new modest square untrimmed collars. No more flamboyant beribboned lovelocks or Brussels lace collars rising to the ears over deep-piled velvet. Not in public, anyway. This was not a good idea in the new Puritan England.

Times had changed. England was now at peace, but never again as before. There was no king, courtiers, or House of Lords. Those of the royal family still alive had fled, impecunious, to their relatives in France and the Netherlands. Royalists whose property had been sequestered followed, for reasons of health. Those who remained, tended to live very quietly at home and hope for the best: quelled, kingless, and governed entirely by God and the Lord Protector Cromwell. True, he had been surprisingly tolerant rule--so far--considering. So long as one dressed and behaved circumspectly. The lion, having demonstrated claws and teeth, could afford to purr a little, and even initiate some desirable social reforms. But no one cared to take any chances.

They rode silently, reflective: shaken by their first glimpse of Corfe Valley from the gap in the hills, not looking up the hillside above, even for a glimpse of the always-elusive cuckoo. The child riding pillion before his grandfather stirred restlessly.

Verity eyed her little son, his fair hair bright over teal coat. He sported his father's blunt chin, his mother's eyes, eyebrows and challenging expression. It had been a long ride, and he was unusually quiet. Not grumpy. He was merely marshaling some questions.

"Madam Mother, is Protector Cromwell going to be king?"

"I don't think so, dearling."

"Why?"

"He said he'd rather be Lord Protector."

"If he does be king, will he be King Cromwell?"

"No, he'd be King Oliver."

"Why?"

"Because that's how it is. Kings and some titles use Christian names. Your grandfather as an army officer was Colonel Goodchild, but his knightly title is Sir Nathan. Your other grandfather is Richard, Lord Heath. It will all seem quite simple to you one day."

"Oh," said Nathan the Younger, and fell again into contemplation, leaving his parents to raise their brows at each other and go on thinking about the past. The blackbird was joined by a song thrush. Everyone looked at the road, remembering.

The end of the war had been far worse than the start. King Charles, having made every possible and several impossible blunders, had managed to lose most of his most faithful followers, the war, the throne and finally his head! This deeply shocked all of England, for even those who had fought against him would have drawn the line at regicide! (On the other hand, Peregrine reflected fair-mindedly, there really had been nothing else to do with him. Even as a defeated prisoner, he had behaved like an arrogant victor, refusing with contempt the generous terms of a limited monarchy.)

So now they had Cromwell, that man of total contradictions, a tormented man of enormous and unhappy power: passionate and brooding and ruled by a despotic puritan conscience. Striding England like a Colossus, he had abolished the House of Lords, thoroughly intimidated Parliament, (who had innocently supposed that *they* would rule England now) and, wielding more Power than Charles had ever dreamed of, proceeded to rule (aided by God and the New Model Army)--yet with more tolerance than anyone had expected.

Provided, of course, one did not offend the Puritan Ethic.

The vagrant road erupted to the right up to the village square, paused, then headed left to the sea, leaving the half-dozen riders behind in a scatter of summer showers and tentative May sunshine. They reined in their horses and sat surveying Corfe Village very much as three of them had done some ten years before. Nathan, who had never seen it, stared wide-eyed and curious.

The village still sat solid on eternal hills. Late afternoon sun gleamed across the Purbeck stone. The church at the far end had been repaired--but not as it was before. No stained glass now bejeweled the blue-gold stone, for the Presbyterian God did not approve.

The sounds and movements of a drowsy village crept into awareness. A baby cried and was soothed, a woman laughed, a loom clacked and a game of tag chased itself across the square followed by a scatter of puppies. From the hill to the left, chickens chuckled busily, a robin sang a silver trill and a blackbird a throaty one. From the inn on their right came a bawdy song Cromwell would never have approved. The square was at the moment occupied only by one man, who sat peacefully in the stocks as if he had never left, looking not a day older, still wearing the unlined child-face of one with no cares because he had no conscience.

Nathan Lennox had his father's need to know, his mother's passion for accuracy and his very own determination to spread knowledge as seed upon the world. He had not yet looked up the hill, for his attention was fixed on the stocks.

"Who's that and what did he do?"

Verity sighed. "It's Salamon Soames and he probably stole something."

"Why?"

Why, indeed? Though she argued less with God as she got older, she still could not comprehend the workings of His mind. Probably He did not intend her to. But if He deliberately created amoral souls like Salamon--which presumably He did--*why?* How could He justly send him either to heaven or hell?

A woman who might be Mistress Abbot grown seven years stouter and with no brood, appeared in a doorway across the square and stood peering nearsightedly. Verity smiled, but then her gaze followed that of the others, unwillingly, across the inn roof to the castle towering just behind.

Less than eight years ago it had been a stone jewel crowning that perfect cone. It was now a stark ruin, looking more like a battered dragon sprawled in death agony, with a huge jagged fang where the keep had risen in pure splendor. Verity--all of them--had thought they were prepared for the sight. They were not. The stricken silence that had held them all the way from the distant view from the gap in the northern hills, now held them even more powerfully with this better view. They had, to be sure, been told that the castle was destroyed by Parliament's order--but they had not taken this literally, because they had known it was not possible. How could it be? A very large cannon might in time breach a smallish wall--but Old Wat's cannons had overheated themselves to extinction without making more than a scar on those walls. Now some power had literally rent the inner gatehouse in two, causing the towers to lean precariously sideways; had so thrown down, blown up and mangled the gloriette, inner bailey, and even outer walls and towers and the formidable outer gatehouse, that it was no longer certain where anything had been. It looked as if a giant Hand had reached down, gasped the entire hill in its palm, and crushed the impregnable castle like a child's toy.

Like Jericho.

God being omnipotent, incalculable and undoubted, all of them shivered uneasily. Only the retired-Colonel Goodchild, who had seen much war destruction, and his eldest grandson who had never seen any, gazed with composure. And even the Colonel's face was grim, and Nathan's blue eyes round and wondering. Someone came out of the inn and rushed back inside. White fluffy clouds began to gather purposefully, challenging anyone to suppose they were out of season. Not in England!

Sowerby spoke. "Happen Parliament were in a right hirdum-dirdum," he observed.

Happen they were.

"No army could do't," breathed the youngest man-at-arms with low-voiced conviction. "Never, nohow. Must've had help from Satan."

Nathan the Younger leaned forward, disapproving but interested.

"Is that where you lived and Grace got borned, Father? How did it get like that? Did God tell Joshua to walk around and around it for seven days and then blow the trumpets to make the walls fall down? I don't think that was very nice of Him."

"God had little to do with it," his grandsire observed dryly. "And trumpets, even less. 'Twas the work of men, and it took mines, sappers, tons of gunpowder. Parliament spent as much time, skill, money, munitions, thought and sheer anger on destroying this castle than on winning a major battle, if that's any comfort."

It was not. Staring upward, three of them remembered vividly that autumn of '43, when they seemed to have won everything. The siege was defeated, both fathers had been won over, Sir Walter Erle and his savages had retired. The future promised to be, if not victorious, at least reasonable.

Peregrine and Verity had wed at Christmas, and 1644 promised fair. Mayor Bastwick and his wife, murmuring that the Lord had given and the Lord had taken away, adopted five ruddy-cheeked children orphaned by the assaulters. Dorcas bore a daughter, and Verity became pregnant. The civil war still raged near--but there was not another actual assault. Only sorrow when young John Bankes died in Oxford that summer, followed six months later by his father, leaving young Ralph first the heir and then the owner of Corfe Castle. Lady Bankes never flinched visibly, only went with her daughters to the funeral and to make sure Ralph was being cared for.

She had found him in the custody of Peregrine's Grandmama, better known as Madam Dragon, whose pet hobby was collecting and controlling people. Considering the child owner of Corfe Castle to be spoils of war and a suitable husband for her youngest grandchild, she had had no intention of giving him back--until she met Lady Bankes.

The Dowager Dragon, to the awe of Oxford, had never stood a chance. It had been a defeat like that of David over Goliath: hardly even a contest. The victorious Lady Bankes bore her relieved son in triumph to the care of his elder sisters, and returned to Corfe. All seemed fine--until Dick Brine laid bitter complaints to Parliament that the castle garrison had pulled down two houses and carried all the stones in to the castle. They might easily have verified that he had only one house, which he was still occupying. Instead they turned their postponed anger back to that infuriating castle. Letters went to Colonel Butler, the governor of Wareham, who began harassing them and seizing cattle and provisions, until he was neatly captured and imprisoned in the castle.

And then--in the dreadful spring of '46--both Oxford and Corfe fell to the armies of Parliament! It was really the end of the civil war--except that King Charles, true to form, fled to the Scots, who promptly took him prisoner and began a second war. It was certainly the end of Corfe Castle.

Peregrine and Verity were still thinking in the same mind. "I mind me you did say when first we saw it that it could be taken only by treachery," he murmured.

She had. And it was. First Lady Banke's trusted officer and neighbor Captain Lawrence had turned his coat and helped Colonel Butler escape through the sallyport Verity knew so well. Then an officer of the castle garrison admitted some seventy Roundhead soldiers in the middle of the night--and by the time they all awakened to the sound of battle from within the walls, it was all over, and nothing for it but to surrender. They could, even those like Dorcas and Fulke with homes in the village, consider themselves fortunate to keep their lives, and merely be driven away with only what they could carry, leaving behind the richness, the gilded green leather, blue silk damask, Turkish carpets, crimson velvet--and Sir John's priceless library! Even Naomi!

Memory had held them only a moment or two, while their son carefully considered all the new information presented to him. The pretty little white clouds gathered themselves into a thin grayish one, which began tossing wetness downward. Colonel Goodchild sheltered Nathan with his own cloak. A freckled young man with jug-handle ears came from the inn and hurried toward them.

"Is't thee at last? Is Dorcas come? And Fulke?"

The boy had become a man! Peregrine dismounted and turned to him. "Gaston? You've grown up! You've had our letters, then? Does your uncle expect us?"

"Ay, two letters. Uncle Soames be old: I'm running t'inn, and there be places for horses and servants, but you and yours will be guests of Mayor Bastwick. Dorcas be well?"

"Sends her love," said Peregrine regretfully. "She's breeding again, and stayed with the children. She and Verity have seven between them. And with us away, Fulke, too, is needed at Fairview Manor."

The thin cloud began a determined drizzle. A plaintive squawk from the stocks caused someone from the nearest cottage to come let Salamon out. A familiar voice came from the elegant manor house behind them.

"For these my children were lost and are found. Luke."

Verity slipped from her horse, turned, stretched affectionate hands to Mayor Bastwick. "Set me as a seal upon thine heart, as a seal upon thine arm: for love is strong as death. Proverbs. I'm so glad to see you! Your letters to Lady Bankes arrived in Ruislip, and she sent word to us, but we've had none--"

It was hardly surprising. Mail had been unreliable enough before the war. Now, in a still-ravaged country with terrible and mostly un-signposted roads, few messengers would spend much time wandering the hills seeking secluded estate like Gracewood or Fairview Manor near bucolic hamlets called Hungerford or Hazelmere.

They regarded each other with pure pleasure. The fierce little Puritan maiden was now a vivid young women, eyes as blue and challenging as ever. Mayor Bastwick still wore green, but in that subdued shade known, regrettably, as goose-turd. He had aged much in seven years. Verity, shocked, pretended not to notice. His once-portly figure was lean and stooped, his face lined, and there was bleak emptiness behind his eyes--but, she perceived, his smile was--peaceful? Not Salamon's irresponsible peace, but the tranquility, perhaps of coming through grief to the other side?

"Come thee in, friends, from the wet, for 'there is a sound abundance of rain'. First Kings."

Peregrine nodded. "In a moment. Sowerbutts, will you help Gaston see to the stabling and all? And, Gaston, may we order dinner for tomorrow for all our old friends here?"

The toothy grin displayed itself. "Oh, ay; I thought ye would. All's prepared and Sarah busy and excited."

"My girls are nigh grown now," said the mayor, taking Verity's arm and leading he way to the house she remembered so well. "D'you remember Sarah? My oldest. Married Gaston last Michaelmas. You won't recognize Judith here: she was four when you left. Go help Hannah and Martha prepare refreshments, pet. Come in, Colonel Goodchild: is that Verity's babe you're carrying?" he added to the indignation of Nathan the Younger. The daughters, respecting his wounded dignity, swept him off to be cosseted.

His wife was not visible, nor had he mentioned her. Verity, dismayed, tugged at his arm and raised speedwell-blue eyes to his. He replied. "Ay; she went to be with Miles and the babes, two-three years ago. She was content. And I'm fortunate in my daughters."

Verity, unsurprised, was nevertheless stricken. Peregrine came close behind her. "Not fortune, sir. You cast your bread upon the waters, I think, and found it after many days. Buttered." He grinned across her shoulder at Hannah, who giggled and curtseyed and rushed into the kitchen after the other girls. They were nothing at all like the fragile Miles, but healthy and uncomplicated. Good.

The big sitting room had changed little. Bastwick waved them to be seated. An old cat with one blonde eyebrow uncurled herself from the softest chair, yawned, blinked, got down, came to Verity and invited a scritch. Verity, deeply moved, obeyed. Naomi arched, purred, rolled over, swore, and went back to finish her nap. Bastwick confessed that he had never quite got scritching to suit Naomi. The girls returned with ale, cold lark pie, a dish of comfits and Nathan.

"Is that Naomi?" he asked eagerly. "May I scritch her? Does she miss poor Dinner? Can I go look at your garden?" Given permission, he trotted off with Judith, giving his elders a chance to talk.

"Tell me, then, what happened to you all after you rode away from Corfe with little more than what was on your backs?

"It could have been worse," said Verity. "'Twas Father's letters that saved us, you know."

The colonel did not smirk, for it would not have befitted his rank--but it was a near thing. "From Generals Essex *and* Fairfax," he murmured. "Suggesting that all Parliament men protect my daughter and her friends from any incivility, lest they incur serious displeasure."

"I do think," Peregrine mused, "that that did indeed save us. And Lady Bankes and the others, as well. Sir Wat was still furious enough to eat cannon balls, and certainly to hang his least-favorite Malignants. Even more furious when he read the letters and found his hand stayed. Did he turn his ire on you after we left? " he asked Mayor Bastwick. "We've always feared it."

"No, just on the castle. Before destroying it, they stripped it of everything: furniture, carpets, tapestries, clothing, paintings, all the linen and blankets and feather beds, the pewter and brass and porcelain, even the big trunk with Milady's crimson satin petticoat."

"The books?" asked Peregrine wistfully.

"Alas, I believe Erle looted almost everything. Still, he didn't take the entire library--did he? How many books did you manage to smuggle out in place of your clothing and effects?"

"Too few," said Peregrine, regretful. "Our own, of course, and all the Shakespeare, because he's rare these days, and Euripides and Aristophanes and Plato and Ovid--"

"And did you make the whole trip without a change of garment? What did Lady Bankes say?"

Verity looked austere. "She *told* us to take as many as we could manage. Dorcas and Fulke and Sowerbutts managed a few, as well."

Bastwick observed in awe that no wonder some of the horses had looked ready to founder. The girls looked enchanted. Not, it was understood, for the books, which none of them cared for, but that Old Wat was cheated of some of his loot.

"What befell you then?" begged Judith.

"Not very much. Well, we all stopped at Gracewood, which is on the way to London, and all stayed for a bit. M'mother and her parents and my youngest sister Lark were all there then. Then Lady Bankes and her children went on to her family in Ruislip, and Sowerbutts and Dorcas and Fulke and the babes stayed with us, and then came when we moved to Fairview Manor."

"But after all was lost--? Bastwick paused delicately.

It was always hard to know how much of adult conversation young Nathan understood. Usually, it seemed, more than anyone expected. Now he raised his silver-gilt head.

"King Charles had his head chopped off," he informed them. "At the Banqueting Hall, and he wore his warmest clothing in case he should shiver because it was winter, and people think he was afeared."

Peregrine waved his errant eyebrow. "Indeed. 'Nothing in his life became him like the leaving of it.'" No one quite winced. Only Verity knew the quotation. The others, used to those two, ignored it. Nathan, suddenly uncomprehending, listened, intent, working at it. Peregrine, who, with his father and brother, had had close personal knowledge of that monarch, went on mercilessly. "He was the classic Tragic Hero: a man of high status who brought about his own downfall with *hubris*. Dying was the best thing he ever did for England," he finished, and flicked a challenging glance at the Colonel, who instantly accepted it. If Peregrine could savagely criticize his own leader, so could his father-in-law.

"He means, England is very much shocked at what we did to ourselves. We--subjects and Parliament--are quelled by that and by Cromwell's stern hand, and even by the reforms he seems to be making. But not forever. We struggled for too many centuries to have a say in our own government, to give it up. One day--perhaps not in Cromwell's life nor in mine--but some day-- we'll demand it back. Possibly even a new form of monarchy. And a new Parliament, of course.

"If Prince Charles manages to survive," Peregrine mused, "he might do nicely. He was a nice lad. More brains than the rest of the family put together--"

"And after all that's happening to him, being poor and every princess in Europe snubbing him, perhaps he won't have any silly ideas about his Divine Royal Rights," added Verity.

Judith, understanding very little more than Nathan, felt that they all needed to be comforted, and passed the comfits. Hannah ventured a question.

"But the seques-- sequestrations-- Did they let you keep your family's home?" And she instantly blushed at Peregrine's smile.

"Oh yes. They were ordered not to offend my wife, remember. And though some of my family later went to France for their health--".

Nathan came alert. "No, Father, it was because Uncle Bevil and Grandfather Lennox were very important king's men, so they might have been beheaded, too."

His parents rolled their eyes slightly. The colonel gave him a look which subdued him briefly. Peregrine went on.

"That wouldn't have happened, son. Your grandfather and also your Uncle Evan saved Gracewood for the family. So Bevil can return some day--"

Nathan, unsubdued after all, felt the need to Inform. "Because he's heir. But I'm heir to Fairview--" He received a severe glance from that gentleman and backtracked. "Well, Mother is, but I'm next, and not Grace, because she's only a girl and boys come first-- " Another glance, another backtrack. "I mean, she'll get married and go live somewhere else, won't she? And I'll inherit Fairview Manor." He leaned against his maternal grandfather with an air of calm possession.

Over his oblivious head, his parents and grandparent silently agreed that any incipient *hubris* in this lad needed to be nipped in the bud--as soon as they returned home. They all looked out the front casements and found the clouds defeated, the ruins lit by the sun and all the visible foliage viridescent with May; each new-minted leaf separately luminous.

"I want to see your nice ruined castle," Nathan announced. "Can we go up in it?"

The adults exchanged glances. "Why not?" said Bastwick. "You've time today to see the Outer bailey. 'Tis safe enough: anything that could fall, has, these past seven years. My girls will take you. Tomorrow the Powl lads can show you further: they all know it well. I'm a little past it, myself."

"I'll stay with you," said Colonel Goodchild. "I dare say we'll find something to talk of, we oldsters."

They sat comfortably on the front porch as the young folk crossed the square and vanished behind the inn. The villagers, who knew already just who had arrived, now came bustling about, ostentatiously busy. The mayor pondered. The comfortable silence became a reflective silence.

"Tis a fair distance here from Fairview."

"Ay."

"Just for Verity wishing for to see us again?"

Goodchild looked rather like Naomi having a scritch. "Ay. She had too few to love until she came here, and you mean much to her. I'd not deprive her further. I mean to see she's wealthy in love for as long as either of us lives."

Mayor Bastwick tried not to look overwhelmingly gratified, and failed. It seemed that, after all, they had much in common, those two. The lowering sun to their left shone slantways on the tortured stones above. The destruction was shameful; the hatred behind it, worse. But Corfe Village still rested secure on eternal hills, as did the slain castle above it. Hills, village and ruins would be unchanged long after the very names of those who savaged it had passed into nothingness. The gaunt beauty rising before them must surely lie there unchanged for--what? A hundred years? Five hundred? A thousand? While England lived?

Colonel Goodchild and Mayor Bastwick smiled, not altogether discontent.

The End

HISTORICAL NOTE

Many Americans have never noticed that England had a civil war, too. Well, three of them, actually, which isn't bad for a country many times the age of ours. Stephen and Matilda in the 13th Century settled their battle over who was to be monarch with compromise. Stephen took the throne but named Matilda's son as his heir--the redoubtable Henry II.

The dreadful Wars of the Roses in the 15th Century were ended by Henry Tudor, a most unprepossessing, stingy, ruthless man whose only claim to the throne was through a bastard grandmother a few generations back--and by invading England with the help of France. Still, he had one virtue: he ended the war very effectively--by killing the anointed king, Richard III. Then he pre-dated his reign--so any who fought for the legitimate King Richard could be executed for treason to Henry. Nice touch, that--and typically Henry. Then since the least of the Plantagenets still had a better claim to the throne than he, he systematically wiped the rest of them out.

That almost certainly included the little princes in the Tower. The much-maligned Richard has been blamed for that, ever since--quite idiotically! Richard had neither motive nor proclivity for such actions. Henry had both. Richard, in fact was one of England's best kings. In only three years he proved himself to be a wise, kindly and just ruler, who introduced the right to bail, and prohibited the intimidation of juries, and was much loved. But done was done. And after some fifty years of intermittent war, any peace, however draconian, must have been welcome. (Except, of course, to the Plantagenets).

The final home war--known as The Civil Wars--began in 1642 and culminated with the execution of King Charles I in 1649. It was extremely complicated, and I haven't tried to get into it much beyond the needs of this story. Probably Peregrine put it rather neatly when he said that everyone involved mistook themselves for God and tried to behave accordingly.

Still, all the history and geography in this book is, if sometimes truncated, as true as I can discover, as well as many of the characters. Jarvis, Sydenham and Skuts were the very real names of the very real captains of Sir Walter Erle, who was indeed called Old Wat. For the reasons given. All that part of the story, except for Verity's role, is historically accurate. Including the 'sow and the boar' incident, and Erle's eventual part in the looting of the castle. Peregrine, Sowerbutts, Dinner, Major Rawlins, the Gypsies, and some of the villagers are fictional. Dick Brine and Captain Lawrence are not. (Nor is Naomi: she lies buried in my back garden.)

My description of the castle furnishings, from crimson velvet to gilded green leather, and the 'white dimity bed and canopy with the whole furniture wrought withe black' of Lady Bankes' bedroom, came directly from the long and detailed list that Lady Bankes made, hoping to get some of it back. In 1661 after the Restoration of the monarchy, Sir Ralph Bankes wrote to Sir Walter Erle, listing the items and asking that they be returned. I have a copy of the letter and Erle's answer which was long and florid, and boils down to (a) He didn't destroy Corfe. (b) Well, anyway, he never looted a single thing. (c) And he won't give any of it back, so there.

One primary contemporary source of information is the fairly lengthy account in the well-known diurnal of the day: the *Mercurius Rusticanus.* So of course any writer on this subject must certainly read it.

And again. And again. It presents difficulties. For one thing, the narrative is convoluted. Well, this in itself can be overcome; the problem here is that when one unconvolutes it and tries to make a sequential narrative, one discovers that it abounds in contradictions, unlikelihoods and what seem to be downright impossibilities. (That's aside from being just a teeny weeny bit partisan.)

For instance, events come in one order one one page, another on the next. Again, it says of Lady Bankes that 'understanding that the king's forces, under the conduct of Prince Maurice and the Marquis of Hertford, were advancing toward Blandford, she by her messenger, made her address to them to signify unto them the present condition in which they were'. (That condition being that they were surrounded by hostile garrisons and defended by only five men-at-arms, the maids and the family.)

Very straightforward, yes?

No.

It wasn't until I started trying to fit this into the book that I began to wonder how in blazes she (a) knew that the king, way off in Oxford, was sending troops to the west country? (b) why she thought they'd detour through Blandford? (c) and when? and (d) how she contrived to get her messenger (e: who?) just to the right place at the right time through all that hostile country? And all without cellphones, too.

As you'll notice, I fiddled it into something that I could put down without my readers wondering if Sally Watson had suddenly forgotten how to write a sane plot.

The matter of the cows was worse. This is while Erle's 600 or so men have tightly surrounded the castle, which in turn was tightly sealed against them. 'Therefore, not compelled by want, but rather to brave the rebels, they sallied out and brought in either cows or a bull into the castle without the loss of a man or a man wounded. At another time five boys fetched in four cows. They that stood on the hills called to one in a house in the valley, crying 'Shoot, Anthony.'

Well, I came all-a-bits with this one! For who could resist including such a good bit of action? But who could make sense of it? Many sleepless nights failed to produce any notion of how *any* of it could have been done, given the historical situation--including the fact that all the boys in the castle had been sent off to safety except Baby Will, still in swaddling clothes. So, craven, I turned it into a bit of war propaganda--and if somehow it was actually true, I hope the writers of *Mercurius Rusticanus* won't show up to haunt me. (On second thought, if they could tell me how it was done, I wouldn't mind a little haunting.)

Still, much of the *Mercurius Rusticanus* account was useful and useable, and worth all the hard study.

These were the real names and relative ages of the Bankes family--I think. Sir John and Lady Mary were as portrayed. I frankly invented the children's personalities--but I think no one these days has a notion what they were like. I had a terrible time discovering even their names and ages, beginning in the mid-sixties when I first tried to write this book. I came up with several contradictory versions. Finally, my wonderful researching friend Gill Freeman, who lives in London and has trotted all over England for me, produced a definitive list of offspring, names and ages, after I'd made a good start on the story.

Uh-oh! Alice and Mary were much older than I'd made them! And the youngest ones were in a different order. So I had to rewrite a good deal. By then, I'd already established their personalities, and incorporated them into the plot--so, I confess, I diddled the ages of Will, Bridget, and Arabella. *Mea culpa!*

John matriculated at Oxford in July, 1643, died the summer of '44, and was outlived by his father, Sir John, who died Dec. 28, 1644.

Lilbourne followers were not generally called Levellers until a few years later, after '46. I'm pretending he called himself that earlier. Privately, of course.

179

QUOTES
(often very roughly translated)

Aeturnun servans sub pectore vulnuis: Holding a grudge:

Agenti incumbit protatio: The burden of proof is on the accuser:

'A man may smile and smile, and be a villain': Hamlet

Amantes amentes: Lovers are mad:

Amicus certus in re incerta cernitur: A friend in need is a friend indeed.

Anagke oude theoi machontai: Even the gods don't fight necessity:

a priori: a conclusion reached by self-evident propositions.

Audendo magnus tegitur timur: Great fear is covered by an act of courage.

Aude sapere: Dare to be wise:

Audi alteram pertem: Hear the other side.

Cadit quaestio The argument collapses for want of proof.

Cave quie dicis, quando et cui: Be careful of what you say, and when and to whom.

Concordia discors: Armed truce:

Daimon: this was Socrates' 'spirit advisor'

Damnant quod non intelligunt: They damn what they don't understand.

Decipit frons prima multos: First appearances often deceive

En nukti boule tois sophois gignetai: to take counsel of your pillow

Fortus fortuna aduvat: Fortune aids the brave.

Gnothi seauton! Know thyself

'--how ill all's here about my heart': Hamlet

Inter canum et lupum: caught between a dog and a wolf I

Ira furor brevis est: Anger is a brief madness

Hubris: Overweening pride: the usual tragic flaw in Greek tragedy.

181

Kalokagathia: An ideally good and beautiful woman--according to Athenian men

laese majestas, lesé majesty: An offense against majesty's dignity

Lupus pilum mutat, non mentem: The wolf changes his coat but not his nature.

non culpabilis: Not guilty;

non sequitor: It does not follow

Pax: peace; truce

Phtheirousin ethe christh' homiliai: Evil communications corrupt good manners

Quae nocent docent: It is demonstrated

Quot homines, tot sententia: There are as many opinions as there are men:

sang-froid: cold blood

'Then, as mankinde, so is the world's whole frame quite out of joynt.' John Donne.

'The time is out of joint; O cursed spite that ever I was born to set it right. Hamlet

Throng: busy

Touché: Ya got me.

Vanitas vanitatum, et omnia vanitas: Vanity, vanity, all is vanity.

Varium et mutabile semper femina: Woman is a changeable and fickle thing.

Vis comsili expers mole ruit sua: Force without counsel is crushed by own weight

Vox popula, vox Dei: The voice of the people is the voice of God.

BIBLIOGRAPHY

Ashley, MauriceEngland in the 17th Century

The right Honourable George Bankes family history

John Murray, Albemarle St. 1853, The Story of Corfe Castle

Brooke, IrisA History of English Costume

Burton, ElizabethThe Pageant of Stuart England

County of DorsetColorful Isle of Purbeck

Tilsed & Son, High St. Wimborne DorseGuide to Corfe Castle
 (bought in 1958, price one shilling)

Ellis, E. A. The Countryside in Autumn

Fraser, AntoniaWeaker Vessel

Goodwin, Tim Dorset in the Civil War

Hardy, EmelineThe Story of Corfe Castle

Hansen, H. H.Costume Cavalcade

Irwin, MargaretThe Stranger Prince

Ladybird BooksBritish Birds and their Nests

Ladybird BooksWhat to look for in Spring

The National Trust, 2002Corfe Castle

Norman, AndrewBy Swords divided

Pomeroy, ColinCastles and Forts: Dorset

Quennell, MarjorieEveryday Things in England 1500-1799

Sancha, SheilaThe Castle Story

Tiarra, MichaelThe Way of Herbs

Varley, Frederick JohnThe Siege of Oxford
 (Oxford University Press)

Wedgewood, C V The King's Peace

Wedgewood The King's War

and-- *Mercurius Rusticanus*

Castle Adamant *l*

Breinigsville, PA USA
29 December 2010
252365BV00003B/102/P